She s **k,**
hu

'Oh, David…' She sighed. 'We'll have to get married now.'

He tensed.

Well, she'd been prepared for that. He must be shocked to learn that she was the woman he'd just ravished.

But before he could say anything someone flung up the sash window and stepped into the orangery.

She didn't have time to do more than lift her head and swivel it in that direction before the light of two lanterns flooded the scene, clearly showing the unmasked faces of the three people standing there.

The Neapolitan Nightingale, her mouth agape.

Marianne, her hands clasped to her bosom.

And worst of all…David—*not* the man currently embracing her!

Annie Burrows has been writing Regency romances for Mills & Boon since 2007. Her books have charmed readers worldwide, having been translated into nineteen different languages, and some have gone on to win the coveted Reviewers' Choice Award from *CataRomance*. For more information, or to contact the author, please visit annie-burrows.co.uk or you can find her on Facebook at facebook.com/AnnieBurrowsUK.

Books by Annie Burrows

Mills & Boon Historical Romance

Brides of Waterloo

A Mistress for Major Bartlett

Silk & Scandal

The Viscount and the Virgin

Stand-Alone Novels

Regency Candlelit Christmas
'The Rake's Secret Son'
Devilish Lord, Mysterious Miss
A Countess by Christmas
Captain Corcoran's Hoyden Bride
An Escapade and an Engagement
Gift-Wrapped Governesses
'Governess to Christmas Bride'
Never Trust a Rake
Reforming the Viscount
Portrait of a Scandal
Lord Havelock's List
The Captain's Christmas Bride

Mills & Boon Historical *Undone!* eBooks

Notorious Lord, Compromised Miss
His Wicked Christmas Wager

Visit the Author Profile page
at millsandboon.co.uk for more titles.

THE CAPTAIN'S
CHRISTMAS BRIDE

Annie Burrows

Published in Great Britain 2015
by Mills & Boon, an imprint of Harlequin (UK) Limited,
Eton House, 18-24 Paradise Road, Richmond, Surrey, TW9 1SR

© 2015 Annie Burrows

ISBN: 978-0-263-24820-3

THE CAPTAIN'S
CHRISTMAS BRIDE

To my brand-new daughter-in-law Emily.
Welcome to the family.
And special thanks to Joe for the brainstorming on this one.

Chapter One

Christmas Day, 1815

'How long do you think it will take? To make sure I am thoroughly compromised?'

Lady Julia Whitney observed Marianne's face turn a little pink as a frown flitted across her brow. But then Marianne disapproved of the whole venture and was uncomfortable being dragged into it.

'You only need to leave us alone long enough to be sure he is kissing me,' Lady Julia pointed out. 'And then you can burst into the orangery and find us.'

'Yes, but how will I know he *is* kissing you?' Marianne yanked hard at the laces in her valiant, prolonged struggle to do up Lady Julia's masquerade gown. 'The mistletoe didn't work. And we hung kissing boughs *everywhere*.'

Lady Julia winced. Not only had they hung mistletoe everywhere, but almost everyone else was making good use of it.

'I'm sorry,' said Marianne. 'Did I pinch you? This dress is rather tight, isn't it?'

'I shall hold my breath until you get it done up,' said Lady Julia, unwilling to admit that it was chagrin that made her wince, at the reminder that after all the hours spent gathering mistletoe, fashioning it into dozens of kissing boughs, and getting footmen to hang them all over the house, she hadn't managed to coax David to stand still underneath a single one of them.

'Thank you,' said Marianne. 'I didn't realise how difficult this would be. I mean, you do *look* about the same size as the Neapolitan Nightingale. I didn't think we'd need to make any alterations when she agreed to lend you her gown for the evening. But actually, you are rather more… um…robust.'

She gave another hard tug. 'There. All done,' she said.

'Oh, my goodness,' said Lady Julia, studying her reflection in the mirror with awe, as well as a touch of dizziness from having held her breath for so long. 'But it was worth it.'

'Lawks,' said Marianne, her eyes widening as she peeped over Lady Julia's shoulder.

Lawks indeed. The peacock-blue silk gown was a lot more daring than even she'd suspected it might be. On the Neapolitan Nightingale—the opera singer from whom she'd borrowed it—it hadn't looked any more daring than any of her other gowns. But with Lady Julia's bosom hitched up like that, and overflowing the straining bodice, it was teetering on the verge of scandalous.

'Lawks,' she echoed faintly, staring with astonishment at the impressive cleavage which had never before had a public airing.

'Well, that puts paid to any worries that people might recognise you,' said Marianne tartly. 'Once you put the mask on, not one single man there will be able to raise his eyes from the front of your gown.'

'And don't forget the wig,' came a muffled voice from behind the screen where the Neapolitan Nightingale herself was changing into the costume supposedly made for Lady Julia.

Marianne and Lady Julia exchanged a guilty look. Just how much might she have heard? They'd been whispering to start with, but the sight of that cleavage had shocked them both into indiscretion.

'Goodness,' said the Neapolitan Nightingale when she came out from behind the screen—in a

voice that betrayed her far-from-Italian origins—
and saw the way the two young ladies were gap-
ing at Lady Julia's extremely *risqué décolletage*.

'You look far more delicious in that than I ever
did,' she said, with a wry twist to her lips. 'You
can keep it if you like, after the party is over.'

'Oh, no, really, I couldn't…'

'Well, I shan't want it back. It's been my favourite this season, but it's about time I got a
new look.'

Julia took another look at herself in the mirror. The idea had been to make herself look irre-
sistible and completely unlike her rather demure
self. Well, she'd certainly done that!

She stroked the shimmering blue-green silk
lovingly. She couldn't imagine ever having the
nerve to wear such a revealing gown again. But
she would rather like to keep it as a memento.
Of this party, and the woman who'd lent it to her,
and, she hoped, the successful conclusion to her
campaign to make David propose.

'Then, thank you. Thank you very much.'

'Now, the best way to trick everyone,' said the
Nightingale briskly, 'is to let me do all the work.
I've got that rather mannish stride of yours down
pat. And some of your other little mannerisms.
And your stock phrases.'

'Stock phrases? I don't use stock phrases,' Lady Julia objected.

'Everyone uses stock phrases. Marianne is always saying, *"Oh, dear me, no. Really, I couldn't,"*' said the Nightingale in a voice uncannily like Marianne's. 'And you are always saying, *"Stuff!"*, and then sniffing, and tossing your head.'

'I don't toss my head.'

'You do,' said Marianne, trying not to giggle. 'Really, Nellie has you down to a T.'

Lady Julia was on the verge of saying *stuff* before recollecting that she'd objected to having it pointed out that she was always doing so. Her neck muscles clamped up as she resisted the urge to toss her head, or sniff, or do anything else to express her irritation at learning she was so predictable. It was a funny business seeing someone as talented as the Nightingale learn to impersonate you. She'd had Marianne in stitches over the past couple of afternoons, aping attitudes Lady Julia had no idea she affected. Like the way she shrugged just one shoulder, apparently, and made a little moue with her lips when she was struggling to be polite to some crashing bore.

'Now, Marianne,' said the Nightingale briskly. 'Your part is to stick close by me all night, the way you usually do with Lady Julia. And you mustn't forget to call me Cuz now and then, just to reinforce the idea that it is Lady Julia in this modest white gown.'

'I know,' said Marianne in a resigned tone of voice. They'd been over all this dozens of times. And spent several hours, on the pretext of working on their costumes for tonight's masquerade, rehearsing.

'Now for the wigs!'

Nellie the Neapolitan Nightingale lifted a glossy blue-black wig from its stand, and placed it on Lady Julia's head.

'I wish my hair was really this colour,' said Julia, fingering one of the rather coarse-feeling ringlets. Her own was that depressingly dull shade of brown that, were she not the daughter of an earl, people would decry as mousey.

'Nobody really has hair that colour,' said the Nightingale prosaically as she tied Lady Julia's mask over her face. 'Not unless they get it out of a bottle. There.'

Marianne and the Nightingale stood staring at her, while she stared at her own reflection in the mirror. The mask was made of the same silk as the dress, with just the hint of a beak to disguise the shape of her nose, and was topped off with a plume of peacock feathers that made her look several inches taller.

Actually, she was several inches taller anyway, thanks to the heels of the shoes Nellie had lent her.

'Now for the finishing touch,' said Nellie, reaching for a pot of blacking.

With a little brush, she dabbed at the upswell of Julia's left breast, recreating the distinctive diamond-shaped mole that nestled provocatively upon the Nightingale's own bosom.

'There, all done,' said Nellie. 'If anyone can tell that we've swapped places under these costumes, I'll eat my hat. But look,' she said, turning to Julia with a frown. 'If you find any of the men behave a bit too free, thinking you are just me, then we'll stop the charade at once. I wouldn't be able to live with myself if you got into trouble.'

Julia and Marianne looked anywhere but at each other. The whole purpose of swapping identities was so she *could* get into trouble. Naturally, they hadn't let Nellie into the whole of the plan, else she'd never have agreed to go along with it, or been so helpful coaching them. As far as she knew, they'd just thought it would be a lark to try to get everyone thinking that Nellie, the opera singer who'd been hired to entertain her guests, was Lady Julia Whitney, daughter of their host, the Earl of Mountnessing, and vice versa. They'd reminded her of the tradition of having a Lord of

Misrule at Christmas, who upset the social order by taking a crown and ordering his betters about, and how everyone thought it a huge joke.

They'd neglected to tell her that the Earl of Mountnessing had never unbent enough to permit a Lord of Misrule to form *any* part of the Christmas festivities.

'I shall be fine,' she said, to Marianne and Nellie, who were both looking at her with a touch of concern. 'You go off now, together, and I shall come down to the ballroom in a moment or two.'

'By the backstairs,' Nellie reminded her, before tying on her own white-satin mask, which sported a set of cat's whiskers, and pulling up her velvet hood, which was topped with a pair of pointy ears.

Marianne was the only one of them not in costume. She'd agreed to don a plain black-silk mask, but that was as far as she was prepared to go. Julia hadn't argued with her for long before realising that actually, her stubborn refusal to have an expensive costume made up would help her achieve her goal. Everyone would recognise Marianne instantly. And would assume that the woman she shadowed, who was dressed, very primly, as a white cat, must be Lady Julia.

Once they'd gone, Julia was able to add the last, final touch to her disguise.

From her reticule, she withdrew the bottle of perfume she'd taken from Nellie's dressing table earlier. Normally, ladies dabbed scent behind their ears and on their wrists. But she couldn't get at her ears through the mass of false hair and peacock feathers. Neither was she going to risk pulling off her elbow-length evening gloves. She'd never get them buttoned up again without help from a maid.

Finally, in desperation, she tipped the bottle between her breasts, hoping she didn't spill too much on her gloves in the process. The cloud of scent which billowed out made her eyes water for a second or two. But at least it would mark her out as the Nightingale. Nellie had this perfume specially made, so rumour went, by one of the most exclusive *parfumeurs* in Paris. There was a lot of musk in it. Not at all the sort of light, floral scent a young girl like Julia would normally use, if she were to use scent, which she didn't. Plain soap and water was enough for her.

Lifting her chin, she opened the door and stepped out into the corridor. As she made her way to the back stairs, she concentrated on the languid way Nellie had taught her to walk, swaying her hips in what felt like an exaggerated manner, but when viewed in a mirror simply looked sensuous. They'd only practised for a couple of afternoons, but the heels, as Nellie had promised, did help her to avoid striding out the way she usually did. Though she wasn't *mannish*. She walked with a purposeful *manner*, that was all. She'd taken on a lot of responsibilities since her mother had died, and she'd never get the half of her duties done if she dawdled about.

She clutched at the handrail all the way down the stairs. The last thing she wished to do was trip and tumble headlong into the hall below.

'Nellie, my love,' cried a man's voice, as she descended from the last step. 'You look sublime!'

It was a slender young man, dressed as an Elizabethan courtier. She was just basking in a sense of achievement at having fooled him, when he shocked her by walking slap up to her and kissing her cheek, just where the mask ended and her skin began.

She'd sniffed and turned her head away before she realised the gesture might give her away.

'Beg pardon,' said the courtier, raising his hands in apparent surrender. 'Didn't think. Must have taken you hours to get into costume. Don't want it spoiled before you go into the ball.'

Thank heaven this young man didn't know her very well. She slid him a sideways glance, wondering exactly who he was. At this time of year the house always swarmed with all sorts of extra staff, from Nellie the famous singer, to the humble artist brought in to chalk fabulous yet ephemeral decorations on the ballroom floor. He couldn't be one of the extra servants, even though she'd met him in the service corridor, or he wouldn't be all dressed up and ready to attend the masquerade. From the familiar way he'd spoken to her, it was more likely he was one of the troupe of players who worked at the same theatre as Nellie. Wasn't he the one who played romantic leads? Eduardo something or other—that was it. Though the name was patently false. This man was no more Italian than Nellie, for all that people called her the Neapolitan Nightingale.

Still, he would lend credence to her disguise if he escorted her into the ballroom. So she took his arm and drifted down the corridor beside him, thankful that she'd bitten her tongue when he'd accosted her. The moment she opened her mouth, her disguise would fall apart. No matter how hard she'd tried, she simply couldn't imitate the mellifluous tone of Nellie's voice, let alone capture the way she peppered her speech with vulgarisms.

But at least if Eduardo had been fooled by the way she'd moved, the fake mole on her bosom, and the cloud of perfume hanging round her, then it looked as though her plan stood some chance of succeeding.

'Uh-oh,' murmured Eduardo into her ear, a few moments later. 'Here come your admirers.'

She froze as the gentlemen guests of the house party all turned to peruse her through their eye-glasses, detached themselves from the respectable females they were supposed to be escorting and headed her way. Her stomach lurched. Was this what Nellie felt like every time she went onstage?

'Don't worry, I shan't cramp your style,' said Eduardo, letting go of her arm. She was just about to beg him not to desert her, when he slapped her bottom with an earthy chuckle.

Making her wish him at Jericho.

Five minutes later, she realised he was no worse than any of the other men. They all seemed to think her *derrière* existed for the sole purpose of being patted, or pinched, or squeezed. It wasn't long before she was sure it must be a mass of bruises. How on earth did Nellie put up with this kind of treatment? She was sorely tempted to sidle into an alcove and keep her back to the wall, only that might mean losing sight of David.

She'd hoped he would have been amongst the crowd clustering round Nellie. But, bother him if he wasn't being particularly attentive to her tonight—at least, the woman he thought was her, since she was dressed as a white cat, and attended by a girl who was very obviously Marianne.

Oh, but he did look splendid in the full-skirted coat, long dark wig, and tricorne hat of the seventeenth century. The telescope he held in his hand told the world that he was dressed as Sir Isaac Newton. Well, of course, David being a man of science himself, he was bound to choose such a costume, rather than something more frivolous, like a pirate, or a Roman emperor, or an Elizabethan courtier.

Her own Uncle Maurice was dressed tonight as Henry VIII, a figure he managed to emulate extremely well, since he was rather corpulent and florid of complexion. She smiled at him in relief when he offered her a glass of champagne, feeling sure her dear old Uncle Maurice wouldn't pinch her, or squeeze her bottom. But her relief was short-lived. First, he tried to manoeuvre her under one of the kissing boughs. Then he asked if she would like to come to his room that night. Of course Uncle Maurice was rather foxed. And he didn't have very good eyesight. Nevertheless, it was with genuine indignation, larded with a good deal of revulsion, that she rapped him over the wrist with her fan.

It was all proving far more difficult than she could have imagined. She'd assumed David would have approached her before now. She'd banked on it. He'd been so fascinated by Nellie, from the moment she'd arrived. So fascinated that she'd even accused him of flirting with the singer.

David had pokered up. Sworn it was no such thing.

'If you cannot tell the difference between flirting, and the conversation of an educated man with an intelligent woman, then I despair of you,' he'd said. 'The Neapolitan Nightingale has a unique perspective on the world. She has travelled extensively, and rubbed shoulders with the very highest, though she comes from very humble origins.'

Nellie certainly did have an entertaining way of talking, Julia had to admit. Though her stories were sometimes rather scurrilous, she always related them so wittily that Julia could hardly blame David for joining the throng of her admirers.

Though now she wished she hadn't reproved him for doing so. He was behaving with perfect propriety, just when she most wished him to stray!

She'd almost given up hope of getting him

on his own, when a gust of cold air swirled into the ballroom, heralding the arrival of a troupe of mummers. At the sound of their pipe, fiddle, and drum, the professional musicians laid down their own instruments, left their chairs, and headed for the refreshments table. With murmurs of anticipation, the masked-and-costumed guests fanned out, yielding the heart of the ballroom to the newcomers.

Julia's stomach constricted into a knot. If she didn't make a move soon, David would leave. Since they'd discussed her father's refusal to countenance David as a suitor, he hardly ever visited the Hall any more. It was only because of the Christmas masquerade ball, to which all the tenants were invited, that he was here now. Once the mummers finished their act, everyone would unmask, go in to supper, and then go home. And he would return to Edinburgh, and it would be months and months before she could see him again.

It was her last chance. If she didn't manage to entice David away from the other masqueraders, in her guise as Nellie, the fallen woman who exerted such fascination over every single man attending this house party—and quite a few of the married ones, too—she would have failed. And she couldn't fail. She just couldn't.

There had to be some way. Some way to indicate she wanted to get him alone without having to open her mouth and say it, thereby giving
away her identity.

But how? How did anyone convey their intentions without speaking?

And then it hit her. She'd hated the way men
had been pinching and pawing at her all evening,
but it had certainly conveyed *their* intentions.

Her heart sped up a little more. Both because
she'd come up with a plan, and because David
had temporarily moved out of sight.

But then she spotted him again. She wondered
that she'd lost sight of him even for those few
moments, because he was half a head taller than
most of the gentlemen present. Especially with
that tricorne hat, worn over that long, curled wig.

He was subtly moving to the back of the crowd
as they all pressed forward to get a better view.
Of course the mummers were dressed up to play
out the tale of St George and the dragon. And
they would include a scene where a doctor was
called to bind up St. George's wounds. It was a
comic scene, which always annoyed David in-
tensely, since he was studying medicine himself
and couldn't bear to see a doctor being made a
figure of fun.

Her heart in her mouth, she edged around the

outskirts of the crowd until she was right behind him. Nobody was paying her any attention. Especially not now the mummers had taken up their starting positions.

The dragon let out a mighty roar, a puff of smoke billowed from his nostrils, and the heroine of the piece let out a piercing scream.

Lady Julia slid her hand between the tails of his full-skirted coat and found the curve of his bottom. His muscles clenched under the palm of her hand.

St George strode onto the scene, waving his cardboard sword.

The guests gave a rousing cheer, which drowned out the gasp Sir Isaac Newton gave when she pinched his bottom, hard.

She kept her gaze directed at the mummers, and their antics, when he turned to see who'd pinched him. It was bright enough, just here, for him to be able to see her fairly clearly, and she only bore a superficial resemblance to Nellie. She had the same soft roundness to her jaw, but anyone looking closely at the uncovered part of her face would surely notice that her mouth was not as generous, nor her lips so full. And it would be fatal to look directly into David's eyes. Even though the upper part of her face was covered, and she was using her cleavage as a distraction, if he looked into her eyes he'd be sure to wonder why Nellie's melting brown eyes had faded to the hue of a peeled grape. And he'd know. And be furious that she was doing something so improper.

But she was done with being proper. It hadn't got them anywhere at all. If only he didn't recognise her then the chances were she could get *him* to behave in a highly improper fashion, too, and then all their problems would be solved!

Only he still wasn't doing anything! St George was stepping over the heroine, who'd just collapsed in an artistically terrified swoon, but Sir Isaac Newton was just standing perfectly still, apparently content to savour the sensation of her fondling his behind.

Now what?

Oh, bother the man, couldn't he just once forget propriety, and act with a bit of dash? Well, there was nothing for it. She was just going to have to take the initiative.

She removed her hand from his bottom, and fumbled her way round the tailcoat until she discovered his hand. She got as many fingers round it as she could, considering it was bunched round the brass telescope, and gave it a little tug.

It was enough to propel him into movement. Meek as a lamb, he followed her to the nearest door, which happened to lead out onto the terrace, then all along its length, and down the steps at the end.

She didn't dare glance over her shoulder, not even when they plunged into the pitch darkness of the path through the shrubbery. And especially not when they emerged again, round the back of the house, where some light did filter out through one or two unshuttered windows, making the glass roof of the orangery glitter as though it was sprinkled with sequins.

She'd chosen to take David to the orangery because it would be lovely and warm in there. It was tacked on to the back of the kitchens where specially designed flues kept her father's collection of rare tropical plants frost-free throughout the winter. Gatley, the head gardener, had locked the door when the first of the house guests arrived, to prevent anyone wandering in and then carelessly leaving the door open when they wandered out again. But the lock on one of the sash windows, which could be raised or lowered during the summer months for ventilation, was broken. She'd made sure of it that very afternoon.

Julia had to let go of his hand while she pushed the sash window up, but that didn't matter. He wouldn't have come all this way only to run away now.

She stepped over the sill, and stood to one side

so he could do the same. Then she carefully lowered the sash again. Gatley would be livid if his precious plants were exposed to a draught. Anyway, she didn't want to be exposed to a draught either. Not when there was so very little gown draping any part of her body.

Goodness but it was dark in here. Only a faint glimmer of moonlight peeked in through the roof. The massed palms at the east end of the orangery curtained the interior from any light that might have found its way this far from the house.

But the darkness seemed to make David uncharacteristically bold. He didn't even wait for her to turn round before sliding his arms round her waist, and bending his head to kiss her cheek. As his lips brushed her skin, sending delicious shivers right down her spine, she felt his tricorne hat tangle with her feathers.

With a low growl, he pulled off his hat, and his wig, and tossed them aside. Then stooped to lay the telescope down on top. She turned round, longing to be in his arms again, but face-to-face this time, so that he could kiss her properly. On the lips. And so, as he straightened up, she flung her arms round his neck and pressed her lips to his before he could say anything, or required her to say anything that would give her away, and have him marching her back to the house, scolding her all the way.

And, oh, joy! He put his arms round her, and kissed her back.

At last. At last. And, oh, it was every bit as magical as she'd ever dreamed. Better. For now she was in his arms, he seemed taller and broader, and so very much more…muscular, and masculine, than she'd expected.

Her heart pounded, her breath shortened as though she'd been running. Actually, her feet were moving, now she came to think of it. For he'd turned her round a bit, and was steering her toward the rear wall. Against which there was a bench. Oh, clever, clever David, to remember the bench where they'd all sat on rainy days, talking of every topic imaginable. Until, that was, her father had warned him off.

He kissed her all the way to the bench, then let go of her with one hand to feel his way down to the cushions. He sat, and pulled her down after him. Not that she needed much of a pull from his hand. It had taken all her resolve to stop herself from flinging herself onto his lap. Except he didn't pull her onto his lap, but onto the bench next to him. Oh, well, it was almost as good. It was heaven to feel his mouth on hers once more. Such heaven, that she put up no resistance at all when he pushed against her, and kept on pushing, until she was sprawled rather inelegantly on her back with him half over her.

Never mind the inelegance of the sprawl, she sighed. It felt too wonderful to feel his weight bearing down on her. She put her arms round his neck, kissing his face and caressing his shoulders to encourage him to keep on doing what he was doing. Because if Marianne and Nellie found them together like this, then there was no way he could deny he'd crossed the line.

Though, ought she to let him be quite so free? His hands were exploring rather more of her than she'd expected. And a deal more roughly. Not that he was hurting her, on the contrary, it was all very stimulating.

She did let out a shocked gasp when he delved into the front of her bodice and scooped out her left breast. But it didn't stop him raising it to his mouth, and lashing it with his tongue.

Heavens, it was as though she'd unleashed a wild animal.

She'd never dreamed David could be so…unruly.

Or so exciting.

At last he'd abandoned all his stuffy principles about the way a gentleman should behave. Where, now, was his declaration that he was beneath her station? That he couldn't aspire to her hand?

Sacrificed, apparently, to his determination to get beneath her skirts.

So forgetful of his station was he, that he was actually reaching down, seizing a handful of her gown and pushing the material up her legs.

All thoughts of Marianne and discovery went up in smoke when he moaned into her cleavage at the exact moment his hand reached the soft flesh of her inner thigh. He was being so eager, so ardent. If anyone dared to interrupt them now, she would probably scream with frustration.

For this was absolutely heavenly. She'd never felt anything so utterly delightful.

Until his exploration became shockingly intimate.

She winced, and yelped, at the startling, and rather painful intrusion of his fingers.

'I'm sorry,' he growled into her ear. 'I thought you were ready.'

Ready? For him to touch her there? How could she have imagined he'd want to do such a thing? Not that she could protest. Else he might stop altogether. Which was the last thing she wanted. They had to be discovered locked in a passionate embrace, not sitting next to each other demurely begging each other's pardon.

While she was still puzzling over what response she ought to make, he dropped to his knees on the floor and pushed her skirts right up to her waist. She almost cried out a protest. It had been hard enough having her bosom on show all evening let alone her most private parts. Not that he could actually see anything in the darkness, nor was he trying to, Julia suddenly realised in shock. What he was doing was lowering his head and kissing her. Nibbling at the top of her tightly clenched thighs, and then, when the sheer bliss of it had her relaxing, he pushed her legs apart so that he could kiss the exact place where his hand had ventured.

Julia almost panicked and pushed him away. Surely he couldn't want to kiss her there? Could he?

Oh, heavens, whatever was she supposed to do now? What would Nellie do in her place? Was she used to men doing this sort of thing? Was she…?

Oh, heavens but that felt…

Oh, goodness, if he kept on doing that…

Oh, goodness, she hoped he would keep on doing that. That was…that was…

Excitement built in her, just as though he'd lit a fuse. It went fizzing through her, burning brighter and brighter, until somehow, she knew, there was going to be some sort of explosion.

It burst through her, startling a scream of pleasure from her throat.

He knelt back with a satisfied growl. Got up, bent one of her lax legs at the knee and propped it up against the wall. He then pushed the other down so that her foot was on the floor and came back down on top of her.

'Unnhhh...' She tried to say something, anything. But she was still stunned by the force of the explosion that had just flung her skyward. She was still floating, somewhere far above the earth, as he settled between her legs.

It was only when he surged forward she realised that at some point he'd undone his breeches and was sliding *inside* her. She tensed, remembering the discomfort his fingers had caused. But this didn't hurt. Not even when he started thrusting into her—clutching at her bottom with one hand, and propping himself against the kitchen wall with the other.

And then he exploded, too. She felt him pulsing deep inside her as his whole body shuddered over her.

She slid her arms round his neck, hugging him in sheer delight.

'Oh, David,' she sighed. 'We'll have to get married now.'

He tensed.

Well, she'd been prepared for that. He must be shocked to learn that she was the woman he'd just ravished.

But before he could say anything, someone flung up the sash window and stepped into the orangery.

He didn't have time to do more than lift his head and swivel it in that direction, before the light of two lanterns flooded the scene, clearly showing the unmasked faces of the three people standing there.

The Neapolitan Nightingale, her mouth agape.

And Marianne, her hands clasped to her bosom.

And, worst of all... David.

Chapter Two

'David?'

No! If David was standing over there, by the window, then who was this man who'd just…who she'd just permitted to…

Her stomach froze into a solid block of ice. David's face contorted with disgust.

'Cover yourself,' he said.

The man on top of her twitched the full skirts of his coat over her exposed thigh. Though there was nothing he could do about her leg from knee to toe.

'If you wouldn't mind giving us some privacy,' he drawled in the hatefully cutting way that identified him at once. 'I can hardly…disengage, with you three standing there staring.'

Marianne gave a little whimper, and sagged at the knees. David put his arm round her shoulder and pulled her face to his chest.

The Nightingale clapped her hands over her mouth.

And Julia clamped her jaw against a wave of nausea. David was standing *over there*. Which meant she had her legs wrapped round the waist of *another man*. And not just any man, but the very last man she'd have suspected of being able to act like…like this.

Captain Lord Dunbar. The dour Scotsman who'd arrived uninvited a couple of days ago and had been acting the part of spectre at the feast ever since—skulking on the sidelines and glowering particularly ferociously at anyone who dared look as if they were enjoying themselves too much.

'Wait!'

As the three witnesses to her downfall turned to leave, the man she'd just seduced by mistake barked out the single word in a forceful way that only served to confirm his identity. Only a man used to command could make perfect strangers stop in their tracks that way. A man who was used to storming enemy ships and cutting his opponents to ribbons. A man who would have been perfectly at home on the deck of a ship tossed by a howling gale, but who'd looked stifled by the social niceties of a drawing room.

'You will none of you speak of this,' he informed them. 'Not until I have had a chance to speak to the young lady's father.'

David swelled and quivered with indignation. 'If you think I would ever stoop to blacken the name of a lady, no matter what her conduct—' he flicked her another disgusted look that flayed her like a whip '—then you are very much mistaken.'

Oh, David. She'd lost him. Irrevocably. She'd never be able to look him in the face again, after this, never mind persuade him that, despite the difference in their stations, she'd make him a good wife.

'And I could never, never speak of it,' added Marianne in woeful indignation.

'I definitely don't want anyone knowing I had a hand in any of this,' added the Nightingale.

'Would it be too much to ask for one of you,' Captain Dunbar said in the sarcastic way that never failed to set Julia's teeth on edge, 'to leave us a lantern?'

Marianne placed hers on the floor. Well, she wasn't going to need her own, since David was holding her in such a protective embrace. No chance of her tripping over a loose flagstone on the way back to the house.

There was an awkward little interlude after the others had left, during which Captain Dunbar disentangled himself from her and briskly readjusted his clothing. Julia just about managed to swing both legs to the floor though they felt all weak and wobbly.

Oh, heavens! Now she knew just what a spent rocket felt like. Two minutes ago she'd experienced a kind of fire-bursting ecstasy. Now she just felt used and shattered.

Damn it all to hell and back! Snared by the oldest trick in the book. By a green girl, which was worse. Lady Julia, if he wasn't mistaken. The two sycophants, who normally trailed everywhere after her, wouldn't have cared tuppence what happened to any of the other guests at this house party.

Just to make sure, though, he untied the ribbons holding the elaborately decorated mask over her face. She barely reacted. Just sat there, shoulders hunched, gazing miserably at the floor, in the position she'd adopted after sitting up and smoothing down her skirts with trembling hands.

She looked as broken as the peacock feathers that had snapped off some time during their frenzied coupling.

Hell. He looked at the bedraggled mask dangling from his calloused fingers. Lady Julia had been a virgin. Of *course* she'd been a virgin. And he'd just treated her as though she was an experienced courtesan.

Though wasn't that what she'd wanted him to believe? Else why sidle up to him and get him all primed, then run him out here and set the spark to the touch hole?

It was her own fault.

He clenched his jaw, recalling her yelp of discomfort when he'd started exploring her. He had been impatient. Rough. He'd probably torn her then, with his fingers. He'd certainly felt no resistance when he'd entered her. Just a slick glide into the haven he'd sought ever since coming ashore two weeks earlier.

But blast it all—he'd have stopped if he'd sensed she was a virgin.

He *would*.

She lifted her head and met his furious gaze full on. 'Aren't you going to say anything?'

Defiance burned from her eyes—eyes that looked too big, too bright. And luminous with unshed tears.

'I'd like to say plenty,' he snarled. 'But the sad truth is, the only words spoken between us tonight have already said it all. We *are* going to have to get married.' There was no other way out. Not for him. His whole future depended on maintaining a spotless reputation. It wouldn't have mattered so much during the height of the war. An able, hard-working, skilled captain would always have been able to get command of a ship. But now?

And it wasn't just his own career he had to consider. He couldn't afford to become one of those officers who were only considered safe at sea. If it got about that he went about debauching unmarried, titled ladies he wouldn't be welcome anywhere. Which would cast a cloud over Lizzie's reputation, too. So far, his sister had done really well for herself. Sending her to that exclusive, expensive school had meant she was rubbing shoulders with girls from the best families. She'd even gained an invitation to this Christmas house party because of a connection to one of the Earl of Mountnessing's nieces.

But if word got out that her brother was a rake, what would that do to Lizzie's standing in society? To her chances of making a good match?

'No,' Lady Julia whispered.

She couldn't marry this man. She was going to marry David.

David.

'No…' she moaned as the truth hit her squarely in her midriff. David would never marry her now. He had such high ideals. He could never marry a girl he'd caught with her legs wrapped round another man's waist. No matter how highly he'd esteemed her before.

Alec squared his shoulders, remembering all the promises he'd ever made to his little sister. His promise that no matter how little they saw of each other, he'd always look after her. His promise that she would never go hungry, nor fear being made homeless. But most of all, his promise to be the kind of man on whom she could depend—unlike their scapegrace of a father.

He'd kept his word all these years. And he wasn't going to break it now. He'd always done whatever necessary to shield Lizzie from the worst excesses of their father. And now he was going to have to do what was necessary to shield her from his own excesses, tonight.

'Ye cannot say no to me like that as though you have a choice,' he snarled. 'D'ye think I want to marry you either? Hell, you're the last woman alive who would make a suitable wife for a man like me. You're too young, too foolish, and entirely too untrustworthy to leave alone while I'm away at sea.'

'How dare you—?' she began, getting to her feet.

'Don't waste those hoity-toity manners of yours on me. We're not in some drawing room now, where you can get away with looking down your nose at me, just because you think I'm uncouth.'

Though she looked as though she would dearly love to answer back, she restricted herself to a toss of her head, and a disapproving sniff. Because he'd hit the nail on the head. She'd queened over the tea table too many times to be able to refute his accusation. She'd looked down her aristocratic little nose at him when he'd been rude to one of the dozens of simpering misses infesting her father's house. Though being rude was the only way he'd found of fending them off. If he was polite, they kept on cooing over him. And batting their eyelashes at him. And sighing over his supposed heroic exploits, which they claimed to have heard all about.

And trying to manoeuvre him underneath one of the kissing boughs.

Julia alone had turned her nose up at him. He'd assumed it had been because she was too high in the instep to look twice at an impoverished sea captain, no matter how heroic the newspapers made him out to be. Instead, all the time, she must have been planning a far more effective stratagem than the others.

'Though what kind of marriage you think we're going to have when we come from such different worlds I cannot imagine.' Alec turned from her and ran his fingers through his hair, before turning back on her. 'You know nothing about me at all. So what on earth possessed you to make a play for me like this? I can only think it some kind of attempt to prove you could triumph where all the others had failed.'

'You arrogant oaf,' she hissed. 'I didn't make a play for *you* at all. I detest you.'

'Then what the hell was all that...fondling about? You cannot deny you got me all primed up before leading me out here.'

'No, but I didn't know it was you under that wig!' She pointed wildly at the heap of horsehair lying on the floor. 'I thought it was Sir Isaac Newton!'

'You were attempting to seduce a man who's been dead two hundred years?'

'Oh, don't be so stupid. I mean the man who came to the masquerade disguised as Sir Isaac Newton, of course!'

Of course. That made sense. She wouldn't have looked so dejected if he had been the man she was trying to compromise.

But, what kind of man came to a Christmas masquerade dressed as Sir Isaac Newton? What did Sir Isaac look like anyway? And then he realised.

'That man who found us. He was wearing

a full-skirted coat like this.' Though he'd discarded his wig, and tricorne hat—had he ever been wearing one. 'You mean to tell me *he* was the one you intended to seduce?'

'I never intended to *seduce* him,' she protested, clenching her fists as she squared up to him. 'I thought we would just kiss a bit. And then Marianne and Nellie would find us, and because Nellie is an outsider, Father would agree David and I would have to get married.'

'If kissing was all that had happened, it's more likely your father would have paid the singer to keep her mouth shut and have taken a horsewhip to that David.' Actually, he felt like taking a horsewhip to the man himself. The pompous bag of wind had marched out and left her lying in the arms of what any gentleman would have assumed was her seducer. What kind of man abandoned a girl, a sheltered, pampered innocent, just when she needed help the most?

'He isn't worthy of you,' he growled, incensed now that, after the lengths she'd gone to in order to strong-arm him into marriage, all the ungrateful oaf had done was look at her as though she was something nasty he'd stepped in.

'How dare you say that! Just because his parents have no title, and only modest means, it doesn't mean he's a nobody.'

He hadn't said the man was a nobody. So she must be reacting to arguments she'd heard from someone else about the pompous bladder of wind's unsuitability.

'He is the son of a gentleman,' she carried on, indignantly.

Though her anger was completely misdirected, at least she'd cast off that pitiful, dejected air that made him feel like a clumsy great gowk.

'And one day, he *will* be somebody. He's studying medicine. He's going to make great discoveries and become famous! So I wouldn't be throwing myself away on him. And anyway, I love him.'

'Well, he doesn't love you.'

'How can you possibly know anything of the sort? Of course he does.'

'No, he doesn't. Or he wouldn't have looked at you that way.'

'What way? I mean—naturally, he was very shocked. And…and disappointed.'

'But not devastated. Any real man who was in love would have attempted to strangle the man who'd got there first, not turn his nose up as if he'd smelled something bad.'

She reeled as if he'd struck her. He firmed his jaw. Better to get her to face facts now, than have her mooning over the man for months. He'd far rather have her angry and spitting fire when he marched her down the aisle, than drooping on the verge of tears.

'Come on,' he said, gripping her arm and towing her towards the window. 'We need to go find your father and make the best of this.'

'Wait,' Julia gasped, struggling ineffectually to shake off his hand. He had to let go of it eventually, to throw up the sash. Once he'd done so, he held his hand out again, imperiously.

Instead of taking it, she backed away. They couldn't go and tell her father what they'd done! She couldn't bear his disappointment, on top of her own. Or worse, his disapproval. So far, he'd never subjected her to the chilling antipathy he invariably displayed towards her older half-brothers. She'd been prepared to brave it for David's sake. But for this man? This stranger? No.

'Look…' He sighed. 'I know I shouted. And, yes, I'm angry, very angry, but I promise, you don't need to be afraid of me.'

'I'm not afraid of you.'

'Then what is the matter? You've got to face the facts, woman. You cannot very well pretend this never happened. I ken well it wasn't with the man you intended, but the end must be the same.'

'No. No, there must be some other way…'

'There isn't. The only way to make this right is to marry.'

'You think marrying a stranger could ever make *anything* right?'

'It will make it the rightest it can be.' He stepped over the sill, leaned back inside, and hauled her out after him.

She'd already discovered he was too strong to make struggling with him anything but undignified. So, she simply trotted along behind him, though her mind was racing as fast as he was obliging her legs to go.

Thank goodness she'd stopped trying to resist. There was no time to waste. Alec didn't trust any of those three to keep their mouths shut. Not for very long, anyway. And he needed to get this mess straightened out before they had a chance to do any damage. The very last thing he needed right now was a rumour going round that would blacken his reputation. He'd had to work twice as hard to gain his present rank, as men with family sponsors greased their way into promotions and fat prizes. He wasn't going to let this silly girl bring it all crashing down round his ears.

'Weeping and wailing isn't going to make this go away,' he said harshly, when he heard what sounded suspiciously like a stifled sob.

Alec clasped his fingers round her wrist a little tighter as a fresh wave of indignation had him lengthening his stride. If it had been Sir Isaac Newton dragging her through this shrubbery to confront her father, she would be cock-a-hoop. No man liked to have a woman think of him as second best. Second best? Not even that. She'd been looking at him as though he was some kind of ogre ever since he'd removed his mask and she'd seen exactly who he was.

'What…' she panted '…what do you plan to tell my father?'

That brought him to a dead halt. She caught up with him, and stepped in front, barring his path. Though she need not have done. He did need a moment to come up with a story that would satisfy an outraged father, and also prevent their union becoming fodder for scurrilous gossip.

He glared up at the bulk of the immense house Lady Julia's father owned. Light and laughter spilled from its windows. The laughter of the rich, privileged guests the earl had invited into his home. The kind of people who thrived on gossip and scandal. The kind of gossip that would ring a death knell to his career, as well as Lizzie's hopes.

'Listen,' she said. 'I don't care what you say

about me. About my part in…in enticing you away from the party and…and all that.'

He lowered his head to look at her.

She lifted her chin and met his eyes squarely, for the very first time.

'Naturally you are very angry with me. I'm angry with myself,' she admitted with a shake of her head. 'But please, please, don't let that anger spill over to my friends and drag them into our mess. That is, I know you will have to relate how they found us, but you don't need to make it sound as though they knew anything about it. Or…or helped me, do you?'

It hadn't occurred to him before. But now he saw that to carry out a deception of this magnitude, she would indeed have had to have accomplices.

'Nellie—I mean, the Neapolitan Nightingale did lend me her dress and agree to pretend to be me, to throw others off the scent, but she didn't know the whole of it. She just thought it was a jest, to see if we could fool people into mistaking us for each other. She thought we were going to stand next to each other at the end of the evening, and take off our masks, and everyone would be astonished. I couldn't bear it if she got into trouble for a…a prank I played on her as much as anyone else. And I'm afraid that if Papa thinks she was in any way responsible, he will throw her out. Probably do things to destroy her career. And it's all she has.'

Now it was his turn to reel. Up till now, he'd thought she was just another spoiled, petulant society miss. Just like the other empty-headed chits his sister claimed as friends. But that impassioned speech proved she was capable of thinking of others.

It was more than he would have expected of a girl like her. Not that it would do the opera singer any good. Lady Julia's father wasn't a fool. He would have seen her aping his daughter's mannerisms all evening, as well as Julia sashaying around in the opera singer's revealing gown. It was typical of her sort to act irresponsibly and then be surprised when the underlings they'd dragged into their mess bore the brunt of the repercussions.

'I agree,' he said curtly. 'You *should* take all the blame.'

She made a little moue of protest. But then, instead of launching into yet another barrage of protests, she lifted her chin.

'Thank you,' she said, stunning him. 'And... and as for Marianne...' Her whole face creased in concern. 'She didn't want any part of it. She told me it was wrong, but I...I took no notice.'

'Your father won't hold that against her,' he grunted. 'I only met any of you two days ago, but it's clear even to me that she has no influence over you whatsoever. You do as you please and expect her to trot along at your heels like a spaniel.'

'I do no such thing! Marianne is my friend!'

'Oh? I thought she was some sort of poor relation.'

'She—well, yes, she did come to live with us when her parents died. Because she had nowhere else to go, but I absolutely do *not* treat her like a spaniel. And she doesn't behave like one, either.'

He shrugged. 'It's of no concern to me. You want to shield both her and the opera singer from blame. That's commendable, I suppose, if a touch impractical.'

'Impractical? How?'

'Never mind how,' he said, irritated that somehow she'd made him share even a tithe of his thoughts. A good officer never let his subordinates into the workings of his mind. It could lead them to believe he wasn't totally infallible. 'Let us just leave it at the point where I agree to leave all the others out of it. Except for the part where they found us *in flagrante delicto*.'

She lowered her head for an instant, as though

discomfited by his brutal reminder of her spectacular fall from grace.

'Then, what,' she finally said in a small, almost penitent voice, 'do you plan to say?'

'You leave that to me,' he growled. 'And just remember, your father isn't going to be the first hurdle we have to leap tonight. We're going to have to walk back into that house and start searching for him. With everyone staring at us, and wondering what on earth we're doing together when so far this week we haven't been able to say two civil words to each other.'

'Oh. Well, I'm sure we can go in a side entrance...'

'If you think we're going to be able to carry this off with either one of our reputations intact, by skulking about as though we've done something to be ashamed of, then you're even sillier than you look.'

'Oh! What a nasty thing to say.'

'But true.'

She opened her mouth to argue. Looked as though she'd been struck by the truth of what he'd said. Shut it with a snap.

'Very well,' she conceded. 'We'll walk in together, stroll around until we find my father, and then—'

'And then I will insist on speaking with him

in private,' he broke in, before she could come up with yet another hare-brained scheme.

She glared at him.

'Fine,' she snapped, after a brief struggle with herself. 'Have it your way.'

'Oh, I will,' he said smoothly, as she laid her arm on his sleeve and squared her shoulders. 'From now on, you're going to find that there are some people you cannot twist round your little finger. No matter how you simper, and smile, and cajole.'

'And you will find out,' she snapped back, as they mounted the steps, 'that there are some women who would rather die than simper and smile and cajole a man. Particularly not a man like you!'

'Then it appears our married life is going to be a stormy one,' he replied grimly. 'We will both be as glad as each other when my business ashore is done, and I can go back to sea.'

She smiled up at him sweetly. Because they'd reached the terrace, where anyone might see them if they happened to glance out of the windows.

'Oh, I think,' she said in a caressing tone, 'that I shall be far more pleased to see the back of you, than you will of me.'

They strolled across the terrace and in through

the same door they'd used such a short time before in silence. It was a good job he wasn't the kind of man who minded having the last word. But then he just couldn't see the point of engaging in pointless debate with her. Not when they were, basically, in agreement. Neither of them, given the choice, would have chosen the other for a life partner. Hell, he hadn't planned to marry for years, if at all. His estates were mortgaged. His ancestral home let out to tenants. His sister living with friends she'd met at the exclusive boarding school that had swallowed up practically every penny he'd ever earned. He had nothing to offer a wife. No home, no money that wasn't spoken for, and few prospects now that Wellington had finally defeated Bonaparte on land, which meant that the war against the French was over.

'You could try smiling, too,' she hissed up at him through a smile so forced it was hurting her teeth. 'To look at your face, anyone would think some great disaster had just befallen you.'

'It's my natural expression,' he replied. 'Better get used to it.'

'I thought we were trying to persuade everyone we hadn't done something to be ashamed of.'

'Aye. But that doesn't mean I need to go about with a fatuous grin on my face.'

'There's a world of difference between a fatuous grin and the murderous look you've got on your face.' Though her own smile faltered as she said it. Because she'd seen Papa. 'And my father has seen us,' she said, pointing towards the fireplace. 'Over there.'

He was standing beside one of the ornate marble fireplaces that were a feature of Ness Hall, eyeing them with one of his bushy grey eyebrows raised in reproof. Hardly surprising. Julia's scandalously low-cut gown was crumpled and stained now, her exposed bosom streaked black with what remained of her attempt to make it look as though she had a mole, her mask gone, her hair straggling round her face. In short, she looked as though she'd just been thoroughly ravished.

Once Papa learned she *had* just been thoroughly ravished, all hell was going to break loose. If he'd been so adamant he wouldn't have her throwing herself away on a perfectly respectable man she'd known all her life, he was going to be furious to learn she'd flung herself at a total stranger.

Nevertheless, they made straight for him. Because she had to face him sooner or later. Better to get it over with.

'I should like to speak to you in private, if I may, sir,' said Captain Dunbar.

'I should think,' said Papa, raking her from head to toe, 'you do.' He drained the glass of wine he'd been holding and set it down on the mantelpiece with a snap. 'My study. Now.'

Lord Mountnessing turned and made his way out of the reception room. They followed close behind, leaving a trail of avid eyes and speculative whispering in their wake.

Alec scanned the inquisitive faces as people made way for them, searching for one of her particular friends. It would be better if he could palm her off on one of them. This was not an interview Lady Julia needed to attend. Both men were going to have to speak bluntly, and it wasn't going to be pleasant. No gently born lady should have to go through that kind of scene.

No matter what she'd done.

'You should make yourself scarce now,' he murmured into Lady Julia's ear, when he failed to spot anyone to take care of her. 'This isn't going to be pleasant.'

'You think I'm going to run away and hide while you and my father decide my whole future,' she hissed back at him. 'I think not!'

'But you agreed to let me handle this." He

couldn't believe she'd changed her mind so quickly." I'm only trying to spare you unpleasantness. Your father is going to lose his temper when he finds out what we've done. He may say things he later regrets. Better for you to face him once he's had time to cool down, and can speak to you rationally.'

She shot him a suspicious look through narrowed eyes.

'I can handle my own father. But if you think I'm going to trust you, or meekly do as you say, at a time like this, then you have another think coming!'

'I might have known,' he muttered, as the earl opened a door to their left, and went into a book-lined room. 'He is the one who has spoiled you, isn't he? The one who has made you think you can have whatever, or whomever, you want for the crooking of your finger?'

'He has done no such thing,' she just had time to spit back at him, before the earl reached yet another fabulously intricate fireplace, turned, and took up the very same position he'd adopted in the ballroom. Legs apart, with his back to the writhing Greek demi-gods.

'Well?'

'I have to beg your pardon, sir,' replied Alec

stiffly, 'but also to inform you that your daughter and I will be getting married.'

'Indeed? And what makes you think that I will grant my permission?'

'We have been indiscreet. And the indiscretion was witnessed.'

The earl's shrewd eyes flicked over the state of Lady Julia. His lips compressed into a hard line for a second. Then he looked at Alec again.

'By whom was this indiscretion witnessed?'

Alec couldn't believe the old man was taking this all so calmly. He'd expected an explosion of wrath. But it seemed that the earl was the type to weigh everything up, and take his vengeance cold. He stood a little straighter.

'Lady Julia's companion. I forget her name.'

'Marianne,' put in Lady Julia in a woeful, almost penitent voice.

'And the leading lady,' he continued, not sure whether to be annoyed by her interruption, or glad she was doing what she could to soften the old man's heart.

'I believe she goes under the name of the Nightingale,' he said, squeezing Lady Julia's hand hard in the hopes she'd understand he'd rather she didn't interrupt again.

'And a young man, by name David.'

Something flared in the old man's eyes at that.

'David Kettley?'

Lady Julia nodded her head. Then hung it. She looked the very picture of repentance. If he was her father, he might almost have been taken in by it.

But the old man didn't look the least bit compassionate.

'And you, sir, what have you to say for yourself? What do you mean by it, eh?'

'Oh, please, don't be cross with him, Papa,' blurted Lady Julia, before he'd managed to utter a single word of the excuse he'd planned to make. 'It was all my fault.'

What? She was admitting it? For some reason, though he'd said the very same thing not five minutes ago, hearing her try to take the blame didn't sit right with him.

'We are both—' he put in swiftly before floundering to a halt. He may not have come up with a story to satisfy the heart of a doting father, but he knew the truth wasn't going to suffice. 'That is, neither of us—that is—the truth is, sir, that...'

Actually, there could probably be only one excuse he could give that might, eventually, mollify an outraged father.

'Our feelings for each other overwhelmed us.'

That eyebrow went up again. 'Your feelings?'

'Yes, sir. We got carried away.' Well, that was

certainly true. He couldn't remember ever being so completely entranced by a woman. There had been nothing in his head but her. After all the months of oak and muscle and sinew, the sweetly scented softness of her body had been too alluring to resist. He hadn't stopped to think. He'd just wanted to drown in the haven she offered. The heaven.

'And when Lady Julia says it was her fault, she can only mean, of course, in permitting me to take her to a secluded spot when she knew it was not at all the thing. The blame for what happened afterward was entirely mine. As a man, an experienced man, I should not have let things go so far.'

'And how far, exactly,' said the old man in that cold, forbidding tone, 'did things go?'

He felt Lady Julia flinch. He squeezed her hand again.

'I regret to have to inform you, sir, that your daughter could be with child.'

The earl went very still. Not a single flicker of emotion appeared on his face. But in a voice that could have frozen the Thames, he said, 'You have, in effect, left me with no choice.'

Chapter Three

With child? Heavens, that possibility hadn't even crossed Julia's mind.

But of course, doing what they'd just done was obviously what started babies.

And just as obviously, she would have to marry the man who might have started one growing inside her. She simply couldn't have a baby out of wedlock. She couldn't do that to a child.

And no matter what she felt for the father, she would love her own child. She knew only too well how much a child could suffer because of what the parents felt about each other. She'd always known that the main reason her father hadn't been able to warm to his first two sons was because they resembled their mother in looks.

The thought sent a fresh chill down her spine. Captain Dunbar was very, very angry with her.

What if that anger never went away? What if the resentment he felt about having to marry her spilled over to their child?

'It appears,' her father continued, jerking her back to her present difficulties, 'that my daughter has escaped the wiles of one fortune hunter only to fall into the clutches of another.'

Alec's stomach turned over, as her father brought that aspect of the case to his attention. Not only was he going to be saddled with a wife, he was also going to be accused of marrying her for her money. Like father, like son, they'd say. When he'd worked so hard, for so long, to prove he wasn't that kind of man at all. Damn the chit!

'No, Papa!' Lady Julia took a step forward, as though attempting to defend him from the invisible darts her father was shooting his way. 'I told you it was my fault. Entirely my fault. He didn't even know it was *me* in the orangery. Just look at the way I'm dressed.'

'Eh?' The earl stopped trying to send Alec to the coldest reaches of hell by sheer force of will, and turned to look at his daughter.

'He thought I was the Neapolitan Nightingale. I...I deliberately deceived him and lured him out there...'

'You did what? Why?'

'Well…' She swallowed and then started gazing frantically along the rows of books on the shelves, as though she might find inspiration amongst the stiff leather spines.

Yes, what excuse could she possibly come up with to explain this evening's fantastic sequence of events? Without, that is, confessing the whole truth, which would land her friends in the very trouble she'd already declared she wanted to spare them.

Or laying the entire blame upon his shoulders, which it looked as though she was equally reluctant to do. Which came as quite a surprise. He would have thought she'd have been only too willing to throw him to the lions. Instead, she'd drawn the earl's fire down on herself. Although from the look on her face now, she hadn't really thought it through. She'd acted on impulse. And backed herself into a corner.

Alec supposed he had to give her credit for speaking up in his defence. He hadn't expected her to demonstrate the slightest shred of honour over this affair, not given the way it had come about.

'Don't say another word,' he advised her. He'd come in here seething with resentment at the way she'd trapped him. But she'd drawn the line at letting her father think he was a fortune hunter as well as a despoiler of innocence. It would cost him nothing to return the favour.

Besides, he could see she was floundering in a welter of equally unpalatable choices. Whatever lie she might choose to tell her father next was only likely to plunge them both into even deeper water. And he was used to thinking on his feet. Alec knew, only too well, that no matter how meticulously you planned an assault, something always cropped up that you couldn't possibly have foreseen. The success or failure of many a mission had depended on his ability to adapt to such new challenges.

'My lord,' he said, turning to her father, 'I am sure your daughter did not know what she was doing. She is so naïve—'

'No, I won't have you taking the blame, and everyone saying you are a fortune hunter when it is no such thing,' she cut in, hotly. 'I may not have planned for things to go so far, but—' She broke off, blushing. 'Papa—you…you saw how he was with all the ladies. So curt. So dismissive. How he refused to take any notice of me at all.'

The old earl's wintry gaze turned on her. He regarded her coldly for some moments. 'I have spoiled you,' he said. 'You saw a man who wouldn't pay court to you, and decided you must have him, by hook or by crook.'

It hadn't been like that. It hadn't been the least like that. She had detested him.

So why was she implying that it was? Why was she willing to shoulder the blame herself? She could easily have painted him as the very sort of opportunistic fortune hunter her father had taken him for. Instead, she was clearing his name.

And he couldn't even contradict her story, not without exposing what she'd really been up to out there... Ah! So that was it. A matter of saving face. She'd rather her father think *he* was the man she'd wanted to seduce all along, than for him to know how very far her true plans had gone awry.

He gave a sort of mental shrug. If that was the way she wanted to play it—fine.

'Well,' said the earl with weary resignation. 'At least this one is an improvement on the last fellow you fancied yourself in love with. At least nobody will blink at the connection. Only the manner by which it came about.'

'Yes, Papa. He is the Earl of Auchentay, as well as being a naval captain, is he not? And you always did say I should marry within my own class.'

'The title is hollow, sir,' he felt duty bound to point out. 'My lands are mortgaged—'

'But still in your possession?'

'Aye, but not likely to bring in any revenue, beyond what I get for renting the house and land. Which isn't very good land, either.'

'You won't be needing the rent so very much now you are marrying into my family. Julia's dowry will enable you to buy half-a-dozen Scottish properties, I dare say, if you had a hankering for them.'

'I'll not be squandering your daughter's money on foolishness of that sort,' he said testily. A man should take care of his womenfolk, not marry them for their dowry then fritter it away. Making free with his wife's money would smack too much of what his father had done—marrying an heiress then gambling away her entire fortune. Something he'd sworn he'd never do.

Not that lifting the mortgages would be a bad thing, if he could do it.

And he would like to improve conditions for his tenants, too. But...

'I had no thought of that when we—that is when I—'

The earl held up his hand in a peremptory gesture. 'Spare me the details of what you were, or were not, thinking when she took you out to the orangery.'

'Aye, sir.' For the first time that night, he felt his cheeks heat in a flare of embarrassment. He'd been too long at sea, too long without a woman to have been thinking of anything but the glorious release the siren in the blue-silk gown had appeared to be offering. He just wasn't used to being surrounded by so many females, all revealing so much flesh. There'd been nothing but delicate arms, and slender necks, and tantalising bosoms wherever he'd looked, ever since he'd arrived. And all of them belonging to gently reared girls who were out of bounds. He'd been so frustrated, what with one thing and another, that by the time a mature, available woman—or so he'd believed—had offered him the opportunity to do something about it, he hadn't stopped to think.

He'd just followed her out to the orangery like a lamb to the slaughter.

'Whig, I suppose, are you? Like so many of your countrymen?'

'Aye, but—'

'Good, good. You'll be taking up your seat in the House, in due course. When you do, it may interest you to know I have the ear of—'

'No. My lord, it is very good of you to take a concern in my future, but I must tell you right now I have no head for politicking.'

'Then what do you plan to do, now the war is over? England doesn't need so many ships. Nor so many captains. Do you intend to return to your ancestral lands and take up the reins of estate management?'

Alec hadn't thought about it. He'd still been in the process of gutting his last ship when he'd received that letter from Lizzie which had brought him hotfoot to Ness Hall. Getting married and restoring his ancestral home had been the last thing on his mind.

'You didn't expect to be pressed into marriage, did you, by Gad!'

It was as if Lord Mountnessing had read his mind. Not only that, but his cold expression had melted into something approaching sympathy, the words sounding downright apologetic. Having given them both a hearing, he'd clearly decided to blame his headstrong daughter.

And it *was* her fault. *All* her fault.

Yet he couldn't just stand here and let her take all the blame. It wouldn't be the act of a gentleman.

'I did not, no, but I can only say what I always say to men pressed into the Navy. This is my life now. No point in complaining. Just have to make the best of it.'

He felt her stiffen at his side. Probably in outrage that he should speak of making the best of marriage, when she must consider it ten times the disaster he did.

'Quite so,' said the earl drily. 'Julia—' he turned to his daughter '—I need to speak with Captain Lord Dunbar in private.'

'Oh, no, Papa—'

'Oh, but, yes, my girl,' said the earl firmly. 'You need not fear I am about to tear the poor fellow to shreds. But we do need to deal with all the dull, legal matters with our lawyers. Settlements, and so forth.'

'Yes, but—'

'But nothing. I am too disappointed in you to bear looking at you tonight. Tomorrow, when I have come to terms with your behaviour, you may say whatever you wish. I dare say I shall even be able to consider forgiving you once my anger has cooled.'

'Thank you, Papa,' she said in a small, penitent voice. He glanced sideways at her downbent head. If he were a doting father, her pose would have wrung his withers.

As he was not, it made him want to wring her neck.

'We will announce your engagement tomorrow, at the Hunt Ball,' Lord Mountnessing continued. 'Too many people saw you coming in from the garden in a state of disarray for us to prevent gossip. But at least we can turn it into the kind that nobody will very much mind. And then everyone can attend your wedding before they return home. We can fit most of them into the chapel. We even have a bishop on hand to perform the ceremony—'

'Uncle Algernon?' Lady Julia's head shot up, and she wrinkled her nose.

'And there will be no problem procuring a licence. So we can hold the wedding the day after tomorrow.'

'Oh, but—'

He turned a wintry stare on his daughter. 'If you are going to say something about not having time to shop for bride clothes, or anything of that nature, then I have to tell you, my girl, that you should have thought of that before you dressed up like a trollop and all but ruined a man who has so far served his country in a brave and commendable fashion.'

Nothing commendable about deflowering his host's daughter though, was there? Angry with her though he was, still it rankled to hear the man scold her, in his hearing, whilst remaining silent in regard to his own conduct. He'd rather the man had ordered him flogged.

For Lord Mountnessing had been a remarkably generous and understanding host. He hadn't batted an eyelid when he'd shown up two days ago without an invitation, demanding to see his sister. Instead, after hearing a brief, and strategically censored, version of what had brought him here, Lord Mountnessing had told him he was welcome to stay for as long as he needed, to get the business with the wayward girl settled to his satisfaction. True, he'd then proceeded to serve him up as a sort of after-dinner entertainment to stimulate the jaded palates of the lords, poets, and bishops already *in situ*. Nothing like having a serving naval officer, who could provide eye-witness accounts of battles they'd only been able to read about in the papers before.

Though he found it hard to speak about his part in any of the actions in which he'd been involved, he felt he owed it to his host to repay his hospitality by at least answering any question put to him as honestly as he was able. And so, each evening after dinner, when the ladies withdrew, Alec had rendered accounts of various engagements in which he'd fought, drawn verbal sketches of the more famous among the officers with whom he'd served, and attempted descriptions of the various countries where he'd dropped anchor.

It generally ended in them all raising their glasses to him. Which he'd hated. His answering toast had always been to all the other gallant officers and men who'd served with him.

Aye, and died, too, in defence of their country. Though the memory of all the friends he'd lost over the years wasn't all that left a bitter taste in his mouth. It was the fact that these pampered, soft gentlemen felt a sort of patriotic glow from just drinking a toast to the men who'd actually gone out and done the dirty work. That they felt a part of an action they'd never seen, just because he'd told them about it. And though possibly one or two of them might have followed the course of the war against France, the general level of ignorance of the others had been hard to stomach.

They hadn't cared, not really, that men like him had spent their entire adult life fighting so that they could lounge about their clubs and country estates, secure from threat of invasion.

'I shall do all in my power,' said Lord Mountnessing, now, to his daughter, 'to prevent any slur being cast upon his name because of this. And you will do the same, d'ye hear me?'

She hung her head again. And in a small, chastened voice, a voice that might have fooled him had he not known how many lies she'd told this evening, said, 'Yes, Papa.'

One good thing about having been at war for most of his adult life was that Alec was used to surprise attacks from the enemy. Not that Lady

Julia was his enemy, but she'd certainly surprised him. Which meant he'd had to come up with a strategy to deal with the new tack on which he was going to have to steer his life. He'd spoken the truth last night when he'd said that, like a press-ganged man, there was no point in struggling against the inevitable. Marriage, like life on board ship, would depend a great deal upon how a man went about it. So the question was, what did he want from marriage?

He'd had a vague notion of finding a sympathetic companion, one day, eventually, to be a mother to his children. A woman he could trust to run his household while he was away, and make it a place he'd be glad to return to after an arduous voyage.

Instead, he was going to have to make a life with a woman he neither liked nor respected. He was facing a lifetime with a challenging, unprincipled, hot-blooded siren for his wife. Just as she was facing a lifetime with the last man on earth she would have chosen, to judge from the look on her face when the masks had come off.

Well, he'd been faced with seemingly impossible challenges before. He wouldn't have gained promotion to captain without displaying ingenuity and daring. Could making a success of his marriage truly be more daunting than closing with a French frigate twice the size of his own vessel, or leading a boarding party against apparently insurmountable odds?

No. Besides, though his mind balked at spending a lifetime with a woman of Lady Julia's stamp, his body wasn't paying attention. His body was eager to engage with her all over again.

And so he planned to tell her. At least, that his conclusion was that they were both going to have to make adjustments. Huge adjustments, if they didn't want to make each other completely miserable. He had to let her know that he bore her no ill will, that he was willing to put in the effort required to make the match run as smoothly as it could, all things considered. And not just for themselves, but for the sake of any children they might have. He didn't want his children to become casualties of the kind of warfare waged between his own parents.

To that end, he'd decided to go along with the fiction that this was a love match. He was pretty certain she'd see the sense of that. For the one thing he'd learned about her last night was that she didn't want anyone to suspect he wasn't her choice. Which suited him fine. Alec didn't want anyone to know what a tangle they'd landed in, either, nor have any shadow of scandal cast over his children's lives. So he had to speak to her in private, as soon as possible, and negotiate terms.

Lizzie had informed him, when he'd managed to corner her briefly at luncheon the day before, that most ladies took breakfast on trays, in their rooms. She'd offered it up as an explanation as to why he'd not been able to locate her, though it was a poor excuse. She'd been avoiding him. And continued to do so.

Women! He still hadn't got to the bottom of what Lizzie was up to—though he hadn't been in Ness Hall for five minutes before discovering it wasn't what she'd led him to believe—and now he was entangled in another net, cast by another scheming, manipulative female.

But at least he could begin to make some headway with Lady Julia. Though he had hardly seen any female make it to the breakfast table during the time he'd been here, and scarcely more of the men either, she'd always been up, acting as hostess.

Or, as he'd thought of it before last night, queening it over the breakfast table and all its occupants.

Well, he'd have to erase any trace of disdain from his face before he spoke to her this morning. The success of his plan depended on it.

As he descended the stairs, he schooled his features into what he hoped passed for the kind of expression a man would wear, who'd just been granted the hand of a woman with whom he was infatuated.

He was glad he'd taken the precaution. There were decidedly more people clustered around the table this morning. Mostly men. Dressed in riding gear.

Of course—the hunt.

It was a tradition for the guests staying here to join the local hunt on Boxing Day, so Lord Mountnessing had informed him upon arrival. He'd even offered to provide him with a mount, should he wish to take part.

He was glad he'd declined now.

He glanced to the head of the table, where Lady Julia was sitting next to her father. Alec breathed a sigh of relief. For she was dressed in a simple morning gown, which meant she wouldn't be joining the hunt either.

It would give him an opportunity, he hoped, to speak with her alone. Surely, with so many of the houseguests being out of doors, they would be able to find ten minutes in which to negotiate the terms of truce? It shouldn't take much longer than that. He'd already seen signs she might be amenable to his terms when she'd admitted she'd been at fault, and defended him against the charge of being a fortune hunter.

Lady Julia was sitting, as usual, at her father's left hand. She looked pale, but calm. Her eyes were clear. She didn't look as if she'd spent the night weeping into her pillow, at least. Nobody would guess how very upset she must be to have landed herself in this predicament.

He ignored the footman who was holding out a chair halfway along the table, went to where she was sitting, and pulled out his own chair, sitting down on it without taking his eyes from her face.

Which put paid to her pallor, anyway.

'Good morning, my lord,' she said, then, her blush deepening, lowered her head to stare at her plate.

'Good morning, indeed,' he replied, edging his chair a little closer to hers.

One or two people, he noted out of the corner of his eye, were already shooting curious glances their way.

He leaned in close.

'Follow my lead,' he murmured into her ear. Then took a crust of her toast from her plate and popped it into his own mouth.

'Coffee or tea, my lord?' A footman thrust a silver pot between them, dangerously close to his face, obliging him to heel to port. He had to admire the servant's loyalty. And wonder at the devotion she appeared to have inspired in him, since he'd come to her defence from what he must assume was an importunate male guest, with such alacrity.

'Ale, if you have it,' he replied, which made the servant glower at him, since it meant he'd have to desert his mistress, to go to the sideboard and fetch him a tankard.

By this time, all eyes were upon them. And conversation ebbed. Claiming the place at her side, and whispering into her ear had been enough to raise brows. But the fact that she was doing nothing to rebuff him, when he'd previously observed her repelling all boarders with chilling hauteur, was clearly such unusual behaviour that it invited speculation.

'What the deuce,' said Lord Staines, who was sitting on the earl's other side, 'do you think you are about, sir? How dare you treat my sister with such familiarity at the breakfast table?' He blinked as though realising the absurdity of what he'd just said, and added, 'Or anywhere else, come to that!'

'No need to get into a pucker, Staines,' the earl said drily. 'I meant to announce it today anyway. The pair of them have decided to tie the knot.'

Alec carried Julia's hand to his lips, striving

to look as though she'd just made him the happiest man in the world.

'And they have my blessing,' said her father, shooting Lord Staines a frosty look.

Masterly. Lord Mountnessing had concealed his displeasure at their behaviour by turning it all upon his son, for speaking out of turn. Nobody would now guess that he was far from happy about the match. Or the way it had come about. Nor even the fact that he'd had to announce the betrothal at breakfast, rather than at the ball later on, as he'd planned.

'Good grief,' said a man who looked so very much like Staines that he had to assume they were brothers. 'She's finally deigned to drop the handkerchief.'

'No call for vulgarity of that sort, Whitney,' said Lord Mountnessing, confirming his suspicion that they were related. 'Mixed company.'

There were only two ladies present. One of whom was Lady Julia. The other, a matron who was rigged out in full hunting gear, uttered a little gurgle of laughter.

'No need to mince words for my benefit,' she said. 'I think it's marvellous. Especially the fact that I'm clearly one of the first to find out about this sudden turn of events. Your other aunts are going to be green with envy, Julia dear, that I found out before they did.'

She popped a forkful of eggs into her mouth with a cat-like smile.

'So,' said Lord Staines, dourly, 'I suppose this means you are going to break out the champagne.'

'Too early for that,' replied the earl, firmly.

'I didn't mean at the breakfast table,' retorted Lord Staines.

'No?'

Lord Staines glowered at his father. And Alec, who'd put the man's ruddy complexion down to his love of outdoor pursuits, now wondered whether it owed as much to consumption of alcohol.

'We will have champagne *tonight*, to mark the occasion,' said the earl to Lady Julia, turning his shoulder to his heir. 'Instead of making the announcement just before supper, as I'd planned, we'll let everyone know that this year's Hunt Ball will serve as your betrothal ball as well. I am sure all those radicals, who are forever decrying the shocking extravagance of the ruling classes, will applaud the economy of utilising an occasion when all your family are already about you.'

'Just as you say, Papa,' she said, half-rising from her seat to place a dutiful kiss upon his cheek.

Her apparent meekness made him feel a trifle nauseous. The last thing she wanted was to have a ball celebrating her union with a man she detested. And as for being pleased that all her family would be about them—neither the earl nor his daughter, from what he'd observed, seemed all that fond of any of the others.

But perhaps it was as well to know exactly how duplicitous she could be. Alec would be on his guard with her, which would stand him in better stead heading into the choppy waters of the matrimonial sea, than the blinkered hopes and dreams of men who believed their brides were paragons of virtue. He was at least going into this with his eyes open. There would be no shocks along the way. For he'd already seen her at her worst.

'My sweet,' he said, when at last she'd finished pushing a selection of meats and bread around her plate, signifying the end of breakfast. 'Will you allow me to escort you for a walk about the gardens?'

'In this weather?' The man who looked so very like Lord Staines shot a disbelieving glance out the window.

'You're going hunting in it, Herbert,' Julia re-torted.

'Yes but *I* don't care about getting my clothes muddied,' he replied scornfully.

'Plenty of gravel walks in the grounds,' put in the matron, with a twinkle in her eye. 'So she won't need to get her skirts muddy and there are all sorts of convenient little outbuildings, should it come on to rain.'

Did everyone feel they had the right to make observations about how he intended to spend his day?

'Captain Lord Dunbar won't have time for strolling round the grounds this morning,' Lord Mountnessing informed the table at large. 'I've arranged for Benson—my man of business,' he explained to Alec, 'to attend us in the library. We have a lot of documents to sign.'

'Plenty of time for that, I should have said,' remarked Lord Staines.

'No, you really shouldn't,' replied his father coldly.

Lord Staines narrowed his eyes. His lips twisted into the beginnings of a snarl.

'What Papa meant,' put in Lady Julia swiftly, 'is that we are going to marry very soon. As soon as can be arranged. So there isn't much time.'

Lord Staines didn't look the slightest bit grateful to her for attempting to smooth over their father's cutting remark. Instead, he turned his venom on her.

'You? The embodiment of all the virtues? Getting married in a hurry? To a man you only met two days ago?' He laughed rather nastily. 'You do know what people are going to say, don't you? They are going to say you *have* to get married. Lord, if that were only true! I'd give a monkey to hear you'd been knocked off that pedestal on which you stand looking down your nose at all us lesser mortals.'

'That's enough, Staines,' growled Lord Mountnessing, as Lady Julia turned an even deeper shade of red.

'By Gad, I think you've hit the nail on the head,' cried his brother. 'Just look at her face!'

Indignation sent him surging to his feet.

'If either one of you,' he snarled, glaring from one sneering, malevolent face to the other, 'dare repeat such foul accusations again, I shall—' He stopped, recalling that it wasn't the done thing to duel with one's brothers-in-law. Even if they hated her. Which it appeared, from their faces and the pleasure they took in baiting her, that they did.

He didn't know what she'd done to rouse that hatred, but whatever it was, no man who had a sister ought to treat her with such contempt. Especially not in public.

'The reason we have decided to marry so swiftly is—'

'Is none of their business,' Julia said, cutting him off before he had time to manufacture an excuse. 'Don't descend to their level. They'd enjoy nothing better than starting a brawl over the breakfast table.' She gave them a scornful look.

Lord Mountnessing rose from the table. 'Come, my lord. We have more important issues to deal with than petty family squabbles.' He tossed his napkin on the table with the sort of disdain that told everyone present exactly what he thought of his sons.

'I shall have to go,' he said, bending down to murmur into Julia's ear, hoping it looked as though he was whispering an endearment. 'But I must speak with you privately at some time today. When can we meet?'

She twisted her own napkin between her fingers. 'I don't know. I don't know. I have a thousand-and-one things to do today.'

'I won't have you avoiding me,' he growled. This was what Lizzie was already doing—coming up with feeble excuses when what they needed to do was sit down in private and talk.

'If you don't think of a time and place, I shall hunt you down.'

'Very well, very well. Oh, um, how about... as soon as you have finished with Papa and Benson? In the orangery.'

He quirked one eyebrow. Really?

She flushed, and lifted her chin.

'I will be waiting for you there.'

Chapter Four

Captain Lord Dunbar despised her! Oh, he'd been trying to hide it, but he wasn't a very good actor. He'd been wearing a brave, rather resolute smile when he'd entered the room but he hadn't been sitting next to her for more than a minute before she detected the anger and distaste simmering just below the surface. And as for the way he'd demanded she meet him, so that they could *speak privately*. Oh, she had no doubt what kind of things he wanted to discuss. No doubt at all.

Especially after the way he'd looked at her when she'd suggested they meet in the orangery...

Even now she cringed at the message his wintry grey eyes had sent her. He thought she was a trollop. A scheming baggage.

And if he did, she had nobody to blame but herself.

She sniffed loudly, blinked hard, and quickened her flight up the stairs. She had to get to her room, where she could pace up and down, or throw something, or scream into her pillow. She was not going to give way in public. She was not.

Both Papa and Captain Dunbar were doing their best to conceal how they felt, which was shielding her from any threat of censure. She must not be the one to give the game away by giving so much as a hint that there was anything amiss.

Julia got to her room, shut the door firmly, then sagged back against it.

She was going to be married to a man who despised her. In the chapel where, for years, she'd dreamed of marrying David...

Oh, David. Her stomach contracted into a knot of pain.

The way he'd looked at her! She slid to the floor, landing with a bump on the bare boards, covered her face with her hands, and groaned.

However was she going to get through it? How was she going to walk down the aisle to wed another man if David was sitting in the congregation, watching? Remembering her with her bare legs wrapped round Captain Dunbar's waist— yes, for that was the way he was always going to picture her, now. Just as she was always going to remember him with that appalled, disgusted look on his face.

Perhaps he wouldn't attend, though. He wouldn't want to attend, surely? And who was likely to invite him, come to that? The chapel was not all that big. Wouldn't it be filled with all those currently staying as guests in the house itself? Anyway, she would be in charge of issuing invitations, wouldn't she?

So—that was one problem dealt with.

She raised a trembling hand to her brow. Rubbed at the furrow between her eyebrows where a headache was beginning to form.

Oh, but it was tempting to use that as an excuse to stay in her room and hide all day. She didn't know how she was going to face *anyone*, never mind David. But she would have to. Almost her entire family had come to stay for Christmas. Not to mention a smattering of those people in whom Papa was currently interested. The poet whose latest work was all the rage. The brace of scientists who'd discovered something or other. Not only was it her duty to ensure they were all enjoying their stay, but the family would also think it was their right to ask her why she'd suddenly, as Herbert had put it, *dropped the handkerchief,* when until now she'd managed to evade all attempts to get her to the altar.

Her unmarried cousins would also want to know how she'd managed to snare Captain Lord Dunbar when all their efforts to get him to notice them had failed.

When she thought of the way the girls had sighed over whispered rumours of his *prowess* in various naval battles, gazed adoringly at his *rugged profile*, simpered, and giggled, and generally made total fools over themselves, because he was so *manly*, it made her want to scream. Because she'd seen the man behind the reputation. The reputation, she reflected waspishly, that he'd done his best to promote with all those tales he'd regaled the gentlemen with over the port.

And the man behind the so-called hero of the British navy was dour as well as being a braggart. Harsh, and judgemental, too, if his own sister's determination to avoid him was anything to go by. Nobody knew a man quite so well as his own sister. And his sister, Lady Lizzie Dunbar, had been doing her level best to avoid him, even though he'd been away at sea for so long. If he'd been even a halfway decent brother, surely she would have been pleased to see him? Surely she would have wanted to spend every moment she could with him? Instead, her attempts to hide from him had reminded her of the way, as a little girl, she'd always done her utmost to evade her own brothers whenever they'd come home from school in the long vacation.

And this was the man she was going to have to marry.

She pushed herself up from the floor and made her way to her dressing table. Within the many pots scattered across its surface there must surely be one that could help her look as though she was an excited bride, on the eve of her wedding to the man she loved, with such fervour she'd anticipated her vows.

Although—her hand stilled as she reached for a pot of rouge—only a few people knew she'd actually done so. If Marianne, or Nellie, or David, had let the cat out of the bag, breakfast would have been an ordeal of an entirely different nature.

Everyone who'd heard would have dragged themselves out of bed to goggle at the spectacle of Lady Julia Whitney, *in love*. As it was, the half-dozen or so habitually early risers had behaved the way they always did. There hadn't been a keen glance or muttered aside to suggest she'd become the subject of gossip.

Not until Captain Lord Dunbar had made his way to her side and played the part of adoring swain.

She dipped her brush in the rouge pot, idly

swirling it round and round. She still couldn't really understand it. He'd been trying to make it look as though he was delighted to be marrying her. When he was anything but.

Perhaps he'd calmed down overnight, and was now resigned to his fate?

Absentmindedly, she flicked the rouge over her cheeks. No, that couldn't be it. He hadn't looked *resigned* to his fate. He'd looked determined. As though he'd decided to make the best of it. Hadn't he said something to that effect last night? It was hard to recall. She'd been such a seething mass of mortification, and loss, and dread, and anger, and…oh, a dozen other negative emotions.

But later, when she'd tried to get to sleep—oh, heavens! She caught sight of herself in the mirror, her cheeks such a deep shade of carmine she looked like something out of a pantomime. She flung the rouge brush aside, dipped a clean handkerchief in water, and began to scrub it off. She had no need of rouge when she recalled the thoughts that had slid into bed alongside her last night. Far too many of them involving searching hands, and determined lips, and the feel of a large, masculine body pressing down on her. Pressing into her.

Not even now she knew exactly who it had

been doing all those wickedly exciting things. And that was another thing. Modesty dictated she should have felt ashamed, not excited. So excited that she hadn't been able to lie still. She couldn't understand herself. Even thinking about it *now* made her feel all...

She wrung out the handkerchief and dabbed at her heated cheeks in an attempt to reduce the redness that the rouge, and the blushing, and the scrubbing had produced. Though perhaps a natural blush wasn't such a bad look to wear. Didn't they talk of blushing brides? People would expect her to blush, and look a little uncomfortable when they began to congratulate her over her marriage.

And they would congratulate her. Everyone considered Captain Lord Dunbar to be a terrific catch. His name had often been in the papers, in connection with some great naval victory or other. Nobody cared that *he* was penniless.

Oh. She sat up a little straighter. Hadn't Papa said something last night about him now being able to buy as much property as he wanted? She'd been so angry that he wasn't going to cut up stiff over the settlements, the way he'd threatened to do when she'd told him of her intention to marry David, that she hadn't taken any notice of Captain Dunbar's reaction to the news he was about to become a wealthy man. But perhaps that was why he looked more cheerful this morning. He'd had all night to consider what it would mean to be able to spend her fortune however he liked.

Well, she thought, shrugging one shoulder, he'd obviously decided that her money was some compensation for the fact he hadn't wanted to have anything to do with her, let alone marry her.

Something cold landed on her lap. She looked down to see that she'd squeezed her handkerchief so hard a rivulet of pink water was trickling over her dressing table and onto her gown.

She'd have to get changed. Bother. Now he'd think she'd done so just to impress him—if he was the kind of man who noticed what a woman wore.

She'd pick something as close to this morning gown as she could, then. And hope he couldn't tell the difference between muslin and cambric.

It was only as she went to ring for a maid that it struck her that on any other day Marianne would normally have been in here by now. Julia wouldn't have needed to ring for a maid at all. Marianne would have helped her to change. But Marianne was clearly too embarrassed to face her this morning.

And no wonder.

* * *

Alec paused and narrowed his eyes as he left the ballroom through the door on to the terrace. Though whether it was the bright sunshine, or his reaction to Lord Mountnessing's attitude that made him blink, it would be hard to say.

Not that he'd been surprised to find the old man so keen to get his wayward daughter off his hands. Alec hadn't been surprised either, all things considered, to find her money tied up in such a way that if he had been a fortune hunter, he'd have been mightily disappointed.

He was surprised, however, by the amount left over, free and clear, to dispose of exactly as he saw fit. For the first time in his life, there wouldn't have been any need for him to take out a loan in order to fit out a ship—had he a command awaiting him. He could have bought the best supplies, silver buckles for his shoes, new lace for his uniform—hell, he could have gone the whole hog and purchased a new uniform altogether while he was at it.

And still be able to leave his wife living in the kind of luxury she'd always been used to enjoying.

Of course, he'd never be sure who she'd be enjoying it with, but that was a risk all men who spent most of their lives at sea had to run.

Shaking his head, like a dog caught in a shower of rain, he set off across the terrace with the measured tread his officers and crew called his 'mulling' walk—behind his back, naturally. Any landlubber who saw him would have assumed he was just out for a stroll. But the way he clasped his hands behind his back and the angle of his downbent head were a certain sign to those who knew him. He was mulling over a plan. A complex plan, if his completely wooden expression was anything to go by. The deeper his thoughts, the less they always showed on his face.

Or so his crew had believed.

Right now the thoughts uppermost on his mind concerned the woman he was about to marry. In particular, did he stand any chance of making such a spoiled, society beauty pay him any heed?

He didn't hold with beating wives, though it was within his legal rights to do so, should she misbehave. It might make a certain kind of man feel better, but he wasn't that sort. And yet her father had just informed him that he was relying on his son-in-law to discipline his *lively*, *self-willed* new bride.

'I've always been too soft with Julia,' the earl had admitted ruefully. 'Could never deny her anything. She was such an affectionate, demonstrative sort of child, you see. As well as being the first fruits of my second marriage. I was terribly in love with her mother.' He took a pinch of snuff then shut the box with a snap, as though he was annoyed with himself.

'She gave me another brace of sons, as well as those I had from my first wife.'

Had there been just a hint of distaste about his lips?

'But you cannot mollycoddle boys if you want them to grow up to become men.'

'Indeed not, my lord,' he'd agreed wholeheartedly. He'd gone to sea himself at the tender age of twelve. If his own father had 'mollycoddled' him, the harshness of those first few weeks on board his first ship might well have destroyed him.

'When my Maria died,' the earl had continued, 'I suppose I switched all the affection I felt for the mother to the daughter. Very much like her, you see.' He sighed. 'Now, of course, I see that it was disastrous to appear to favour her over my other children. But at the time…' He shook his head.

'However, since she claims to love you, I have no doubt she will do her best to be a good wife to you.' He frowned. '*Her* idea of a good wife. It will probably not be your idea of what a good wife should be, but then, women, you know…'

He'd finished with another of his grimaces of distaste.

Captain Dunbar had made no response. If Julia really had been in love with him, it would have been the act of a scoundrel to complain about the way she'd entrapped him. Especially since her poor old father was trying to encourage him to hope the union might bring him the same kind of happiness he'd experienced with her mother.

Nor could he very well explain that Lady Julia had been as appalled as he when their masks had come off. He hadn't needed to question her assertion that she hadn't been trying to trap *him*. He'd seen his own shock mirrored on her face. She didn't love him, but another. The last thing on her mind was making him a good wife. No, for her, it was all about saving face.

So why the hell had she asked him to meet her in the orangery? His heart started skipping like a frigate in a stiff breeze as it hove into sight. But he kept his pace even and steady. He wasn't going to betray, by any outward sign, just how much it affected him to approach the scene of last night's tryst, in broad daylight.

Which was a foolish resolution to make. The moment his mind turned to the astonishing events of the night before, his body began to behave in a most unruly manner, springing enthusiastically to attention. Giving an all-too-visibly outward sign that he was far from reluctant to be meeting her in such a secluded spot.

So it was with a frustrated growl that he tried the handle of the door, and with a scowl on his face that he knocked on it.

She emerged from behind a screen of foliage, and gestured to one of the windows. Then she went to it and threw up the sash.

'Gatley—that's our head gardener—keeps the door locked when we have guests,' she explained, beckoning him over. 'You will have to climb in through this window, as we did last night. The lock is broken, you see. But hardly anyone knows. So we won't be disturbed.'

So that was why she'd suggested they meet here. It was just as he'd thought. She was going to try to fuddle his mind with memories of last night, so that he wouldn't see whatever trap she'd laid for him today until it was too late. He'd laid enough traps, himself, when he'd needed to sneak up close to an enemy in order to inflict maximum damage, to recognise one.

Well, if she thought he was going to be tricked by a slip of a girl—again—she'd got another think coming.

The scent of tropical foliage assailed his nos-

trils the moment he'd got one leg over the sill.
And with it, a barrage of memories. The taste of
her lips, the softness of her skin, the cry of pleasure she uttered as she'd welcomed his touch.
And then the warm, wet welcome she'd given
him. The encouraging way she'd risen to his
rhythm as he'd thrust into her.

And just like that, he was ready to take her
again. Even though she no longer looked like
the siren he'd followed out here last night. Today
she was wearing one of those insipid gowns that
seemed to be the uniform with which all the girls
at this house party had been issued. Pale, and
formless, only hinting at what it concealed.

But he knew what it concealed. Had seen, or
felt, every delectable square inch of it. The palms
of his hands tingled with remembered pleasure.
He curled them into fists, refusing to allow them
free rein.

She saw the gesture and flung up her chin, as
though assuming his action was one of aggres-
sion and was squaring up for a fight.

'You wanted to talk to me?' She met his gaze
boldly. For a moment he admired her courage.
But then her eyes flickered towards the cush-
ioned bench which ran along the back wall. And
she quivered. And lowered them.

'Yes,' he grated. Seeing her standing there,

looking torn between defiance and wariness, so covered up, within inches of the place he'd stripped her, taken her, was creating a maelstrom of conflicting feelings to surge within him. Though uppermost was the desire to do it all over again. Which was out of the question.

He cleared his throat. 'We need to reach an understanding.'

She sighed, as though relieved. 'Yes. Indeed we do. But before we go any further, I just want to thank you for your forbearance.' She glanced at his clenched fists again. This time they tightened in genuine anger. What kind of man did she think he was?

'My...forbearance?'

A frown flickered across her face. 'Yes. You could have told my father exactly what I'd done, last night. Destroyed his fondness for me at one stroke. Instead, you...tried to shield me. I noted the number of times you tried to take the blame. Saying I didn't know what I was doing—'

'You didn't,' he said brusquely. 'Only a complete innocent would have lured a man out into a place such as this, dressed the way you were, and think he'd stop at a few kisses.'

'Well, I—that is, thank you.'

'I didn't mean it as a compliment,' he retorted. 'It's just the sort of hen-witted scheme Lizzie would come up with. Dressing herself like a whore, teasing a man who's been so long without a woman he's practically cross-eyed with the wanting, and then expecting him to make an honest woman of her when he does what any red-blooded man would do in the circumstances.'

'You're very cross. I understand that—'

'Do you? Do you really understand how *cross* I am?' He marched over to her and seized her upper arms. Shook her a little. 'I didn't come here to get tangled up with the likes of you. It was bad enough having to come here in the first place. And now I am here I should be dealing with my sister, not—' He broke off, shaking his head as he considered the wild goose chase Lizzie had led him on from the moment he'd come ashore.

'Is she in some kind of trouble?' Lady Julia peered up at him as though she really cared what happened to his sister.

'I didn't come here to talk about Lizzie,' he growled, thrusting her away from him. God, what the nearness of her did to him. The scent of her. The feel of her soft flesh, even through layers of cotton, or whatever it was she was wearing.

'You were the one who brought her into the conversation. I thought that perhaps that was what you wanted to talk to me about. Her future. If I can be of any help—'

'You? You are the very last person into whose care I would entrust a high-spirited lassie like Lizzie. As if she isn't enough of a handful.' He spun away from her, thrusting his fingers through his hair, not caring for once that by his gesture he was betraying his agitation. Not only to her, either. Anyone looking at him five minutes from now would know he'd done it, because it would be standing up in a spray of disordered spikes.

'I beg your pardon,' she said, coldly. 'What did you wish to speak to me about, then?'

He whirled back to her.

'Aye—that's just it. Just like her. Standing there looking at me as though butter wouldn't melt in your mouth, when you are probably hatching some devilish scheme.'

'I'm not hatching any kind of scheme.'

'Of course you are. Everyone plots and schemes, in my experience, from the lowest rating trying to get extra rum to the Admirals of the Fleet jockeying for public recognition.'

'I'm not like that!'

'You are. If that…' he gestured to the bench expressively '…wasn't the result of some devilish scheme, intended to entrap some poor man, then I don't know what is.'

She coloured. 'It wasn't a devilish scheme. David has been in love with me for ages—'

'Hah!'

'But he couldn't pluck up the courage to propose. Papa was set against the match. Because of the…the discrepancy in our fortunes, our stations.'

'I've never heard anything so maudlin, or so unlikely, in all my life.'

'You may very well sneer,' she said, her eyes kindling. 'But you make your own living doing far worse things.'

'I do not.'

'Yes, you do. I've heard all about how you hoist false colours to deceive some poor French boats, then blast them out of the water. How is what you do so very different from me…flying under false colours to…overcome the difficulties besetting David and me?'

The fact that he'd thought something very similar on the way here touched a raw nerve.

'Dear God,' he blustered defensively. 'If you cannot see the difference, then…'

'Well, come on then. Explain it to me.' She planted her fists on her hips. 'I didn't kill anyone. I didn't even intend anyone the slightest bit of harm.'

'But you did harm in the end, didn't you?'

She flinched as though he'd struck her. Then rallied, lifting her chin. 'You may not have wanted to get married, but it won't do you any harm to have control of my fortune. You have, in fact, captured a rich prize, have you not?'

It was the worst thing she could have said.

'Lower your voice.'

'I will do no such thing. How dare you try to order me about? Is this the way you intend to behave once we are married?'

When they were married? When they were married, he would…he would have the right to… all that soft flesh…

He couldn't keep his hands off her a moment longer. He strode back to her, seized her in his arms, and stopped her impudent mouth with a kiss.

Lady Julia wasn't used to such ruthless treatment. *That* was why she froze instead of slapping his face. Which was a mistake. The nearness of him, the heated pressure of his mouth on hers pitched her right back to the night before. Her stomach flipped, and an ache sprang to life between her legs. Where he'd gone the night before.

Instead of struggling to break free, like any woman with an ounce of pride would have done, she found herself melting into his embrace.

Even when he broke off, to breathe into her ear, she couldn't seem to raise a single objection.

'There's someone walking along the terrace,' he murmured hotly. Then nibbled his way along her jaw. 'And I told your father I'd do my best to make it look as though this is a love match.' He mouthed the words against her lips, so that it felt as if he was kissing her. With tiny, breathy little kisses.

'They won't think that if they find us quarrelling, will they?'

It was only when the backs of her knees hit an obstacle that she registered he'd been steering her over to the bench. She sank down onto it, the pressure of his arm round her shoulder sufficient to overcome the spongy consistency of her knees.

She heard a burst of girlish laughter, caught a flurry of pale muslin through the steamy windows, then the patter of several pairs of slippers tripping back to the house.

'That should serve to perpetuate the myth,' said Captain Dunbar.

'What?' Julia blinked up at him.

'Aye, the dazed expression on your face is very convincing. But you can drop it now. They've gone.'

Convincing? Oh! He'd kissed her because he'd heard her cousins coming. He'd done it to make

it look as though they were madly in love. It had
been bad enough when she'd assumed he'd just
been trying to stop them arguing.

But this?

All the excitement she'd been feeling curdled
and went sour.

'I suppose,' she said tartly, 'you expect me to
be grateful to you for trying to make it look as
though you are as keen on this marriage as my
father believes *me* to be.'

The moment the words left her lips, she realised they were nothing less than the truth. She
should be grateful to him. He didn't need to cover
for her. If he'd been a peevish kind of man, or a
man with little honour, he could have denounced
her from the start. And everyone would be sali-
vating over her scandalous conduct. Her reputation would be in shreds.

And she'd be embarking on a disastrous, miserable marriage.

'You should,' he snapped as he removed his
arm from her shoulder and stood up. 'But since
you do not appear to be, perhaps we should go
for that walk you promised me, rather than lingering here. This place appears to have a delete-
rious effect upon your behaviour.'

The beast! He was the one who'd swooped
down and kissed her. All she'd done was turn

up. And last night—he'd been the one doing all the swooping and kissing then, too.

'And it is no use looking at me like that,' he informed her sternly. 'Dagger looks won't have any effect upon me, any more than getting me out here, with the intent of trying to work your wiles on me again. Just because I lost my head last night when it was too dark to know who you were, I won't have you thinking you can twist me round your little finger any time you like.'

'I didn't get you out here with *any* intention,' she retorted. 'You were the one who said you wanted to talk to me in private. And you don't know the estate well enough to have arranged to meet anywhere else. Not without involving a footman. I just didn't think you'd forget how to find your way *here*, that's all.'

He glowered at her for a moment. Shook his head.

'I will never know whether you are telling the truth or not.'

'Then there's no point in talking to each other at all, is there!'

She flounced over to the window with the broken latch and tugged it up. She was halfway along the terrace before it hit her that he hadn't made any attempt to prevent her leaving. How insulting! After the readiness with which she'd agreed to his request for a private meeting, too.

She was almost at the top of the stairs before it occurred to her that she hadn't found out what he'd wanted to talk to her about. All he had told her, apart from cataloguing her every fault, was that he'd agreed to make it look like a love match, which couldn't have been what he had intended to say since he'd asked for a meeting *before* he'd gone to see her father.

Now she wished she hadn't lost her temper and flounced off. But she didn't slacken her pace. Walking swiftly was about the only outlet available for her if she didn't want to make an exhibition of herself.

But really, how much was she expected to bear? He'd insulted her, and kissed her, and accused her of getting him to the orangery so she could work some kind of wiles on him.

Wiles? She didn't have any wiles. She'd learned that the hard way, with David.

Captain Lord Dunbar was utterly impossible.

And arrogant. And overbearing. And touched in the upper works if he thought she'd enjoyed what had happened the night before so much that she'd lured him to the same spot for a repeat performance.

And when she next saw him, she vowed,

reaching her room, entering it, swirling round and slamming the door behind her as hard as she could, she'd tell him so.

'J-Julia?'

'Oh. Marianne.' Julia turned, slowly. This was all she needed. One look at Marianne's woebegone face, and the way she was wringing her hands, was enough to tell her that her companion was on the verge of bursting into tears.

And it would fall to her, as it always did, to smooth her ruffled feathers. As if she didn't have enough to contend with—she was having to act as though she was thrilled to be marrying a man who was a total brute. A brute who resented being forced into the marriage. Whilst still struggling with the grim reality of forfeiting the regard of the man she'd loved almost all her life.

Mouth tightening, she made for her dressing table and pulled out a fresh handkerchief. For when Marianne indulged in a fit of sobbing, it always took a great deal of mopping up.

Chapter Five

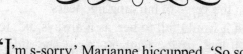

'I'm s-sorry.' Marianne hiccupped. 'So sorry!'

And then the floodgates opened. So Julia pressed the handkerchief into Marianne's hand and led her to the bed, sitting her down on it and putting her arm round her slender shoulders.

For two pins she'd have indulged in a fit of crying herself. But then Marianne had enough tears for the both of them. And it had always been Marianne's role to weep, hers to offer the shoulder upon which to do it. Because by the time Marianne had come to live with them, Julia had given up the habit of crying. She'd learned that it only made things worse. Papa became uncomfortable when he saw her crying, and sent her out of the room until she was calm again. Her older brothers mocked her. And her younger ones took their cue from her and started crying as well, which earned her a slap from their nurse.

All of which had made her vow that Marianne, at least, should have a shoulder upon which to weep should she need it.

'I…I never meant for it to happen! I swear!' Marianne lifted tear-drenched eyes to her imploringly.

'I know,' said Julia, giving her a comforting squeeze. 'You couldn't have known I'd mistake Captain Lord Dunbar for David.'

'Oh, it wasn't that! I was…I was distracted, you see, and didn't notice you going off with the wrong man. Indeed, I never thought you would go off with anyone, when David was…that is… I should have been watching you! I can't think how you came to make such a mistake! When I saw you in the orangery, with that man *on top of you*…' She gave a theatrical shudder and went off into a fresh burst of noisy sobs.

'It wasn't your fault,' Julia repeated soothingly, over and over again, to the crown of Marianne's dark head and shuddering shoulders.

Suddenly, Marianne flung up her head, and gazed at her with incomprehension.

'But how came you to make such an awful mistake?'

'Don't you recall, at the start of the masquerade, how there was a pirate prowling about the ballroom? Blackbeard the Pirate wore a tricorne hat, and a long, Cavalier-style wig, and one of those full-skirted coats. He even carried a telescope. Of course, he also had a bushy black false beard, then, but I suppose at some point he must have taken it off.' He most definitely hadn't been wearing it when she'd sidled up behind him. She distinctly recalled admiring the plane of his freshly shaved jaw.

'And to be honest, I couldn't see all that clearly through my mask. We concentrated on concealing my features, not making it easy to make out where I was going. It's hardly surprising I mistook Blackbeard for Sir Isaac Newton.'

'Yes, but to leave you out there for so long that…' Marianne shook her head, and pressed her hands to her cheeks. 'And if it hadn't been for Nellie, trying to find you so that she could stand beside you at the unmasking, it would never have occurred to me you'd gone missing. Of course, I took them straight to the orangery, as agreed, when I saw what must have happened. But…' Her eyes filled up again. 'Too late! Oh, how can you ever forgive me?'

'It was all just a series of terrible mistakes, Marianne. You warned me often enough I shouldn't attempt to force David's hand. But as usual, I wouldn't listen. So the last person to bear any blame in all of this is you. So stop crying. I can't have you crying all over the place, or people will start to think you are jealous of me getting married, or something.'

'Jealous!' Marianne looked horrified. 'How could anyone think I might be jealous of you having to marry a man who isn't David?'

'Well, you know what Nick and Herbert's relatives are like. Always trying to stir up trouble between us. Besides, they don't know how I truly felt about David, do they?'

Felt about David? Was her love already a thing to speak of in the past tense? A little perturbed that she'd just done so, she went on hastily, 'We won't give them any excuse to make snide remarks about us, will we?'

Marianne sniffed, and blew her nose, and attempted a brave smile.

'That's the spirit,' said Julia bracingly. 'There is too much to do today to worry about what the Caldicotts think about our friendship. We have a betrothal ball to organise. And then a wedding.'

'Yes. And we don't want anyone knowing that you aren't getting exactly what you want, do we?' said Marianne brightly. 'So I shall smile, and pretend I am pleased for you, and nobody will suspect a *thing*.'

With Marianne on board, she did actually feel a little better. She could certainly manage to go about her duties with a more-or-less clear head. And if her nerves did get to screaming point she could always pick up something breakable and throw it against the wall.

The Meissen figurines she detested so much remained safe until luncheon, mainly because she didn't have a spare minute to indulge her secret promise to herself to relieve her feelings by wreaking vengeance on them.

Though there must have been something about the way she approached the table that revealed the simmering broth of emotions she was striving to conceal.

'Your sister-in-law Ellen should be doing more,' observed Aunt Frances from her sofa, as Julia stalked past with her eyes fixed on the cake stand. 'Staines ought to spend more time here, so she could learn how to run a household of this size, rather than leaving it all to you. And you with a wedding to arrange, too.' She shook her head in a reproving fashion. 'No wonder you look so hagged.'

Hagged? Julia froze with her hand outstretched. 'Thank you for your concern,' she replied politely, and picked up a plate. Though what she would dearly have loved to say, was *Why don't you get up off that sofa and do something to help instead of criticising everyone else? And couching your criticism of my appearance under a cloak of concern for my health?*

But that was just typical of her aunts. They'd always all been too busy scoring points off each other to get round to doing anything useful.

'And as for poor Ellen,' Julia continued, helping herself to a generous portion of pastries and sandwiches, 'I wouldn't burden her with anything more than she has on her plate already.' Being married to Nick was a fate she wouldn't wish on any woman.

'Speaking of plates,' said her aunt. 'Do you really think you ought to put so much upon yours?' She eyed Julia's selection of cakes. Then smoothed a hand down her own, almost ethereal figure.

'Well, as you pointed out, Aunt Frances,' she replied with a tight smile, since there was no point in arguing with a woman who was never happy unless she had someone or something to criticise, 'I do have a lot of work to do, what with one thing and another, and nobody but my dear Marianne to help me. So I need to keep my strength up.'

'That girl,' said her aunt with a disdainful sniff. But was prevented from saying anything else, when *that girl* herself came in, looking as harassed as Julia felt. Marianne hurried to Julia's side, one hand fluttering to tidy her rather wind-blown hair after Aunt Frances, having raked her from head to toe, raised her eyebrows and pulled down the corners of her mouth.

'You took the message to Gatley about the flowers then,' said Julia, eyeing a smudge of what looked like moss on Marianne's gown.

'Oh!' Marianne took out a handkerchief and dabbed frantically at the stain. 'Yes,' she said, blushing, and looking anywhere but at Julia's Aunt Frances.

'Well, one thing you have to say for holding your wedding at Christmas, while your family are already all about you,' said Aunt Frances, as though Marianne wasn't there, and hadn't spoken. 'It will save you having to write out and post the invitations.'

Once again, Julia had to bite back a pithy retort. She was sick of Marianne having to endure such slights. And not only from the Caldicotts. For some reason, the only thing upon which all her aunts agreed, from whichever side of the family they sprang, was that Marianne was an encroaching hussy. A foreign encroaching hussy at that. As if she was somehow to blame for having a French father. And worse, a father who'd died penniless. They acted as though Marianne had deliberately pushed her way in at Ness Hall when the truth was she'd been brought here when she'd been far too young to have any say in the matter.

'Indeed it will,' was all she deigned to reply, though she would have liked to add that it would also deny anyone the chance to think up a refusal, too. Nick for one would have been sure to have found some excuse to avoid setting foot in Ness Hall. Let alone to attend her wedding.

Still, she had far too much to do to allow Nick's constant state of warfare with their father to distract her. Which was just as well. Organising a wedding, as well as tonight's ball, left her with no leisure to worry about her marriage. Let alone take time off to throw porcelain shepherdesses against marble fireplaces.

She didn't have time to think about Captain Dunbar, or the argument they'd had that morning, or the way he'd made her feel the night before. Not for more than a second or two, every now and then. And there was always some task on which she could concentrate, which prevented her wallowing in the shame, or the anger, or the more treacherous, quivery flashes of excitement.

In fact, there had been so many tasks that, had she not had Marianne to help her run the more tedious errands, by the evening she would have been in no fit state to attend the ball she'd spent so much time that day adapting to the circumstance of her betrothal. As it was, she would still rather have gone for a lie down, then had a tray sent to her room. But people were travelling to Ness Hall from all over the county. Invitations to the Hunt Ball had gone out weeks ago. It couldn't be cancelled, any more than she could refuse to attend.

And so Julia donned the gown she'd had made for the occasion, when it had merely been the Hunt Ball, with gritted teeth. Though she had to admit, as she checked her appearance in the mirror before going down, that it was a splendid creation. The crossover bodice flattened her bosom and then the rest of the gown swirled down in such a way that it disguised her defects, rather than clinging to them.

Although more than thirty members of her family plus assorted houseguests were going to be sitting down to dine, the first person she saw when she entered the salon where they were all assembling, was Captain Dunbar. And the minute she saw him, her whole body seemed to go on the alert. Her breasts felt full. The bodice now felt as if it was caressing her bosom, rather than confining it. Her lips parted and her heart thumped. Her legs felt too quivery to carry her all the way across the room to where he stood. She could only assume that it was all because she'd been intimate with him. No matter what her mind thought of him as a person, her body had enjoyed his body.

It could be the only thing to account for it. For she'd never reacted to a man like this before.

Not even David.

She fixed a polite, social smile in place and forced herself to walk across the room to the man she was going to have to marry, because she'd become so impatient with another.

He didn't smile back. But the look in his eyes was so intent, so focused upon her progress towards him that she felt as if he was stripping her naked in his mind. Which, instead of embarrassing her, simply made her wonder what he'd look like unclothed. She'd felt the power of his broad shoulders, the roughness of his thighs, and the skill of his calloused hands, but it had been dark. Besides, he hadn't removed a single item of clothing, not completely.

Not that she'd wanted him to!

By the time she reached his side, her face was aflame.

As he reached out and took her hand, bowed

over it, kissed it, she dimly heard someone laugh. Someone observed caustically, 'Right off her pedestal...'

Someone else chimed in with, 'It's what she always wanted, though, isn't it, a love match...?'

And the first voice again, laced with bitterness. 'And the old man let her have her way, as usual, instead of arranging something suitable and sensible, the way he did for us...'

Nick and Herbert. Seething with resentment against her, *as usual*. Though how they would crow if they knew this wasn't what it appeared at all.

From the sudden tension in Captain Dunbar's jaw, she suspected he'd heard the comments, too. But it was what he wanted, wasn't it? Or at least, what he'd agreed. They were trying to convince everyone this was a love match. That they were so in love they couldn't keep their hands off each other. So that if the story about what had happened in the orangery ever did get out, their behaviour would have an excuse everyone would accept.

It was a far cry from the truth. Which was... was... Her face grew even hotter. It was something that made it extremely hard to get through dinner. Only the occasional word or phrase broke through the daze she was in, the way Nick and

Herbert's comments had done. But she couldn't really follow the thread of any conversation, because her body was in a state of melting excitement, simply because he was sitting next to her. It was so vexing. She'd sat next to dozens of men, at hundreds of dinners, but never before had she been so aware of the muscular build of a man. Nor become flustered by the way his long, supple fingers wielded his cutlery.

She wasn't sure how she got through it. But somehow it was over and it was time to remove to the front hall, to welcome those guests who hadn't been invited to dine, and who were starting to arrive for the ball.

He stuck to her side like a limpet. Not that she made any attempt to shake him off. Though the feel of his hand at her elbow drove her half-demented. Because she couldn't help recalling where else that hand had been. And what it had done. And how it had made her feel. Just a touch to the back of her waist, or a brush against her hip sent her well on the way to feeling exactly the same.

She supposed he was doing his best to look like an adoring fiancé. And at least her blushes, coupled with his proprietary air, were enough to convince people they were madly in love. At least when her father introduced him as her fiancé—

with such a proud and pleased expression anyone would have thought he'd had a hand in arranging the match—everyone congratulated them. Even if they did so with sly barbs and knowing smiles.

Her own cheeks ached with the effort of smiling back at everyone. Her neck was stiff with the effort of keeping it still, instead of tossing her head, or shrugging either of her shoulders. And the tension that had started to form between her brows that morning was working into such proportions that she was sure to have a splitting headache before much longer.

It didn't get any easier when it was time to abandon their post and go through to the ballroom where they walked out, arm in arm, to form part of the opening set. She always felt a twinge of sadness when she was one of the first to dance upon a floor so beautifully decorated for a ball. Because the very first dance would obliterate the work of the artist who'd spent all day on his knees chalking it out. But tonight it felt especially poignant. Her own designs, for her own life, had been just as swiftly erased.

When the set ended and Captain Dunbar escorted her to a chair at the edge of the room, she noted sadly that there was nothing left of the artist's work but the tail of what had once been a comet, and the crowned hat of one of the huntsmen he'd drawn leaping over a five-barred gate. The rest was just smears on the floor, and smudges of chalk dust on the hems of the ladies who'd danced all over his best efforts.

And suddenly, it was all too much.

'If you will excuse me,' she said to him. 'I need to go to the ladies' retiring room.'

His grip on her arm didn't slacken. For a second or two he gave a very good impression of a man who couldn't bear to be parted from his bride-to-be for more than a second. Probably because he suspected her of getting up to mischief the minute she was out of his sight.

'You do not need to look at me like that,' she snapped. 'I really do need to take a few minutes to…collect myself. Or I am going to end up prostrate with a headache.'

He let her go with grudging acceptance—for, really, what mischief could one get up to in a ladies' withdrawing room? There was always at least one maid in attendance, ready to pin up torn flounces. As well as a steady stream of ladies making use of the chamber pots handily situated behind a bank of screens.

Julia made straight for the table upon which various restoratives and emergency provisions were laid out, and reached for the bottle of lavender water. She tipped a generous amount onto a handkerchief, and pressed it to her temples. Closed her eyes, and gratefully, deeply, breathed in the calming scent.

She felt someone sit on the stool next to her.

'I've been wanting to speak to you all day,' said the woman in a low voice.

Julia opened her eyes, and met the concerned ones of Nellie in the mirror before which they sat. Nellie picked up a pot of rice powder, placed there for any lady who needed to counteract the redness of a face overheated from her exertions on the dance floor. She began dabbing it on her face, though she didn't look the slightest bit flushed, and spoke, moving her lips as little as possible.

'I don't know what to say…' she began.

'Please, don't say anything,' replied Julia.

'But, last night…that wasn't meant to happen, was it. I mean…'

Julia sighed. Braced herself for the lie she was about to utter. 'I do apologise for dragging you into one of my schemes. It was infamous of me to use the disguise you lent me to lure poor Captain Dunbar out to the orangery. You mustn't blame yourself for anything that happened.'

'Yes, but I might have known *some* gentleman would try and cross the line. I should have kept a closer watch on you. Everyone will think so,' she finished gloomily.

'Well, if anyone *says* so, you just let me know, and I will deal with them. I shall assure them that you had no idea what I planned. That you were an entirely innocent party in all this.'

'Nobody has said anything iffy to me,' she said. 'But I still can't help feeling responsible. You couldn't have planned *that*. If only I'd known exactly why you wanted to swap costumes with me. I could have warned you that it wouldn't work out the way you wanted. Men don't treat me with the respect they accord a young lady of your quality.'

'I found that out for myself,' she said drily.

'Yes, I could see on your face what a shock it was to you.'

'Mmm,' she said vaguely. For her shock had been at seeing the man she thought was lying on top of her, standing in the doorway instead.

'I certainly didn't expect Captain Dunbar's, um, ardour,' she admitted with complete honesty. 'But indeed, he didn't do anything I didn't like. I mean…' She flushed and reached for the rice powder herself. 'I could have stopped him at any time, I'm sure I could. He didn't…force me, if that is what is worrying you.'

From the relief on Nellie's face, it clearly had been worrying her.

'I heard you arguing in the summer house this morning, you see. Then saw you running away. And I wanted to tell you that if you couldn't bear to marry him, then I could speak out, if you like, and see if we can't put a stop to it all…'

'No!' The thought of stopping the wedding filled her with panic. 'There is no need for that,' she said as calmly as she could. 'It was a tiff, what you overheard this morning, that is all.'

'Well, if you're sure?'

Nellie still looked a little worried. So Julia patted her on the hand, and summoned up her most sincere smile. 'I'm sure.'

'There's just one other thing. When Eduardo realised it was you wearing my costume all evening, he started saying some very peculiar things. And now I'm worried your father is going to be so mad about it he'll send the lot of us packing.'

'Good heavens, no! Your troupe is central to most of the entertainment over the next few days. We need you to keep the younger ones busy with rehearsals for the play, during the day, as well as continuing with your musical items for the rest of the family at night. Besides which,' she added, thinking of the hostilities simmering between

Nick and Papa, Nick and his wife, and all the aunts in varying, fluctuating combinations, 'if we were left to our own devices, someone would be strangling someone well before twelfth night.'

'Well, good.' Nellie sighed. 'That's good.'

A sudden horrid thought struck Julia. 'You… you haven't told anyone what you saw, in the orangery, have you? When you said, about Eduardo—'

'No, no, nothing like that. He just got worried because of some liberties he said he took with you, without knowing who you were, is all. I won't *never* tell what I saw in the orangey. Don't you worry about that.'

Nellie's gaze flicked to the bottle of lavender water, then back to her reflection in the mirror. 'I see a lot of things you gentry don't expect anyone to see.' She shook her head and clucked her tongue. 'Which I suspect you'd all blame on the mistletoe anyway.'

'I wasn't the only one misbehaving last night?'

Nellie grinned. 'Lawks, no. You wasn't the worst-behaved neither,' she said, lapsing into her rather less-refined accent.

'Really? How…? I mean… But…'

'Well, put it this way. Neither of you was married, was you? Not hurting anyone else with what you was doing.' She shrugged.

'Oh. Oh, my goodness.' Though she was a little shocked by what Nellie implied she'd witnessed, for the first time that day, some of her guilty shame lifted. She'd felt wretched that her plan to force her father to allow her to marry David had gone so badly awry. But at least she hadn't ended up with someone else's husband in the orangery. Her stomach hollowed out. How dreadful that would have been. She truly couldn't have lived with herself if that had happened.

Which wife had betrayed which husband, though? She ran through the various family members, and the local gentry who'd been at the ball last night, a swirl of disquiet eddying through her. Such things happened at house parties like this. All the time. Because marriages in her class were generally arranged for financial or dynastic reasons, rather than for love, which was why she'd been hoping never to have to make such a match herself.

What could be taking her so long in the withdrawing room? Alec pulled out his watch, and glared at it, then back at the door through which she'd vanished more than a quarter of an hour before.

He wouldn't be a bit surprised if there was another exit to the room. He wouldn't be a bit surprised if she'd sneaked out of it, to escape him, and further some nefarious scheme she was hatching.

After last night, he wouldn't be surprised by anything.

'Do you have to stand there glaring at the door?' The plaintive voice drew his attention to the speaker.

'Lizzie!'

'Nobody dare visit the ladies' retiring room,' she continued, 'because it means getting past you first.'

'Never mind what I'm doing standing here, right now. Where the devil have you been all day? And yesterday?'

'Avoiding you, of course,' she replied with an impudent smile.

'You admit it then? You have something to hide? I knew it. What have you done? And more importantly, where is the man in the case?'

'Oh, that,' she replied with an airy wave of her hand. 'Oh, there was never any man.'

'Never any man? Then why...?'

'Well, it was the only thing I could think of to get you here.' She tucked her hand in the crook of his arm, and tugged him to one side. 'If I'd told you that I wanted you to come and meet my friends,' she said, lowering her voice, 'you wouldn't have even bothered replying. So I had to resort to a little deception.'

'A little deception?' He flung her arm off, and turned so that they were standing face-to-face. 'You wrote that you were involved with a man. You wrote that you were going to meet him at Ness Hall, no matter what I said. You wrote…'

'I wrote what I had to, to get you here.'

'You lied to me,' he growled.

'Not exactly. I am involved with a man. A man I love very much.'

'What? But you just said—'

She giggled. The minx actually giggled. Then laid her hand on his chest, smiled naughtily up at him, and said, 'You, you nodcock.'

'Me?'

'Yes, you. I've been so worried about you. You hardly ever come ashore, and when you do, you always look so grim. And here was I, invited to the kind of place where I knew you were bound to have some fun, for once, and perhaps even meet someone who could make you happy *all* the time.'

You could have knocked him sideways. He'd never dreamed she could have lured him here because she'd been trying to make him happy. It was his job to make her happy, not the other way round.

'The more I thought about it, the more determined I became to get you to Ness Hall, in spite of your stupid objections about being too busy. You're always too busy to have any fun, or meet anyone suitable to become your countess.' She pouted. 'But you have to admit, now, that I did the right thing by you.'

Yes, he supposed he did have to admit that he'd completely misinterpreted her motives. But then, he'd been a fighting man for so long he saw enemies everywhere.

'As soon as they announced your betrothal I knew I didn't need to avoid you any longer. Oh, you are a clever man. You only needed a little nudge in the right direction, didn't you? Here only two days and you've secured just about the richest prize on the marriage mart!'

'Lizzie!'

They both started guiltily at the sound of Julia's disapproving voice. Neither of them had noticed her come and join them, so intent had they been on their quarrel.

'You make it sound as though your brother deliberately valued all the girls here and then cold-bloodedly seduced me! When you know full well he had no intention of marrying *anyone* when he came here.'

Lord Dunbar blinked at Julia. Was she actually defending him? Although…it wouldn't be the first time. Last night, when her father had accused him of the same crime, she'd hotly denied it.

Well, well. She might not love him. She gave no sign of even feeling anything as lukewarm as liking him. But she didn't like anyone laying false charges against him.

It was…a start.

'I didn't mean that,' Lizzie was continuing.

'Well, you should be more careful about what you say, when anyone can overhear you. Think how dreadful it would be should anyone think you believe your brother is a fortune hunter.'

Julia went to stand at his side, and tucked her hand through his arm, presenting a united front.

Alec could only surmise that whatever she thought of him, whatever she chose to say to him in private, at least in public, he might be able to hope for her support.

'But I can't be sorry you're so rich,' Lizzie protested. 'It's about time he had the means to enjoy his life. So far he's spent every penny he has on me. Don't think I don't know what sacrifices you've made, Alec,' she said, when he took a breath to protest. 'It's about time I did something for you. And I've met so many girls, wealthy girls, at the school you sent me to, and all of them wanting to marry someone dashing, and brave, and handsome, like you, I thought the least I could do was introduce you to some of them. And they did all like you. You could have had any of them for the crooking of your finger.' By this time, tears were filling her eyes, almost ready to spill over. 'Why shouldn't I be glad you've managed to capture the heart of the richest?'

He opened his mouth and then closed it. For there was nothing he could say to Lizzie, not with Julia standing right there. He had to settle for glowering at her.

'Oh, Lizzie,' said Julia, letting go of his arm to delve into her reticule for a handkerchief. 'It was sweet of you to try and help find your brother a wife. I can see that you only did what you did because you are so very fond of him.' She nudged him sharply in the ribs while Lizzie was distracted, blowing her nose.

'Aye,' he admitted brusquely. 'But a man likes to find his own wife, you know.'

'You would never have bothered even looking if I hadn't given you a nudge,' Lizzie retorted, stuffing the used hanky in her own reticule. 'You'd have gone on saying you hadn't the money or the prospects to marry, when all the world knows that any girl would swoon with delight to have a genuine naval hero paying her court, when society is so full of dull, overweight, pompous men. And any parents would be thrilled to have you for a son-in-law.'

'Well, let us all say no more about it,' put in Julia hastily, before he could refute any of her assertions. Besides, how could he? The girls here *had* all swooned over him, whenever he'd walked into a room, in what he'd found a highly embarrassing manner. And Lord Mountnessing *had* been pleased that his spoiled daughter was marrying him. Ridiculously so.

But then that was because the poor old fool thought she was in love with him.

'Especially not,' Julia continued firmly, 'if it pertains to my fortune, or your brother's lack of it. We met, we suit, and we are marrying. Never mind how it came about.'

'But I cannot condone your behaviour, Lizzie,' he growled. 'Nor the way you have meddled in my life.'

'She meant it for the best, my lord,' Julia reminded him.

'So you think,' he said, glowering at Lizzie, 'that is sufficient excuse for sending a letter that worried me, and brought me charging down here post-haste. For lying to me—'

'I didn't tell any lies. Not real lies!'

'You deliberately caused me to believe something that wasn't true.'

'But she did it,' put in Julia, 'in a good cause. She thought she was doing it for you.'

'Aye,' he scoffed. 'I might have known you would take her part in this. That you would sympathise with such behaviour. You're clearly two of a kind.' For hadn't she done the same sort of thing? Disguising herself in that dress, and luring him out to the glasshouse? And she hadn't been doing it for anyone's good but her own. Unlike Lizzie, who, he conceded, had been trying in her misguided way to be of benefit to him.

Lizzie, far from looking chastened, actually beamed at him. And then at Lady Julia. 'I've always wanted a sister,' she said.

'How lovely,' Julia answered, looking slightly baffled by the way Lizzie could smile at him when he was still glowering at her. Though he knew it was because Lizzie knew he couldn't be angry with her for long. He loved her far too much. Had always striven to provide her with everything a young lady could want.

That was the moment it hit him, the same way it must have hit Lord Mountnessing the night before: he'd spoiled her. Indulged her so much that she had no fear of him whatsoever. He'd taught her she could get away with anything. Fortunately for him, she loved him back, so was unlikely to use his fondness for her against him.

Julia, though? All she had was that same sublime belief that she was always right.

He'd never have any say over anything she did. Never know what she was planning.

She was going to be as unpredictable, and as uncontrollable, as the sea itself. He had a brief, but chillingly vivid vision of spending the rest of his life hanging on to the rigging, and hoping he didn't end up capsized and drowned.

Chapter Six

Eventually the ball ended, and the guests who'd only been invited for the evening went home. Julia fell into bed feeling completely drained. And yet sleep eluded her. Her heart was heavy. Her limbs restless. And her mind whirling.

It was easier to understand why Captain Dunbar assumed she was a natural-born schemer, now she'd seen the way his own sister behaved. Since he'd spent the last few years steering his ships up and down the coast on the alert for foreign invaders, and then getting tangled in her own plan to compromise David into marriage the minute he stepped ashore, it was hardly any wonder he'd started to think women did nothing but plot and plan to trap men. If she was him, she'd probably be wary of what she was about to get up to next.

Such a depressing conclusion made it even

harder to get to sleep. In the end, Julia gave up. She got out of bed, wrapped her eiderdown about her shoulders and went to the window seat to watch dawn raise its reluctant head over a bleak and empty horizon. The few clouds which had ventured out were scurrying, shivering across the sky. Here came her wedding day. A day when she should be marrying a man she loved. A day when she should be rejoicing.

Instead, the man she'd loved for as long as she could remember no longer loved her back. And because of a series of disastrous mistakes, she was going to have to marry a man she hardly knew. And she was going to have to smile as though she was deliriously happy about it, or she'd look like the world's biggest fool.

Even worse, she'd make her father look like a fool. Everyone knew he'd decided not to arrange a match for her the way he had done for his heir. He'd declared Maria's daughter should only marry for love. If anyone got so much as a hint of the truth of what lay behind her marriage to Captain Dunbar, Nick, and probably Herbert as well, would rub her father's nose in it every opportunity they got. She simply refused to hand her brothers that kind of ammunition to use against Papa. She'd let him down badly enough as it was.

So, no matter how miserable she felt, she was just going to have to put a smile on her face, and keep it firmly in place until this whole wretched day was over.

As soon as it was light enough to make it acceptable, she rang for her maid to bring her breakfast.

To Julia's surprise, Mabel came in with Betty, rather than wait for her summons. And she was beaming—well, both of them were.

'Ooh, 'tis no surprise to see you up so early,' observed Betty with delight. 'I'm sure you can't wait to get your handsome captain to the altar.'

'Betty! You forget yourself,' snapped Mabel. And then ruined her haughty stance by rushing to Lady Julia's armoire and drawing out the dress she'd planned to wear for the Twelfth Night celebrations. 'You must wear this.' She sighed, draping the confection of gauze and spangles over the footboard of Julia's bed. 'You look so lovely in it.'

'You'll dazzle 'im, right enough,' said Betty, completely unabashed by Mabel's reproof.

'Are you sure I should wear that? I mean, it's a ball gown.'

'You will look like a fairy princess in it.' Mabel sighed, flaring the demi-train out into a fan.

A fairy elephant perhaps, thought Julia as she buried her nose in her cup of chocolate. But, since the maids were so excited at the prospect of dressing her up like a Christmas goose for her handsome groom, she voiced no objection.

As they chattered and fluttered round her, she strove valiantly to emulate their excitement. But the more animated they became, the greater her sense of guilt grew.

When she was finally ready, and they stood gazing at her with hands clasped at their bosoms and tears in their eyes, she managed a watery smile for them.

'Oh, my lady,' gulped Mabel. 'There is no need to feel nervous. You make a beautiful bride.'

The dress was certainly beautiful. And the jewels she wore were magnificent. And most people wouldn't look beneath the trappings.

She instantly felt ten times more guilty. The maids both believed it was nerves making her so unresponsive. Though, in a way, wasn't it? Wasn't she nervous about marrying a man she barely knew? For the most shameful of reasons?

There was a soft knock on the door, and her father came in. The maids bobbed respectful curtsies, and scurried out, eager to find good places in the choir loft, from which vantage point as many of the staff who could squeeze into it would be watching the ceremony.

For the first time that morning, she didn't feel as if she had to wear any sort of mask. Papa didn't expect her to be all smiling and excited. He knew she'd misbehaved and felt guilty. And from the stern look he bent on her, he still hadn't quite forgiven her, either.

'Oh, Papa, I do hate it when you are angry with me.' It was such a relief to be able to drop all pretence, and speak the complete truth, she had to sag down onto the nearest chair.

'I am sorry I have disappointed you,' she said, gazing up at him for some sign of softening.

He walked over to her and patted her shoulder, which was as demonstrative as he ever got.

'There, there,' he said gruffly. 'You are headstrong, like your mother. And I have indulged you, rather than curbing you. So the fault is as much mine, as yours.'

'No, indeed it isn't. You are the best papa a girl could have!'

'Well, let us say no more about it.' He sighed. 'Indeed I do not have it in me to remain angry with you any longer. Not today, of all days.' He darted her a wry smile. 'Not when you are looking so pretty.'

She wasn't pretty. He was looking at her

through the veil of affection he'd felt for her mother, as he'd always done.

'It was very wrong of you to entrap that poor man the way you did,' he continued. 'But since he appears to have forgiven you, how can I do less?'

She reached up and seized his hand and kissed it in the relief that he'd decided to forgive her. Even though what he was forgiving her for wasn't exactly what she'd done. If he had known the complete truth… A chill struck to her core. Would he be so understanding then? How could she bear it if he really did cease loving her? If he became cold and critical with her, the way he was with Nick, and Herbert?

She really did have cause to be grateful to Captain Lord Dunbar. If he had told her father the truth…

Julia immediately decided to forgive him for speaking so harshly to her whenever they'd been alone. Didn't he deserve some outlet for his frustration? As long as he kept his true feelings hidden from the world—or, more specifically, her father—she could forgive him any amount of unkindness in private.

'He is a decent man,' said her father.

Yes, she had to admit he was, which made her wince because while she'd done nothing but complain, and flounce off in huffs, and that after dragging him down into her mess in the first place, he'd behaved like a complete gentleman.

'And he really does appear to be coming round to the notion of marriage.'

Yes, she had to give Captain Lord Dunbar credit for his acting ability. Anyone would think he really was smitten if all they had to go by was his demeanour at the ball last night.

'And I have to say, he is just the sort of man I would have chosen for you, had I been inclined to arrange a match for you. I believe he will make you a good husband.'

Julia was certainly not going to complain about him if he wasn't, she vowed. For the rest of her life, she was going to have to put a brave face on it.

Tears sprang to her eyes. Her lower lip quivered as she faced the possibility of ending up just like so many society wives, married to men they couldn't stand, taking lovers from amongst the dissatisfied husbands of the *ton* or eyeing up their footmen.

Just what she'd always sworn she would never do. She'd never seen the point in marrying, unless it was an improvement on the life she led now. Unless she could exchange a life of duty for one of love and warmth.

She blew her nose, and smiled at her father in a watery way. Then she took the arm he extended to her and left her bedroom for the last time as a single girl. Julia lifted her chin and put on a smile, which she kept firmly in place until she reached the family chapel.

It was full to the rafters. She'd never seen so many people crammed into the ancient pews. Was there nothing more interesting to do today? No—apparently she, so used to organising the entertainment for Papa's guests, had become the entertainment. She could understand her female cousins—who were all studying her gown, whispering behind their fans and sighing over what they thought was a whirlwind romance—wanting to attend a wedding. Anyone's wedding.

But what on earth was Nick doing here? And Herbert? Sitting right at the front? She would have thought they'd rather have all their teeth drawn than get all dressed up to witness her wedding—especially when they believed it was to a man she loved. Because neither of them got on terribly well with the 'suitable' wives Papa had arranged for them. And if her half-brothers were miserable in their marriages, they surely wouldn't see any reason why she should be spared the same fate.

And as for all the other guests—well, Aunt

Frances had been correct in saying that just about every member of the family was here. But they wouldn't have filled the pews like this. As she and her papa made their stately progress down the aisle, Julia realised that not only the family and most of the other guests who were attending the house party had come to witness her humiliation, but also a fair sprinkling of locals. She spotted the vicar and his wife squashed into one of the rear pews; the master of the local hunt, and his wife in another. Even Nellie's theatrical company had been allowed to come in and stand along the walls on either side.

Nellie nodded to her as Lady Julia walked past. As though to reassure her that all would be well. It was amazing how much that woman could express with just a nod and a sort of glimmer to her eye. No wonder she was such a hit on the stage. No wonder she had the entrée to so many homes, too. Just that one look had put more heart into her than anything anyone else had said today. Somehow, it reminded her that Captain Lord Dunbar was a decent man. That many people went into marriages knowing far less about their groom than she did, and had to face the terror of a wedding night with men who were practically strangers.

At least the wedding night would hold no fear for her.

Just as she reached that conclusion, she also reached the altar rail, where her reluctant groom stood waiting for her, his back ramrod straight, his eyes fixed forward—as if he didn't want to acknowledge that any of this was happening to him.

Captain Lord Dunbar barely glanced at her throughout the ceremony either. And he barked out his responses in a brisk manner that made even Uncle Algernon wince.

Papa gave him her hand, and Uncle Algernon gave them his blessing, and it was done. They were man and wife. With a sense of acting out a part in a play, she laid her hand on his sleeve and turned to face the congregation, and the world, as a married woman.

Marianne, who was sitting on the second pew, took one look at her and burst into noisy sobs. Julia had been aware of her sniffling all the way through the service, but not until that moment had she realised just how upset her best friend, and cousin, had been.

As their eyes met she tried to convey the message that she didn't bear her any ill will. How could Marianne even think it? As Captain Dunbar had so scathingly remarked, Marianne had never exerted the slightest bit of influence over her. She'd always followed in Julia's shadow. Looked to her for guidance, if anything.

She really should have spent more time consoling her friend.

Just as she was cursing herself for her lack of foresight, she noticed someone passing her a clean handkerchief. It was David.

David was sitting next to Marianne.

Her step faltered. Who had invited him? And why hadn't she noticed him when she'd been walking down the aisle? Because she'd been concentrating on her husband of course! Though— no, that wasn't right. She'd noticed Nick, and Herbert, and even Nellie on her way to the altar.

She stared at him for a moment in complete bewilderment. If she loved him, shouldn't she have sensed he was there? The way she always sensed the presence of Captain Dunbar whenever he was in a room?

Though what did it matter? David could be nothing to her now. He was there for Marianne, clearly. Which was a good thing. Yes, a very good thing. Marianne needed a friend today.

And wouldn't it have been terrible if this incident had deprived Marianne of that friendship? The three of them had been firm friends since shortly after Marianne had arrived at Ness Hall.

Even though she'd forfeited David's regard, she was glad he clearly didn't blame Marianne for any of it. No, all his anger, to judge from the look on his face, was directed solely and squarely, at her. Which was exactly where he should direct it, of course. Marianne had urged her not to try to trap David into marriage. Begged her not to borrow clothes from Nellie and comport herself as a woman of easy virtue. And Julia had brushed all her scruples aside.

Yes, she was glad he was there to comfort and console Marianne, until she had the opportunity to discuss her companion's future. Because now she came to think of it, Marianne must be worried sick about it. Her status in this house had become that of a sort of unpaid companion. She must be wondering what would happen to her now.

She glanced up at her new husband, wondering if she would be able to persuade him to take Marianne into their household. And then realised she had no idea what their household was to be like, or even where they were to set it up. They hadn't talked about anything of that sort.

Oh, how she wished she'd held on to her temper, yesterday morning, and had a sensible talk about practical issues. That was probably why he'd asked to speak to her privately. To discuss such things.

Her husband's arm stiffened under her hand. Even though he was looking resolutely forward, somehow she knew he'd noticed her staring at David and Marianne. And to judge from the stern set of his jaw, had drawn entirely the wrong conclusion. Oh…bother!

She forced herself to look straight ahead as well. And saw the servants, jostling each other and leaning over the gallery to catch a glimpse of her in all her finery. As she looked up, they burst into a spontaneous round of applause. Which made her lower lip start quivering, and tears spring to her eyes. For she'd caused them no end of extra work, by getting married in such haste. And not one of them had complained. On the contrary, they'd flung themselves into the preparations with a goodwill that put her to shame. Even the gardeners had done her proud, stripping half the herbaceous borders, to judge from the amount of greenery decorating the chapel.

She felt about two inches tall.

To crown it all, as they passed through the door that led from the chapel into the great hall, where the wedding breakfast was laid out, Captain Dunbar bent and growled into her ear.

'He isn't worth it, you know.'

'Pardon?'

'That medical student.'

He was referring to David. She took a breath to explain that she wasn't getting teary-eyed over him, but at the touching loyalty of the staff. when he continued, 'You may have thought yourself in love with him, but he wasn't in love with you.'

And just like that, she forgot all about explaining anything at all.

'Just because you despise me,' she hissed between clenched teeth, 'it doesn't mean to say some other man couldn't be in love with me.'

'That wasn't what I said. Some man may be stupid enough to fall in love with you one day. But that one didn't. A man with a broken heart doesn't sit through the wedding of his true love with an expression like that on his face.'

She drew a breath to make a pithy retort, when something about what he'd said struck her. Very forcibly.

Oh, not about David not loving her. She'd seen his love for her die the moment he'd walked into the orangery and discovered what she'd just done.

No, it was the bit about what someone with a broken heart would feel like, watching someone they loved marrying another man. Because it surely applied to a woman, too.

And Julia had to face the fact that she hadn't

been devastated when she'd made her vows. Nor, at any point, had she felt the slightest inclination to run to David and weep and plead for his forgiveness. She hadn't felt the slightest bit jealous of him giving Marianne so much attention during her wedding, either. On the contrary, she'd been grateful that Marianne still had one friend upon whom she could count.

Which meant that her own heart wasn't broken at all.

Her pride was bruised. Her self-esteem crushed.

But she most definitely wasn't suffering from a broken heart.

She wasn't sure what that meant. Hadn't she loved David at all? Or had the love she'd felt died in the same instant as his?

Or...

Oh, what a time to be thinking about another man.

She had to stop it. It was insulting to her husband. Even if they'd only met a couple of days ago, she'd just made vows before God and Uncle Algernon. And she intended to keep them. If at all possible.

No. More than that. She *would* keep them. No matter what. She'd dreamed for so long of a marriage that didn't involve seeking consolation in

discreet *affaires*. And though nothing else about
this marriage fulfilled any of her girlish promises to herself, she could at least hold on to the
one where she never succumbed to the temptation to stray from her husband's bed.

'You look like a medieval martyr on the way
to the stake,' said Captain Dunbar, later that evening, when he came to claim her for the waltz.
The day had been long and arduous, but at last
they were entering the final stretch. Only the im-
promptu ball to endure, and then she could go up
to her room and hide.

'You need to do better than this.'

She took a deep breath. Counted to ten. And
then waited another couple of beats before making her answer.

'People will just think I'm nervous about our
wedding night,' she flung at him as he took hold
of her hands for the march. 'After all, I'm renowned for being particularly prim and proper.'

'Good God! Really?' He looked down at her
with the first genuine smile she'd ever seen on
his face. It made him look like a different man.
A man she could, perhaps, talk to.

The way she used to talk to David.

'I must say,' he said softly, bending to murmur
in her ear as he snaked his arm round her waist

and turned her into the pirouette, 'I find it well-nigh impossible to think of you in that way. Prim, you may look, at this very moment. But proper? No. *Im*proper is what you are…'

Annoyingly, she felt her cheeks heating again. Why was it that she did nothing but blush, or lose her temper around this man?

'And that, I think, gives us the perfect excuse to leave,' he said. 'You look delightfully flushed and nervous, and I'm sure I look like an eager bridegroom.'

'But—'

'Haven't you had enough?'

'Yes, but—'

'Then let's leave.'

'Very well.' She sighed. 'But—'

To her shock, he did away with any further protests by hefting her into his arms, right in the middle of the dance floor, and striding out of the room with her. His action was greeted by a series of gasps, and catcalls, and one or two ribald comments from the uncles who'd been imbibing a little too freely.

'Put me down.'

'No.'

'You will be exhausted, long before we reach our rooms, if you don't,' she warned him. 'I'm not exactly made of thistledown.'

'No, you're very nicely rounded,' he observed. 'But perhaps you have a point.' He stopped at the end of the hall and set her gently down at the foot of the staircase. 'I wouldn't want to expend all my energy getting you to the bedroom.'

'What do you mean?' She shot him a suspicious glance as he grabbed her hand, and tugged her up the stairs.

'You know very well what I mean.'

She was very much afraid she did. And her suspicions were confirmed when he made straight for her bedroom, and pushed the door open.

'You cannot come in here,' she protested, wondering how he even knew where her room was. Had he bribed one of the footmen? No—there had probably been no need to do any such thing. Her own maids had probably volunteered the information, thinking they were furthering the cause of some grand passion.

'Of course I can,' he said, ushering her inside, and following her in. 'I'm your husband now.'

Yes. He was. But it still felt like an invasion. No man but her father had ever come in here.

'I thought...that is...' She shook her head. She didn't know what she'd thought about the sleeping arrangements. Actually, she'd tried not to think about it at all—her wedding night, that was. Apart from that fleeting moment on the way out of the chapel when she'd vowed never to stray from her husband's bed. And even then, she'd never imagined him in hers.

'You don't expect me to stay up in that chilly little room your housekeeper found for me, do you? Not tonight?'

He stalked across the room to the bed. Sat down on it. Lay back, and clasped his hands behind his head, crossing his feet at the ankles.

'Ahhh.' He sighed. 'This is more like it. Very comfortable.'

She stood there glaring at him. Just glaring at him, making himself at home in the room she'd always considered her sanctuary.

And counted to ten again. She was so tired. She hadn't slept last night. She'd been at everyone's beck and call all day. And now, instead of being able to rest, it looked as though he was going to force some sort of confrontation. And she just wasn't up to it.

He sat up.

'Come now, no point in standing over there all night. Time to come to bed. Wife.' He held out his hand.

'I don't...I don't want to,' she said mulishly.

'Don't be a hypocrite.' He sprang up off the bed.

'I'm not a hypocrite—'

'Yes, you are. You're standing all the way over there, pretending to be shy, when we both know you're nothing of the sort.'

'That's not why I'm standing over here.'

'No?' All his good humour evaporated. 'Then it's because you're wishing I was another man, then.'

'No!' She shook her head with some vehemence. She didn't want him thinking that, when it wasn't true. Why, she hadn't spent a tenth of the time, thinking about David, than she had thinking about him, today. Her body kept on leaping to attention whenever he was around. And whenever he'd touched her in the dance, her insides had gone molten. When he'd picked her up and carried her out of the ballroom, a sort of bubbling excitement had erupted on top of the molten feelings, so that when he set her on her feet again it was all she could do to stand up on legs that felt like blancmange. 'That's not it.' She forced the humiliating admission between reluctant teeth.

'Good,' he said, stalking over. 'I'm relieved to see you don't intend to be dishonest about this.' He set his hands on either side of her waist. 'For this is the one real thing we have. Passion. Besides...' his voice dropped to a low snarl

'…you're my wife now. And you are not going to deny me my wedding night.'

She'd had no intention of denying him anything! How dare he suggest she would short-change him? And why was he so angry?

'Now, look here—'

'No. You look here.' He threaded the fingers of one hand into her hair, and tipped her head back. 'I never wanted to get married. But since I am married, I may as well get the one thing from it, from you, that I want.'

His words stung. There was no need to remind her, not right this minute, that she was the last woman he would have married, if he'd actually been on the lookout for a wife.

'I hate you,' she hissed.

'But you want me.'

The arrogance of that statement made her want to slap his face. Especially since she couldn't refute it. She *did* want him.

Anger, and wanting, and resentment, and excitement, went swooshing through her veins, making her heart beat like a galloping horse. She found she was breathing hard, as though she'd been running.

Her one consolation was the fact that he was breathing hard, too. Looking at her with all the turmoil she could feel swirling through her own being.

'And hell,' he growled. 'I want you, too.'

His admission was all it took to snap the restraints. She wasn't sure which of them moved first. But all of a sudden, they were kissing each other. Hard, desperate kisses, which would have rocked her off her feet if he hadn't clamped his arms round her so tightly.

Until he started tearing at her clothes. And backing her towards the bed. She fell onto it, with him half on top, his mouth fused with hers even as he let go of her to remove his own clothes.

And then his hands were everywhere. Everywhere. As if he couldn't get enough of her. Couldn't decide which bit of her he wanted most. And since he was making free with her body, she didn't see any reason why she shouldn't do the same with his. He felt marvellous. Hard, and hot, and peppered with hair that felt wonderful against her own softer, smoother skin.

She knew what was coming, this time. Was eager for it. Desperate for it. So much so that the cry she gave, when he drove into her, was one of completion. She clutched at his shoulders, then his buttocks as he pounded into her, urging him on. It was gloriously reassuring, the way he dominated her, possessed her, so completely. If he'd shown any hint of reluctance, she didn't think she could have borne it. But this…

Even as she was revelling in it, she erupted into a sort of wild ecstasy.

And so did he.

He collapsed to one side of her, his breathing ragged. As ragged as hers. She was sweating. The eiderdown was all bunched up in the small of her back.

'I didn't mean for it to be like that,' he said with what sounded like regret.

A shaft of cold uncertainty pierced to her core. It had felt spectacular to her. Hadn't he wanted it to be?

'Not on your wedding night. I meant to take it slow. Get you to liking it. But it was over as quick as last time.'

What did he mean? Couldn't he tell how much she'd liked it? If she'd liked it any more her heart would probably have exploded.

'Never mind,' she said in a voice that didn't sound as though it belonged to her, it was so husky. 'It wasn't as if it was my first time, was it?'

He reared up and looked down at her. With what looked surprisingly like concern on his face. 'That's why I wanted to make it a bit more…' he shrugged '…tender, I suppose, tonight. But you…

the way you looked at me, all resentful and angry. It...it made me want to just...'

She lifted one hand to pat his shoulder. 'I know. We strike sparks off each other, somehow, don't we?'

'Sparks?' He huffed out a laugh. 'It's more like lightning striking a powder keg.'

She didn't know what else he might have said, had she not yawned.

'Here,' he said, getting up and turning back the covers on the side of the bed he'd been lying on. 'Get in. You're all gooseflesh.'

Charming.

Though at least, she supposed, he was attempting to be considerate. Which was certainly unusual, for a man.

She half-rolled, half-shuffled across the bed, and pulled the covers up to her chin. To hide all the acres of gooseflesh from his discerning, offended eyes.

In next to no time he'd dived in on the other side, put his arms round her, and hauled her into his side.

'Don't worry,' he said, when she stiffened in surprise. 'I'm only warming you up.'

And he was lovely and warm.

In spite of the newness, and the strangeness of the situation, a wave of sheer exhaustion had her snuggling down and closing her eyes. Another yawn roused her, briefly. But then she simply couldn't keep awake a moment longer.

It was dark when she woke again. For a second, she wondered why it felt as if she was sleeping on a hillside. A very warm hillside, that was wrapped all round her.

And then drowsily realised it wasn't grass tickling her legs, but the rough hair of the man who had his arm round her waist, whose greater weight had made her roll into the depression in the mattress and fetch up against his side.

The candles had burned down. The only light in the room came from the fire that was still smouldering lazily in the grate.

The arm about her waist moved. A large hand reached up to cup her breast.

'Mmmhhh,' her husband growled appreciatively into her ear. Sending a shiver of excitement flashing down her spine.

He kept on kneading, gently. All the while kissing her ear. Or just breathing into it.

And before long she didn't feel sleepy any longer. Indeed, she was so awake, and aroused, she couldn't keep still.

But when she would have rolled over, to face him, and kiss him, and press her eager body up against his, he prevented her.

'No,' he murmured. 'Stay like this.'

'I can't,' she whispered frantically. 'I need… I need…'

'Here, then,' he said, gliding his hand down her body, until it came to rest exactly where she needed him to touch her.

And touched her. Stroked her.

'Oh…' she sighed. 'Yesss…' as he slid one finger inside her.

'You're so responsive,' he said, with a tinge of amazement. 'I've hardly started trying to rouse you, and you're ready for me.'

'Nobody could be more surprised than me,' she said, with a touch of bitterness. 'I've never… that is…not even…'

'Never?'

'You can talk.' She huffed indignantly. 'You're just as keen.' She flexed her bottom against the proof that he was, indeed, as aroused as she.

'It's a mystery, right enough,' he agreed, grinding into her. And delving a bit deeper. And then adding a second finger to the one already inside her.

'Don't,' she moaned. 'Don't keep doing that, or…'

'You can't pretend you don't like it.'

'No, I…that is…I like it too much,' she panted. Writhed against the pressure he exerted with the heel of his hand. 'I'm going to…I don't know what it's called, but it's going to happen,' she cried. 'Oh, oh, heavens!'

He clamped her tightly to his body as waves of pleasure swelled up and rippled through her. Murmured soothing words into her ear as she drifted back to sanity, removed his fingers, then his hand and turned her into his embrace, kissing her mouth. Gently.

So gently, she wondered if this was the same man who'd done nothing but growl at her, and criticise her since they'd become betrothed. What was more, he was still hard, and ready. He must want to…and yet he was taking the time to kiss her.

To be gentle.

She reached up, and ploughed her fingers into his hair.

She kept saying she hated him, but how could she, when he kept on being so…considerate? Even though he had every right to be angry with her. And it wasn't just in bed, either. From the very first, he'd demonstrated a kind of innate chivalry that no other man had ever shown her. He could have ranted and raved at her the moment he'd pulled off her mask. Instead, he'd sort of…yes, she could see it now—he'd swallowed it all back down, and just declared he would make it right by marrying her. He'd even tried to shoulder some of the blame when they'd gone to see Papa. And had acted—in public—as though he was besotted with her, so that everyone could think it was a love match between them. So that nobody would ask awkward questions about why they were marrying in such haste. Every step of the way he'd protected her from the consequences of her stupid, rash, desperate behaviour.

Nobody had ever done that for her before. Not even Papa. If she ever fell short of his exacting standards he didn't hesitate to tell her so. No matter who might be listening. Which was why she'd learned, as a very little girl, to always be on her best behaviour.

But now…Alec Dunbar was making her feel…

Was it possible he could be the kind of husband who…?

He sighed then, and smoothed her hair from her face in a way that felt almost tender.

And then began to roll away from her. Even though he hadn't experienced the wonderful release he'd just given her.

'Don't you want to…?'

'You can surely tell I want to.' He flexed his hips against her so she could feel his manhood, hard, and hot, and ready.

'Then why don't you?'

Chapter Seven

He heaved a sigh. Rested his forehead briefly against hers.

'I told you I wanted to give you the kind of wedding night a lady like you expects. Your first experience, out in that greenhouse affair…' He shook his head. 'You got more than you bargained for. Part of it was because I'd been at sea a long time. And since I've been ashore, I've had no chance to get myself a woman. Lizzie put paid to that with her damned letter. And then when I got here, and all Lizzie's friends kept fawning over me…and all of them so pretty. And I couldn't—*wouldn't*—touch any of *them*. I suppose it was like dangling a juicy steak in front of a dog chained in a kennel. I was worked up into such a pitch of frustration, that when I thought a mature, experienced woman was giving me the signal, I went straight into action without pausing to get the lie of the land. And the result was, I hurt you. I know I did.'

She didn't know what to say. No man had ever apologised to her. Let alone explained what had been going through his head.

Not that she could like what had been going through his head. No chance to get himself a woman? All Lizzie's friends so pretty? While she was more in the nature of a juicy steak?

Still, she had to give him credit for making the *attempt* to apologise.

'What's done is done,' she said in a practical, no-nonsense tone.

'And I'm about to do it again,' he growled, stopping her mouth with another of his hungry, demanding kisses.

If he'd given her the chance, she would have told him she had no objection. If she was a juicy steak, then he was...ooh, a rich plum pudding. He didn't need to flatten her to the mattress, or pin her arms above her head. She'd have put them round his neck as he licked, and suckled at her breasts.

Though there was something thrilling about the determined way he was holding her in place. The weight of his leg across her thighs, when he started a more thorough exploration of her body than he'd attempted so far.

By the time he entered her again, she was so desperate for that nameless crisis of pleasure he'd brought her to before, that it rippled through her after he'd only thrust deep a couple of times.

He stilled. Waited till she'd calmed down.

Then began to glide slowly, in and out of her. As though he was savouring the sensation of being inside her. There was no racing to the finishing post, this time. Instead it was languorous, and indulgent. Like floating naked in the lake on a hot summer's day. Enjoying the contrasting sensations of cool water, and hot sun that made every inch of her tingle with various pleasures.

Only nothing measured up to the pleasure he was creating now, with his slow, gliding thrusts, the lazy sweep of his hand up her flanks, round to the curve of her buttocks.

Oh, the feel of him—if only he'd let go of her wrists, which he'd shackled with one of his great powerful hands. She wanted to explore him, too.

Well, she couldn't touch him with her hands, but there was nothing to stop her tasting him, was there? She raised her head and swiped her tongue up the column of his throat, swirling it round his Adam's apple.

He gave a guttural cry, drove deeply into her one more time, then shuddered with the force of his own release.

It created an answering surge of pleasure deep inside her, making her grind up against him as it crested.

Plum pudding? Plum pudding smothered in custard, she sighed. Or maybe brandy sauce.

He groaned, and rolled away.

'I think we should try to sleep for a bit...' he panted '...before doing that again.'

What a strange thing to say. She turned over and curled up on her side without saying a word.

Though, after a moment's reflection, she worked it out.

She'd worn him out.

But he wanted to do it again, as soon as he could.

Her mouth curved into a smile of purely feminine triumph.

If they'd been in love, she might have confessed that she wanted to do it as soon as he could manage it as well. But it wouldn't do to admit it. She had no wish to appear besotted with him. A woman who allowed her husband the upper hand too soon invariably ended up crushed. She had only to think of Nick and Ellen. Which brought another unpleasant thought to mind—she might have vowed to stay faithful to her husband, but she had no guarantee he would do the same.

No—as things stood, it was as well to let

him think he was the one in greater need of... of steak and plum pudding.

It seemed a pity to wake her again. Her little face was all scrunched up in the pillow, her hair half-up and half-down as though she'd been on deck in a hurricane. Alec's lips twitched in a half-smile. Last night had felt like going through a hurricane, to him, too.

He closed his eyes and inhaled her perfume, just to see if he'd imagined, last night, that she smelled just like a wife should. But, no. She definitely didn't smell like sin this morning. Not a bit like she'd done when she'd been wearing a mask and dressed like a whore. All he could smell was pure woman.

He gently removed a hairpin that was about to slide into her ear. Her hairstyle was so elaborate, she must have a maid to put it up in the morning, and another to take it down at night. He probably should have let her take it down before taking her to bed, so she wouldn't wake up feeling like a hedgehog—with hairpins all over.

But then again, if he'd given her time to prepare for bed, she'd have had time to think about what they were going to do. He'd seen the look on her face, seen her mind working nineteen to the dozen, trying to come up with reasons why they shouldn't. No, on the whole, it had been better to storm her before she could muster enough objections to repel him.

His smile broadened. Far from repulsing him she'd practically torn the shirt off his back.

And speaking of shirts, he needed a fresh one. He'd have to go up to the room he'd been allocated on arrival, and collect his belongings. Even though he'd come to this room last night, as though he had a perfect right to do so, nobody had moved his things down here.

He shrugged into as many of his clothes as he could locate, scattered as they were about the chilly room. The fire was almost out, but there was still a little coal in the scuttle. Kneeling down at the hearth, he shot the last of the fuel onto the embers, and blew gently, to rouse them to life.

There was a movement from behind him. He looked over his shoulder to see if he'd woken... his wife. But, no, she'd just turned over.

He'd worn her out. He grinned.

Unless she usually slept like the dead. His smile slipped. For he didn't know.

Well, then, he'd find out.

As long as he managed to stay in her room every night.

He got to his feet, a determined frown furrowing his brow.

The only hope he had of getting to know his wife, and thereby standing some chance of coming to a working arrangement with her, would be to dog her steps night and day. Especially night. Which was why it would be as well to move into this room with her. No fashionable marriage for them, not yet. Not until they'd come to a better understanding than the one they had now.

Understanding? He trotted up the stairs to the tiny room under the eaves where the flustered housekeeper had placed him when he'd turned up unannounced. He didn't understand anything about her. About women in general, come to that. They were almost like a totally different species to men. And since he'd lived in a world totally populated by men, since he'd been a snotty-nosed midshipman, he'd never had a chance to study them.

All the more reason to keep a close watch on *her*. As close as he could. He certainly wasn't going to get the upper hand unless he could learn how to keep her in line.

If that was even possible. Even her own father had admitted she was out of control.

Although nobody would know, to look at her. She hadn't wept, or screamed, or torn her hair, the way he'd heard some women did when crossed in love. She'd carried on her duties as hostess, with a smile on her face for everyone. And remained completely composed when she'd walked down the aisle to him.

Her mask of poise had only been in danger of slipping once. When she'd walked past the man she'd been attempting to compromise, he'd felt her tense. But she hadn't slowed, or given *him*—his lip curled in scorn—a languishing look, or anything of that nature. He'd only noticed her brief reaction because he'd been half-expecting it.

In many ways, he admired her ability to put on a brave face. It was just that it smacked of deception. The kind of deception that had tumbled them both into this mess.

It only took a minute or two to gather up his things and stow them back in his valise. He put his overcoat on over his shirt and breeches for the return trip. His room was like an icehouse. And the corridors weren't much better.

At least he'd got the fire going in her chamber. Their chamber, now, he vowed, stowing his dunnage in the little dressing room which led off the bedroom where his wife was still fast asleep.

She looked very tempting, lying there with her hair all over the place, her cheeks flushed. If he got back into bed, and started kissing his way down her spine, he was pretty sure she'd welcome him. The way she'd done last night when he'd woken her. Half-asleep and not really knowing who he was, she'd almost purred like a contented cat. Yes, she'd kept her claws sheathed, unlike the first time he'd taken her, as his wife.

But—he ran his hand over his chin. He had a full night's growth of beard now. And her skin was so delicate, he'd probably leave her grazed and sore. Besides which, did he really want her to enjoy making love so much when her mind was fuddled with sleep?

So he'd shave first. Let her sleep a little longer. Then make sure she was wide awake, and completely sure who, exactly, was making love to her next time.

There was a bell-pull by the head of the bed, which he went and tugged. He would warrant the first person up here in the morning would come bearing a can of hot water. His wife had always appeared at the breakfast table looking neat as a new pin.

In the event, two maids came in answer to his summons. One carrying a can of hot water, and the other a tray bearing a silver pot, and a cup and saucer.

Only the one.

It seemed that while he was determined to make this marriage work, she, the instigator, was still trying to retain her independence.

He thrust the empty coal scuttle at the maid with the can of hot water.

'Fill this up, if you please,' he growled.

She bobbed a curtsy, and blushed as he took the hot-water can from her, as though embarrassed to come across a man in Lady Julia's room.

But, hell, they were married! What did the servants expect? That he'd tup her, then scurry off to the chilly room up in the eaves?

'Oh, you're up.'

He turned to see his wife struggling into a sitting position, as the maid with the tray set it on the night table beside the bed. Lady Julia bit her lower lip as her eyes darted from the can of hot water in his hand, to the blazing fire, to the overcoat he'd slung over his shoulders.

'Do you...?' She swallowed. Clutched the sheets up to her neck. Though her shoulders were still visible. And completely bare.

'Do you like hot chocolate in the morning? Betty can soon fetch another cup. There's plenty in the pot.'

Too little, too late.

'I prefer ale.'

'Of course you do. Well, run along and fetch his lordship a tankard of ale, Betty,' she said, dismissing the maid.

The pair of them scurried out, heads down, stifling giggles.

'I never thought...' she began. Tugged at the sheets again. 'That is, in future, you must say what you want in the morning.'

He raised one eyebrow. She went bright red. 'I mean, what your habits are upon rising.'

He raised it a little higher. She scowled.

'Look, this is all very...strange,' she flung at him. 'I have no idea what it's like for a man and woman to share a room.' She eyed his bag, which was on full view from her position in bed, through the open dressing-room door. 'It never occurred to me, actually, that we would even *be* sharing a room.'

'Never occurred to you? It must have done.'

She shook her head. 'I don't know any other married couples that do so.'

'Well, we aren't like any other married couple, are we? We need to get to know each other. And that means spending time alone. In private.'

'Oh.' She frowned. Pondered for a second. 'You...want to get to know me?' A strange expression flitted across her face. It looked a bit like wistfulness, only he didn't know her well enough to be certain, and it was gone so quickly he might have imagined it anyway.

'Well...' she began, squaring her shoulders and lifting her chin. And he promptly decided he didn't want to hear whatever it was she'd decided to say.

If she was going to start bargaining for some form of freedom, she'd find her pleas landing on deaf ears. He might not have actively sought marriage. But now he was a married man, he wasn't going to make it easy for her to cuckold him.

Before she could say anything he didn't like, or he said anything he'd regret, he strode to the dressing room with his can of hot water, and tipped some into the basin.

'I usually go down to breakfast,' he heard her say, though his back was toward her.

'I think the few people who go down to breakfast,' he said, shrugging out of his coat, 'can manage without you for one morning.' He pulled his shirt off over his head.

'Yes, I'm sure they can, but, I'm still Papa's hostess. And with the house so full of guests, family guests, many of whom are embroiled in long-running feuds, I find it's always a good idea to get down early, to sound things out.'

He rummaged in his valise for his shaving tackle. He could hear her bedclothes rustling.

One glance over his shoulder was enough to ascertain she was struggling to get out of bed without exposing more than one limb at a time. Which was ridiculous, given that he'd seen every voluptuous inch of her, spread out under him, last night.

Though rather endearing, too. Who would have thought the siren who'd lured him to that greenhouse one night, then torn the shirt from his back another, could be shy, in the light of day? It was something to consider. He wet his shaving brush, and began working up a lather.

'You see...' Her voice was coming nearer. He glanced over his shoulder once more. She'd got a slinky sort of wrap round her. Though she was clearly naked underneath.

He took a deep breath, and lathered his face in record time.

'By the time breakfast is over, I can tell what sort of mood Nicholas and Papa are in. And then I go and take tea with Mrs Dawson—that's the housekeeper. And she lets me know if there's anything else I ought to know about. The maids who light the fires, and carry up hot water, are always the first to find out if there's any trouble brewing. And then I can take steps to nip it in the bud.'

She'd drawn up a stool from somewhere,

and was watching him swipe the razor over his cheeks with a sort of rapt fascination. When she wasn't running her eyes over his naked torso.

Julia had clearly never watched a man shaving before. Well, he'd never shaved while a woman— a practically naked woman—was watching him, come to that. Suddenly he felt more masculine than he'd ever felt in his life.

'I'm sure you understand how it is,' she persisted, though her voice now sounded a bit thready. 'As captain of a ship, you need to know everything that's going on with your crew. So that you can keep everything running smoothly.'

'That is a fair point, actually,' he grunted. He swooshed his razor through the water for longer than necessary while thinking through what she'd said.

'You look young to be in charge of such a large household,' he finally said out of the side of his mouth as he tackled his upper lip. 'Just how old are you?'

'Twenty.'

'I didn't make captain until I was much older,' he admitted. 'At your age, I only had charge of about eighty men. And I'd been trained for command for years.'

'Well, I've been trained to command ever since I was born.'

'Hmmm.' He raised his chin to shave the delicate area beneath it.

'I have been meaning to ask,' she said, twisting her fingers together in her lap. 'What you plan to do next? I mean, do you have a ship to go back to? No—' she shook her head '—I seem to recall you saying something about things being uncertain now the war has ended.'

'Yes, they are,' Alec said, tilting his face one way, then another in the mirror, to make sure he hadn't missed a spot. 'Which makes it imperative that I return to London as soon as possible.'

'Oh, but…'

He dipped his head to rinse off what remained of the lather. And paused. He hadn't imagined it this time. There was definitely disappointment written all over her face. She'd even begun to protest.

'There is no point in arguing with me about this,' he said, rinsing his face swiftly, then reaching for the towel to dry himself. 'Any new commands, any decent commissions, are likely to go to those men with connections to the Admiralty. Since I don't have any influence, I need to be there in person. I need to cruise up and down the corridors so people will notice me. See how hungry I am for a new command. They won't see that if I linger here.' He tossed the towel aside with a grimace. 'If they hear I have married. They will think I'm willing to settle down.'

'You are leaving so soon? Leaving me here?'

'Leaving you? Who said anything about leaving you?' Though…hadn't he just been saying *I* need to be there in person, *I* need to cruise up and down? He supposed he could see why she'd misunderstood. And at least she looked disappointed about it. Was she, too, starting to hope they could salvage something from the situation into which her irresponsibility had pitched them?

Or was she merely annoyed about how it would look for her groom to appear to tire of her so quickly after their hasty marriage?

'Well, obviously I cannot leave Papa in the lurch,' she said. 'Not with a houseful of guests.'

He leaned back on the washstand, examining the pugnacious tilt of her chin. Not what he'd expected her to say at all. 'It isn't obvious to me,' he retorted, stung that she thought helping throw a party was more important than his career.

'I just told you, I have duties—'

'You have new duties now. Wifely duties,' he snapped, taking the two steps to close the distance between them, grasping her under the elbows, and lifting her to her feet.

She gasped, but it wasn't a gasp of shock. The look on her face told him she knew exactly what he meant. And that gasp was an admission she wasn't at all averse to what he had in mind either.

So he kissed her.

The moment he let go of her elbows, to wrap his arm about her waist, she put her arms round his neck, and sort of arched into him.

He was glad he'd taken the time to shave. He wouldn't have been able to kiss her so thoroughly if he'd been worrying about scouring her soft cheeks with his rough whiskers.

Which reminded him of his plan to kiss his way down the entire length of her spine.

He broke off the kiss, and turned her round.

'Wh-what…?' she stuttered, and then, when he lifted the hair from the nape of her neck and nibbled gently, gave a deep, shuddery sigh.

Signifying that she liked it.

So he nipped a bit harder. Slid the silken wrap from her shoulders, and slipped his hands down to cup her breasts. Both of them at once.

'Oh, God,' he groaned. 'But your breasts are magnificent.'

She ground her hips back, against his hardness.

He groaned again. Tore her wrap from her arms and tossed it to the floor. Clamped one arm about her waist to hold her still as he began to nibble his way down her back.

Only, the little noises she was making, the gasps and whimpers, were so encouraging he gave up somewhere between her shoulder blades. Straightened up, grabbed her hand and tugged her back to the bed.

'We shouldn't,' she protested. 'I have to get down to breakfast...'

'Not today,' he growled.

Then turned her, and laid her face down on the mattress.

For a second, Julia felt alarmed. What did he mean to do? Was this to be some kind of lesson? He'd sounded so strict when he'd mentioned her duties. And surely this wasn't good—being bent over with her bottom in the air like this? As though he meant to spank her? Just because she'd expressed a reluctance to leave Ness Hall in the middle of a house party?

If he did anything like that she would never forgive him. It might be his right, but nobody had ever beaten her. Not even with the flat of the hand.

But she wasn't going to struggle, or give so much as a hint that she felt even the slightest, faintest, stirrings of alarm. Showing weakness only made bullies worse. She'd learned that from Nick and Herbert, as a little girl. Which was why she'd been able to teach her younger brothers how to deal with them.

But she was so very naked, so very exposed, so very vulnerable, that she couldn't prevent her heart from banging against her ribs. Nor could she help flinching when his hands finally connected with her body.

Though it was the shock of him slowly caressing her bottom that made her jump. For she hadn't expected it. Well, she hadn't known what to expect. But it wasn't that he should stroke, and knead, and squeeze her bottom like this.

'Lush,' he said. 'That's the only word for your behind. So soft, and sweet, and round as it is.'

The alarm she'd been refusing to let him see skipped a beat, and settled into a new, thrumming sort of excitement.

He swept the hair away from the nape of her neck, again. Nibbled. Then took up kissing his way down her spine, the way he'd begun to in the dressing room.

All her breath left her lungs in a whoosh of relief. He wasn't trying to punish her for objecting to his plan, he was just determined to carry it out.

He slid one hand under her body to cup her breast as he reached the very end of her spine. His other slid up the inside of her right thigh. Pushed it aside so that he could insert one of his own legs between hers and nudged them further apart so that he could stand between them.

And then there was a pause. She glanced over her shoulder to see that he was undoing his breeches. She buried her face back in the bedding before she caught sight of that part of him. Or worse, the sight of him as he entered her. From behind. And then crouching over her, and sinking his teeth into the nape of her neck. The way a stallion held his mare while he was covering her.

The image sent a bolt of something purely animal screaming through her. Just about the same time as the hand that had been cupping her breast slid down her stomach. Toyed with her as he plunged into her from behind. And she didn't know whether it was the pressure of his hand, or his hot breath in her ear, or the sheer dominance of his position, but she'd never felt so utterly feminine in her life. Or so glad to be female.

She groaned with pleasure. Gasped, and ground herself against his hand, and finally bit into the mattress to stifle the scream that tore from her as raw, primal excitement exploded through her whole being.

And then he stood up, and gripped her hips with both hands as he thrust to his own completion. While she lay completely immobile. Just letting him. She could do nothing else. She was too limp from the incredible sensations that had ripped through her frame.

When he finished, on a guttural groan that sounded as if it was torn from the very root of his being, he pulled her up, into his arms, and brought her down next to him on the bed, rearranging her while she still felt like a rag doll.

Then he gave a deep, satisfied sigh.

Well, he was bound to feel satisfied, wasn't he? He'd just treated her to a masterly display of masculine dominance.

He hadn't even had to shout at her, or strike her, to get his own way. To make her miss breakfast. He had just kissed her. And her own body had surrendered. No, worse than that, had gleefully gone to him. That realisation soured everything.

'Now that you're done with me,' she said in a waspish tone, 'may I get up and commence the *rest* of my duties?'

He tensed. The way he'd done when she'd slid her hand under his coat and cupped his bottom, that very first night.

Oooh! It made her mad as fire that everything he did made her think about…*that*. Congress. Conversation. Whatever you wanted to call it.

When she disliked him more than any other man she'd ever met!

With an angry huff, she got off the bed—irritated even further by the way her legs felt so weak—and tottered to the dressing room. She sloshed his cold washing water into the bucket, and poured some fresh for herself, with hands that were shaking. Ooh! She couldn't even make her way to the dressing room, and have a wash, with any dignity.

By rights Mabel should be up here, laying out her gown for the day, and helping her with her hair. She soaped the sponge, and gave herself a brisk rubbing down. Well, that was what you did to a mare, wasn't it? After a lengthy gallop.

'Is something amiss?'

She didn't need to turn round to *feel* him, standing in the doorway.

'Can I not even have a wash in privacy?'

'You watched me wash and shave,' he said silkily. 'It's only fair you let me do the same.'

'There's nothing fair about this,' she almost sobbed. 'Most husbands let their wives have their own room.'

'Not when they're first married,' he said with utter certainty.

Could that be true? She had no idea. Nobody had told her what to expect from marriage. Not even one such as this. Not one of her aunts had bothered asking her if she needed any advice—

not that she'd have welcomed it from them. She'd already solved the great mystery of what men and women did with each other if they could get each other's clothes off. So she didn't need a married woman to tell her what to expect on her wedding night.

Anyway, not one of them had the kind of marriage she'd ever wished to endure. It was probably one of them that Nellie had spied, doing what she shouldn't with one of the guests. Or one of the locals.

'Is that why you didn't have my things brought down here? You expected to have the kind of bloodless marriage that high-born society people have?'

'No,' she blurted out. 'That's the last thing I wanted.' She'd dreamed of a marriage in which they could be friends, as well as lovers. 'But...' she turned to look at him, pleading with him for understanding 'I was so busy planning the wedding I never thought about the marriage at all. About where you'd want to sleep.'

'I want to sleep in this room.'

Her heart gave a funny little twist.

And then plummeted when she couldn't see any sign of tenderness in his face. No sign that he'd forgiven her for the way the marriage had come about, or her lack of foresight about making *her* room into *their* room. Just a sort of hard determination. Determination to have his own way.

Which suddenly turned distinctly lustful as he eyed her naked, soapy form.

'The view is much better,' he said, with the start of a wicked smile.

With a squeal of outrage, she flung the sponge at him.

He fielded it. Laughed. And strolled back to the bedroom, where he disposed himself gracefully on the bed.

She slammed the dressing-room door shut on him.

And kicked his valise, for good measure.

Chapter Eight

Julia had never been so glad she had a suite of rooms. By getting Mabel to remove her clothes from the armoire in the bedroom, and taking them into her sitting room, she managed to get dressed without once having to set eyes on her husband. He'd dressed himself…well, she didn't care whether he'd done it in the bedroom or the dressing room. By the next time she saw him he'd made himself decent, which was the main thing.

'You are still angry with me?'

Well, what a stupid question. She glowered at him from the doorway, undecided whether she was more angry with him for making her miss breakfast, or insisting she leave Ness Hall before her father's guests.

Breakfast. Missing breakfast was the worst offence. Because she'd told him how important she felt it was to be there, and he'd ignored her wishes. Would he always ride roughshod over her? Try and reduce her to the status of…of one of his deckhands?

That was what happened in a marriage without love and mutual respect at its core. Two individuals, yoked together, each striving to go the way they wanted and having to drag the other along, instead of both pulling in the same direction.

He got up. Clasped his hands behind his back. 'I've been thinking.'

Something she'd said had made him think? Good grief.

She was pushing out her lips again, the way she did when she was biting back a sharp retort.

He sighed. 'I can see you take your responsibility to your guests seriously. It was the way you likened your post to being the captain of a ship that made me think. Because, as a captain, I would have found it impossible to desert my post.' He'd thought about more than that as he'd listened to her sloshing about in the dressing room in a sort of thwarted rage. It had put him in mind of the way he'd felt when Lizzie's letter had arrived, and he'd had to come tearing down here instead of staying until the task of gutting his ship was finished.

'And there's no saying there will be any new commands for me to take up even if I were to leave Ness Hall and start my blockade of the Admiralty this very day.'

'So, what are you saying?'

'I am suggesting that we stay here until…until Lizzie leaves.'

'Lizzie?'

'Yes.' He didn't want to look weak. He didn't want her to think she could bend him to her will every time they had a difference of opinion. But, upon reflection, he did wonder if he had been a touch unfair.

Just as Lady Julia hadn't considered sharing her room with him, he hadn't considered altering his plans regarding the Admiralty. Marriage had come as a bit of a shock to them both. And it was going to take a bit of time to make the necessary adjustments.

'It was out of concern for Lizzie that I came here in the first place,' he said. 'And now I am here, I may as well use the opportunity to get to know her better.'

So. He wouldn't stay as long as she'd requested. But only until his sister had gone.

Though it amounted to the same thing. Her husband clearly didn't know that Lizzie would only be leaving when everyone else did.

And it was only natural for him to show more concern for his own flesh and blood than for a woman he hadn't even known existed before Christmas.

Besides, wasn't the important thing that he had altered his plans?

'When we do go to London,' she said, 'I can write and have the town house opened up for our use.'

'I am perfectly capable of arranging lodgings more suitable for a married man than a bachelor.'

'I am sure you are, but wouldn't it make more sense to mount your blockade of the Admiralty from a good address? Nothing could better advertise the fact that you now have Papa at your back—'

'I will get a new command on my own merit or not at all,' he snapped.

'I only meant to...'

'You are no longer a Whitney now, with rights to make use of the Whitney property. You are a Dunbar.'

She knew that! Oh, blow him for being so proud and prickly. Julia had only wanted to show she could help him in his career, rather than be a hindrance—which she felt, to be honest, after seeing that she'd made him stay at Ness Hall with her instead of pursuing his next commission.

But at least he had made that concession. At least he was trying to act like a married man, and not a bachelor. Even though he hadn't wanted to get married at all.

And as for being proud and prickly—well, weren't all men? She should have known he'd interpret her willingness to help as a slur on his ability to provide. Men liked women to flutter around like helpless butterflies, while they strode round with their chests puffed out. They didn't like wives who were completely capable of looking after themselves. Reading between the lines, that had been half the trouble between her father and Nicky and Herbert's mother.

She was going to have to make allowances. It would be better than storing up grievances, and nursing them.

'You said you wished to spend time with your sister,' she decided to say, instead of furthering the argument by objecting to the way he'd slapped her down rather than thank her for offering to help.

'I do.'

'She's most likely to be in the drawing room

in the east wing. That's where rehearsals are taking place.'

'Rehearsals?'

'Yes. The younger people, and some of the ones who have little interest in hunting and shooting, are putting on an entertainment for Twelfth Night. It has become something of a tradition over recent years. It is one of the reasons why Papa engaged so many professionals from the theatre this year.'

Papa had said he was sick of having to endure the amateur efforts of the younger set. He'd hoped that the professionals might be able prevent the worst excesses of some of those with the least talent. Perhaps even stop the production running for hours and hours until they'd all reached the limit of their ineptitude.

Her husband scowled. 'Lizzie is too young to perform in front of an audience.'

'She's fifteen.' Julia sighed. 'And this is a private party, not a public performance. Anyway, I don't suppose she will take a lead role. She may sing some songs in a chorus, or play for the older performers if she's proficient on an instrument. Or she may even only be helping paint scenery, or sew costumes. Really, it's just an excuse for the older girls to get together and gossip and giggle should the weather be too dismal for them

to go out for walks.' Which was why the pro-
gramme, in recent years, had been so chaotic.
Nobody had really had the determination to take
charge. 'You cannot expect girls of that age to
be content to stay with the schoolroom party all
the time. Surely?'

His scowl did not lift. 'I certainly don't expect girls like Lizzie to spend their days with
actresses.'

She winced. He was bound to think that
women like Nellie would be a bad influence.
He wouldn't want to hear that she liked Nellie,
very much, and thought he might do so too if
only he wasn't so prejudiced.

'Well,' she said, in as calm and reasonable a
tone as she could muster. 'You may give your
sister your opinion about actors, and why you do
not wish her to spend too much time with them,
or, indeed, take part in any amateur theatricals,
the moment you get there. And then,' she added
pointedly, 'see how well your belated decision
to spend the rest of this house party *getting to
know her* proceeds.'

She turned and walked from the room, without looking to see if he was following her. She
didn't flounce. Because ladies didn't flounce.
They kept their heads erect, their posture correct, and their carriage elegant.

Whereas her husband, she was sure, was prowling along behind her like some great predator. Growling and swishing his tail. Not that he really had a tail. She was just being fanciful, imagining him stalking her.

Because she was walking briskly, in a purposeful manner, they reached the east drawing room before either of them had time to exchange a single word.

'There she is, as you can see,' she said, waving her hand in the general direction of a table under the window, on which lay a heap of costumes. The theatre company her father had hired had brought dozens of wicker hampers with them, containing all sorts of costumes and props—including the mask she'd worn for the masquerade. Though what on earth they were going to do with the stuffed duck, which her cousin Winifred was daubing with yellow paint, she couldn't imagine.

'Wait.' He seized her arm when she made for the door through which they'd just come. 'Where are you going?'

'Since I missed breakfast,' she replied, smiling through gritted teeth, since several people were looking in their direction, 'I am going to Mrs Dawson's sitting room, to take tea with her, so that I can make sure there are no problems that I should know about.'

'But—'

Did she imagine it, or had a faint trace of panic flashed across his face?

'Alec!' Lizzie had just noticed them standing in the doorway. She dropped whatever it was she'd been sewing, and came bounding across the room, her face alight. 'Have you come to help with the play? We're going to perform—' She clapped her hands to her mouth. 'Oh, it's to be a secret. I cannot tell you. Not unless you are going to be one of the troupe.'

Julia tensed. Oh, how she hoped he wasn't going to drag her away, and read her a lecture on proper behaviour. She might be cross with him, but it was rather endearing, the way Lizzie seemed to worship him. It would be terrible for all her faith, and trust, and esteem for him to be destroyed at a stroke. Not that it would do Lizzie any harm to learn what selfish beasts men could be. But it would hurt him, in the long run, to lose his sister's devotion.

Though why should she care? She gave herself a mental shake.

To give him credit, his features softened when he looked at Lizzie. And he didn't immediately order her to stop enjoying herself, but, instead, had a good look round the room. Lady Julia watched his face as he took in what he was seeing. A couple of her cousins, sitting at a desk, copying out what looked like a script. Another pair watching them from the table where Lizzie had just been stitching costumes.

At the far end of the room, on a huge refectory style table, several of the older boys from the schoolroom party were busy painting something—no doubt a piece of scenery—on a huge piece of canvas, under the direction of the artist who'd chalked the decorations on the ballroom floor. And Mr Atterbury, who was currently employed as tutor to Aunt Constance's boys, was sitting on a nearby armchair, keeping half an eye on them from behind his newspaper.

It all looked just as harmless as she'd promised. A productive way to engage the interest of the members of the schoolroom party who were too old for nursery games and afternoon naps, yet not quite ready for more adult pursuits.

It looked particularly innocuous because not one single actor or actress was present. As far as her husband could see, the young people were being supervised by one of the tutors and a couple of matrons who, for one reason or another, preferred to stay within doors than go out riding. They weren't supervising all that closely, but sitting on chairs by the fire, drinking tea and gossiping. But their presence was enough to convey respectability. Of course all that would change after noon, when the actors finally started emerging from their rooms. But by then, her husband might have mellowed toward them.

Or he might have grown bored and gone elsewhere.

'Who is that lanky youth, with the spotty face, waving at you and spraying paint in every direction?' her husband suddenly asked.

Julia looked towards where he'd indicated, her face breaking out into a warm smile as she waved back. 'That is my youngest brother, Benjamin. Though I cannot think what he is doing here. He usually haunts the stables whenever he is home.'

Her answer came when Lizzie blushed, and gave a nervous laugh.

But—good heavens. Lizzie and Ben? Surely Ben wasn't old enough to be noticing girls, let alone dangling after them? Why, it seemed no time at all since she'd been holding his chubby little hands as he took his first tottering steps round the nursery.

'Oh, do come and meet Winifred,' said Lizzie, seizing her brother's arm. 'She's Lady Julia's cousin, you know, and is at my school. I'm sure you recall I have written to you about her...'

Lizzie's chatter faded as she tugged her brother deeper into the room where he was promptly swamped by a wave of feminine enthusiasm. Julia couldn't help smiling as she abandoned him to his sister's friends. They'd all been dying to get their hands on him, from the moment he'd arrived unannounced. At dead of night, too, and all windswept and wet from the storm, the way all heroes in stories should arrive—at least the kind of stories her younger cousins seemed to enjoy reading.

For her part, she couldn't imagine why that image of him, standing in the doorway, his unfashionably long hair whipping round his grim face, had stuck in her mind. She hadn't swooned at the first sight of him, the way the younger girls had. And she'd met many men as handsome as him, during her London Seasons.

Though she couldn't, just at this moment, recall what any of them looked like.

Nor had she ever felt anything more than irritation when any of them had tried to hold her hand a little longer than was appropriate during the measures of a dance. She certainly hadn't gone all…soupy inside watching them walk away from her on the arm of another female. Even if that female was his sister. Or felt the urge to snap her fingers in the faces of the other girls who came clustering round him, just to remind them all that he belonged to her.

She sucked in a sharp breath. Good grief, she was becoming possessive. Even a touch jealous of the time those girls would spend with her husband while she was busy elsewhere.

Turning on her heel, she hurried from the drawing room before she started experiencing any more stupid, weak emotions about her husband. It was bad enough that his domineering behaviour in the bedroom had thrilled her. She would never forgive herself if she started hanging on his coat tails by day, too. The way poor Ellen used to do with Nick, when they were first married. Before she discovered that behind his handsome face—and, yes, she could concede that Nick was a handsome specimen—he was nothing more than a bully and a philanderer.

It had felt like the longest day of his life. Why on earth had he told Julia he'd been willing to spend it getting to know Lizzie? Because Julia had been so upset at the prospect of leaving before the end of the house party, that was why. And then he'd forced her into fulfilling one of his fantasies, instead of permitting her to go and have breakfast. And all just to prove that she couldn't do as she pleased any longer. Not now she was married.

Only after he'd proved she was very married

indeed, her words about being like the captain of a ship had reared up to goad him. While he'd been putting on his clothes, he'd remembered how he'd felt when his last commission had been cut short. It had been most unpleasant, having his entire identity stripped away, just as he'd been stripping the ship in which he'd fought for the past six months, down to a hulk.

Did she feel like that? he'd wondered as he listened to her taking out her temper on the washbasin. Bewildered and adrift? Or as he'd done when marriage had been thrust upon him? Angry and resentful?

He most certainly didn't want to drag an angry and resentful wife with him to London. And then again, something about the way she'd slammed the door on him put him in mind of scenes he'd witnessed as a child. Of his mother accusing his father of doing exactly as he pleased. And his father laughing and saying why not? That it was a woman's role to obey.

And maybe that was so. But it was not a man's role to crush his wife. Which was why he'd suggested the compromise.

Only now it turned out to be no such thing. Lizzie had let slip that she was staying to the bitter end of the house party, so she could take part in the pantomime the youngsters were rehearsing.

He shucked off his jacket and waistcoat on his way to the dressing room, where he poured water into the basin for a swift wash. Someone had laundered his shirt from the night before, and hung it from a peg above his valise, he noted with gratitude. Alec hadn't brought many changes of clothing, thinking he'd only be here for a day or so. Just long enough to wrest Lizzie from whatever man it was he'd feared was trying to seduce her.

Seduce her? Hah! A man would have to get up very early in the morning to stand a chance of besting Lizzie. She had a shrewd head on her shoulders, and total confidence in her own worth. What's more, she was already practising her wiles on Lady Julia's bacon-brained brother. He'd watched her toying with the poor besotted fool all day. Glorying in the power of her beauty. She'd known Benjamin could hardly take his eyes off her, so the baggage had studiously ignored him, for the most part. Only to encourage him to carry on sighing after her by darting him the occasional brief glance, coupled with a slight smile, after which she'd lower her head and probably play with a curl of her hair for good measure.

The idiot boy had spilled more paint down his trousers and on his shoes than he'd managed to daub on the canvas. Which Lizzie's friends had found hilarious.

Frowning, he pulled his shirt over his head, then splashed his face with water. To think that, in the past, he'd regretted not spending much time with Lizzie. Regretted not being closer, not being able to watch over her in person, but instead having to trust her to the care of schoolmistresses and the goodwill of friends.

Well, having spent the entire day with her, he decided it hadn't been such a bad way to go on, after all. Girls of Lizzie's age were extremely tiresome. Their heads were full of nonsense, which they talked about incessantly. If they'd ever actually had the chance to live under the same roof, he'd have been sorely tempted to send her away to school, just to get some peace and quiet.

He rubbed his face vigorously on the towel, as though he could slough off the day's irritations along with the water. He was just wondering whether he should shave again, when the door to the sitting room opened, then shut with a resounding slam.

It could only be his wife. A servant wouldn't dare slam any door anywhere in the house.

He slung the towel over the rail, and went out to see what ailed her now. He was just in time to catch her sweeping the dozens of pots that cluttered her dressing table to one side, bury her face in her hands, and emit a sort of strangled scream.

She clearly had no idea he was here.

She probably wished he wasn't.

Indeed, the door-slamming, and the wanton destruction of all her cosmetics, and the strangled scream might all stem from her frustration at having to own to him as a husband.

He leaned his forearm against the doorframe while he considered his next move. He'd upset her this morning, insisting she bend to his will, rather than go about her duties as though she was still a single woman. Oh, she'd enjoyed everything he'd done to her. But the very fact that she had enjoyed it all so much had angered her, too.

He even understood her anger. His physical reaction to her angered him almost as much. He didn't want to want her. And was guilty of taking out some of his frustration on her.

He should apologise.

He cleared his throat.

The way she started, then lifted her head to look in his direction, confirmed his suspicion she hadn't had a clue he was there. She'd clearly come here to let out her frustration in what she'd hoped was privacy.

She averted her head swiftly, but not before he'd seen tears streaming down her face.

He planted his feet firmly into the carpet, unconsciously adopting the same stance he'd have taken had he been bracing himself against the recoil of a broadside. He had no experience, as an adult, of female tears, not personally. He'd heard accounts from brother officers, or overheard the ratings talk about weeping women. But he'd never come face-to-face with one. Not one who was crying because of something he'd done.

He had no idea what to do.

Because men didn't cry. Not even boys did, more than a couple of times. Because they learned that the ones who snivelled and complained were universally despised. Whereas the midshipmen who climbed the rigging without protest, even though their hands were already raw from the ropes, and were terrified of the swaying of the ship, and the wind whipping across the deck, were admired for their pluck.

Julia clearly hadn't learned that lesson. Because, after that one, brief, horror-stricken glance in his direction, she buried her face in her hands and begun sobbing in earnest.

For his benefit? Was she trying to gain sympathy? Or had she correctly guessed that the sight of his wife in tears was the one thing most likely to drive him away?

Damn women for being so complicated!

Even so, she wasn't going to drive him away. Inexperienced though he was with women's tears, it was something he was clearly going to have to learn to deal with, now that he was married.

How did other men cope? He swiftly reviewed all he'd heard about how to placate and soothe a weeping woman. Which invariably involved the giving of gifts, or apologies, or even cuddles.

Well, he didn't have a gift to give her. And he was not about to apologise. He'd already backed down about exactly when to leave here and go to London. To apologise as well would make her think she could get her own way every time she turned on the tears. And anyway, hadn't her own father warned him she needed a firm hand? And as for putting his arm round her—no. That would only goad her into slapping his face. For, inexperienced though he was with weeping women, he wasn't a fool. There was a deal of anger mixed up with whatever had made her cry.

In the end, Alec did the only practical thing he could think of.

He crossed the room to her side, tapped her on the shoulder, and proffered a clean handkerchief.

'Oh. Th-thank you,' she sobbed, taking it. 'I d-dare say I shall be done in a minute. P-please don't let me st-stop you d-doing whatever it w-w-was…' She made a strange, indeterminate gesture with her free hand.

'I was only dressing for dinner—' he began.

'Dinner,' she wailed. 'D-don't talk to me about dinner! I sh-shall have to go d-down to d-dinner, and sm-smile…'

She broke down into a fresh gale of angry, bitter sobs.

He'd heard the expression *all at sea*. But never had he truly understood what it felt like, until now. He could only stand still, and watch while she cried herself out. He manfully resisted the temptation to look at the clock on the mantel. She'd stop when she was ready, and not before.

Though, as she'd forecast, the storm turned out to be nothing more than a squall after all. Blown out almost as quickly as it had blown in. She gave one last shuddering sob, and blew her nose.

'I beg your pardon,' she said to the surface of her dressing table. 'I didn't mean to make you uncomfortable.'

She could tell? Even though she'd had her

face buried in her handkerchief the whole time? Women must have some kind of intuition where men were concerned. They didn't need to look directly at a man to know exactly where he was and what he was doing—aye, and apparently what he was thinking, too. Hadn't he spent all day watching Lizzie demonstrate just such uncanny ability with young Ben?

'I just...' Julia explained. 'I couldn't think of anywhere else to go.'

'And it doesn't really matter if you weep in front of me anyway, does it?'

She lifted her head to look at him, wide-eyed.

'I am the one person you don't need to hide anything from,' he explained. 'The one person who has already seen beneath your mask.'

She made a moue of annoyance. But she didn't start shrieking at him. On the contrary, after a frown had flickered across her face, she gave a little sigh. 'Yes,' she said. 'That's true.'

It was a strangely intimate moment. An uncomfortable sort of intimacy, which he would have avoided, given the choice. But then who else did she have to turn to, to talk to, about the things that were upsetting her? Nobody else knew that she wasn't in love with him. That she'd had to marry him to save face.

'Would you care for a brandy?' He could think

of nothing else to offer her. She'd finished with the handkerchief now. Except as an object to twist between her fingers as though she needed to strangle something. Or someone.

'Brandy?' She wrinkled her nose. Then shook her head. 'No. I don't drink brandy.'

'You look as though it might do you good, just this once.' It would certainly do him good. He went through to the sitting room, where he'd had a helpful footman set out a tray with a selection of decanters and tumblers for just such an eventuality. Not that he'd expected to have to tip alcohol down his distraught wife's throat. He'd just thought he might want fortification, at some point.

'Here,' he said, going back to her, and setting one of the drinks he'd poured onto the dressing table before her.

She shook her head. 'I don't think it's a good idea. *In vino veritas*, and all that.'

'You feel you need to keep your wits about you, is that it?'

She nodded. Then her face crumpled again. 'God, I feel like such a fool!'

He downed his own brandy swiftly. If she was going to start crying again, he'd need all the help he could get.

'I'm sorry you feel like that,' he bit out. 'I had

thought we were starting to get used to each other.'

'What? No! I mean—' She looked up at him in horror. 'It's not you—why I'm crying. It's...' She gulped. Gave her handkerchief another savage twist.

It wasn't him? Then someone else must have upset her.

'Tell me,' he barked, setting his empty glass down next to her full one. Once he found out who'd caused his wife to break down like that— the proud, spirited woman who'd married a stranger rather than admit to having made a terrible mistake—he'd make them rue the day they were born!

'No, I...really, it's too...painful...' She gave an expressive shudder.

Which was rather a relief. He would have listened, naturally, had she wanted someone to talk to. Even though he'd had a day of gritting his teeth in the face of torrents of inane feminine confidences.

There must be something else he could do to help her through this...whatever it was. He studied her for a second or two as she strove in vain to recover her composure.

Appearances mattered to her. Very much. She'd even married him, rather than have her schemes exposed. And she'd run in here to weep so that nobody would know she was upset.

What she needed was an excuse to hide away until she felt ready to face the world with her composed mask firmly back in place.

Right. He could give her that. Give her the space to recover, at her own pace. Give her a good reason for avoiding whatever, or whoever, it was who'd upset her so badly. So that she could save face.

'I'm going to ring for some tea,' he said, crossing to the bell pull, and tugging it hard. Then he went to the bed, ripped off the covers, tossed them about, and slung them haphazardly back onto the mattress.

That got her attention.

'What on earth are you doing?'

'Creating a diversion,' he informed her gruffly. 'Stay out of sight when the maid comes up with the tea tray, and let me do all the talking,' he told her. 'She'll think you are too embarrassed to face her.'

'What? Why would I be…?' He saw comprehension dawn on her face. 'Oh!'

He nodded. 'Exactly. She'll inform everyone that we cannot keep our hands off each other, and nobody will be a bit surprised when we don't put in an appearance at dinner. Or ask you awkward questions after.'

'That's…that's…'

'The kind of ruse I should have thought you'd appreciate.'

Just when she was starting to think she could like him, he went and said something cutting, like that.

'I don't appreciate having to resort to ruses at all,' she snapped. 'I would rather people would be honest. And not tell beastly lies. And make you believe…believe…'

Oh, good grief. She was going to start crying again.

Just as someone came to the door to find out why her husband had been ringing. He gave her one blistering look, then went to the door and opened it just a crack. She put the handkerchief to her mouth and bit down on it, to stifle her sobs. As little as she wished the maids to think she'd been…frolicking in bed during the afternoon, did she wish any of them to know she'd been crying?

Which they were bound to think, what with her husband angling his body so that the maid could glimpse the bed he'd so artfully destroyed, and the low murmur with which he gave the order for tea and a cold collation, as though he was trying not to wake whoever was lying in that wrecked bed.

And the fact that he was shirtless. Shirtless! How could he wander around the room in a state of undress, when she was here?

Though to be fair, he'd been here first. He'd been changing for dinner, perfectly innocently.

And even though he hadn't been wearing a shirt, he had produced a handkerchief.

And he was doing his best to shield her.

He'd managed to convey a totally erroneous impression of what was going on in this bedroom without telling a single lie.

It was…masterly, actually.

'I'm sorry,' she said, as soon as he'd shut the door on the maid. 'For snapping at you, when you are just trying to help. You must think I'm an ungrateful shrew.'

He didn't immediately contradict her.

Strangely, she liked that about him—that he was showing no inclination to be untruthful with her, not even to spare her feelings. It looked as though she would always know where she stood with him.

Unlike with some people.

'I think,' he said slowly, as though measuring his words, 'that something has upset you very much, something you cannot admit to the world that you are upset about, and you feel the need to lash out in retaliation. And I'm the only one here.'

'Yes, but it's not your fault.' The more reasonable he was being, the worse she felt. 'It's…'

No, it was no good. She couldn't even speak the name without a pang of terrible pain shooting through her. She hadn't realised she'd actually bowed over, and clutched at her stomach until she felt him patting her on the shoulder.

'There, there,' he said. As though completely at a loss as to what to do with her.

'You really don't have much experience with women, do you?' She glanced up and caught an expression of chagrin on his face.

'Is it that obvious?'

'Oh, yes. A skilled philanderer would have a stock of smooth phrases at his disposal. He wouldn't hand me a handkerchief, or pat me on the shoulder and say *there, there*, as though I were a child who'd fallen and scraped her knee.'

'I beg your pardon…' he began stiffly.

'Oh, don't poker up. I didn't mean to insult you. I'm *glad* you aren't the kind of man who finds it easy to tell lies, or pretend to feel something he doesn't. Not like…' She swallowed. 'David.' There. She'd finally managed to force the name between her teeth.

She swivelled round on the stool to face her

husband fully. Studied his face to see how he felt about having the name of his former rival brought into their bedroom.

It didn't look that much grimmer than usual.

Though suddenly, he spun away from her, went to the wrecked bed, and sat down on the edge of it, his hands on his knees. Gave her his full attention.

'You had better tell me the worst.'

Chapter Nine

'He's…' She swallowed. 'He's got engaged to… to Marianne.'

'And…' His brows drew down into a frown so deep they almost met in the middle. 'And you are upset about this? Even though you knew there was never any chance of a reconciliation, now you have married me?'

'Yes, I'm upset. But not because—' She waved a hand between them. 'It's because I've just discovered they've been…been carrying on in secret for years. And using me as cover. And generally betraying me in every conceivable way. And making a fool of me. When I thought they were my friends!' She pressed one hand to her forehead as if she could stuff the terrible thoughts back into place.

'I don't see why they couldn't have told me in the first place. I would have supported them, then. Made sure they could have met each other. Given Marianne time off, or chaperoned them, or…or anything they wanted! They didn't have to make me think that David…that David…'

It was no use. Her emotions were in such turmoil she couldn't possibly sit still a moment longer. Getting to her feet, she paced across the floor to the fireplace. Whirled round.

'When I went to London, for my first Season, he…he…' A wave of humiliation crushed the rest of it up against her teeth.

Alec made for the dressing table, retrieved the brandy glass, and brought it across to her.

'In vino veritas,' he said, handing her the glass.

He wanted her to be able to speak of David's perfidy? And Marianne's? And was urging her to take Dutch courage?

Very well. She accepted the glass, and took a swift gulp.

It burned the back of her throat, making her wheeze.

Then hit her stomach in a warm rush.

Alec didn't press her to continue. He just stood there, watching her with that grim face of his. That grim, yet utterly trustworthy face.

'You'd never speak to a girl of seventeen, on her way to her first Season, of all her faults, would you? And imply she was shallow? And tell her that she was bound to forget her childhood friends, and come back married to some wealthy, titled fop? And make her feel that if she did, it would break your heart? Would you?'

He shook his head.

'I thought he was making a declaration. Instead he...' She closed her eyes and shuddered. 'I don't know what he was doing. What made him try to prevent me from getting married, when even then, apparently, he and Marianne had an understanding.'

She took another gulp of the brandy. She didn't know whether it was the drink, or telling her husband about David, but whichever it was, she was starting to feel less hurt, and more angry. And with the fresh rush of anger came a startling clarity of thought.

'Actually, perhaps I do,' she said, setting the brandy glass down on the mantel with a snap. 'If I'd married, I would have moved away. And probably taken Marianne with me, because I'd promised she'd always have a home with me. I most definitely wouldn't have left her here, alone, because none of the others like her. And I didn't want her to be miserable. I was trying to *protect* her, for heaven's sake! She was my friend. And I was hers. Why couldn't she just have told me she was in love with David, and he with her? Why did she have to be so…sly?'

When she kept on looking at him for a moment or two, as she gathered her thoughts, he spread his hands in open admission of ignorance.

'I couldn't say,' he said, appearing to think she expected an answer.

'Of course you couldn't. No more could I. Though I suppose she did suffer a twinge or two of conscience about…us.'

'Us?'

'Yes. Didn't you notice her crying all the way through our wedding? I suppose I have to give her that much. She was sorry I was marrying someone I didn't know, let alone love. And felt guilty, too, apparently.'

'Guilty?'

'Oh, yes. You haven't heard the best part yet,' she replied bitterly. 'The reason I ended up with you, in the orangery, rather than David, was because the pair of them had taken advantage of the mummers' play to sneak off together. That was why I couldn't find him. Because the pair of them were both up in Marianne's room for…a tryst.' She spat the word out. The word that Marianne had spoken so archly. With a defiant glint in her eye.

'To think that she pretended to be so set

against my plan to make David propose, when all the time she was planning to make use of it herself!'

He took a breath, as though about to say something.

'And don't you dare throw my words back in my face, about using stratagems to confuse the enemy, or flying under false colours, or anything of that nature. Or I shall…'

She couldn't carry that sentence to any conclusion. Because she didn't know what she'd do. She only knew that if he mocked her now, she wouldn't be able to bear it. All Marianne's perfidy, and David's duplicity, could not hurt her as much as having this man laugh at her.

Which was an appalling discovery to make.

Because it meant that in only a few short days, he'd become as important to her, as dear to her, as either of them had ever been.

'I was only going to say,' he said icily, 'that it sounds as though they are well suited to each other. And that you are better off without either of them.'

He turned on his heel and stalked away.

She hoped it was only because somebody had just knocked on the door.

She darted across the room to a point where she couldn't be seen from the doorway, trusting that Alec wouldn't simply walk out and leave her. Though she wouldn't blame him if he did. She'd been much too forthright. Contrary, even—venting her anger on him when he hadn't done anything to deserve it.

He didn't walk out and leave her. He took first one tray, then a second, from whoever was outside in the corridor, setting them down on nearby tables.

'Thank you,' she said, the moment the door had closed on the last servant. 'For organising the smokescreen.' She indicated the tea trays. 'And also…' She took a deep breath. Because humility didn't come easily to her. 'Also for bearing with my tantrum. And pointing out that they are better suited to each other than I ever was to either of them. You are right. For I cannot abide disloyalty. Or duplicity. Oh…' She waved down the protest he might have made before he could voice it. 'I know you must find that hard to believe, given the way I deceived you the night we…the night we…um…first came together. But…'

He frowned.

'Your code of morals is a little tangled, perhaps, but I concede that you do have one.'

The beast! The pompous, judgemental…

'And that it exceeds that of your…well, I was

going to say friends. But they have proved to be no such thing to you.'

Oh. Well, she supposed she couldn't really take exception to any of that. Not unless she was determined to quarrel with him. Which might make her feel better for a little while, but wouldn't do her any good in the long run.

'I think,' he said, lifting the lid from the teapot and peering inside, 'that they took advantage of your generous nature.'

Generous? He thought she was generous? Well that put paid to any lingering shreds of quarrel-someness.

'Would you like a cup of tea, now? Or would you prefer to keep going with the brandy? There is plenty of both.'

'I do not wish to develop a taste for brandy, thank you very much,' she said.

'Then I shall pour you some tea.'

He replaced the lid on the pot, arranged the cup on its saucer, and settled the tea strainer across the rim.

'Milk and sugar?'

She clapped her hand over her mouth.

'What is the matter now? What have I said?'

'You...' She pointed at him. At his bare chest. The delicate china milk jug in one hand. The sugar tongs in the other. 'You look so...incongruous. Presiding over the tea tray without your shirt.'

His face stiffened. 'Do you wish me to put on a shirt to pour tea for you?'

She shook her head. 'To be honest, I rather like looking at your chest. It is such a very well-made chest.' She ran hungry eyes over his beautifully sculpted torso. A sudden thirst made her lick her lips. And it wasn't for tea. Or brandy. She glanced at the bed he'd unmade.

The milk jug slipped through his fingers and landed with a clatter and a splosh on the tray.

'You want me,' he said.

She nodded her head, too shy to admit out loud to having such feelings without the cover of night, or anything else to hide behind.

'That's the brandy talking,' he said, putting the tongs down in the puddle of milk.

'In vino veritas,' she said with a shrug. 'I wouldn't normally have the nerve to admit it. To be so…bold. Or so…open, about what I feel. But with you standing there like that…' She ran greedy eyes over his upper body again. 'And anyway,' she added crossly, when he continued to just stand there, fists clenched, glowering at her. 'It was your idea to go to bed instead of going down to dinner.'

'I only meant it as a ruse. I didn't mean…'

'Oh. You mean, you don't want me, too?'

'Don't be absurd, woman, you can see that I do,' he replied. Then, shockingly, uncurled one fist and gestured towards his manhood, which looked to her as though it was attempting to thrust its way right through his breeches. The sight sent a rush of heat to the very place it was clearly hoping to go.

'Then what's to stop us?' She took a hesitant step towards him. 'We're married. And everyone thinks that's why we're staying up here anyway.' She reached out and placed one hand, rather daringly she thought, on the mat of blond hair at the very centre of his magnificent chest.

To her chagrin, he didn't immediately sweep her off her feet, carry her across the room, and fling her onto the bed, though she could feel his heart racing beneath her palm.

'You're upset,' he bit out. 'And not used to drinking brandy. I don't want to take advantage while you're vulnerable. It wouldn't be the act of a gentleman.'

'That didn't stop you this morning,' she retorted. 'Is it…is it because I'm the one trying to start it, this time?' She snatched her hand away as though he'd burnt her.

'God, no.' He seized her hand and carried it back to where it had been, placing his own over it to keep it there. 'I regret the way I treated you this morning. I shouldn't have obliged you to submit, when it wasn't what you wanted. I was angry. Trying to prove something.'

Good Lord, this was unheard of. A man apologising for acting brutishly? If that was what he was doing. She couldn't be sure since she'd never heard a man making any attempt to explain his actions. Not any man but him, that was.

'What,' she asked in fascination, 'were you trying to prove?'

'That...that you are not the one in control.'

Dominance—he'd been asserting his dominance over her. Well, yes, she'd certainly felt dominated. Deliciously so, to be honest.

But how far did that need for dominance go?

'So it is just that you don't want to...go back to bed, if I am the one to want it? To ask for it?'

'No! That's not what I meant. I meant... God, I don't know what I meant.' His fingers tightened until they were almost crushing hers. She had no doubt that if she complained he'd let her go. At once.

But she didn't feel like complaining.

'And if it comes to wanting...' he breathed, with such a look of pent-up longing and frustration in his eyes that it made her stomach flip with excitement. 'I want you all the time. And I don't know how that can be when I only met you a handful of days ago. And it...'

Ah. She could see it now. He was in as much confusion as she was. And struggling to come to terms with the desire that kept on flaring between them.

'Infuriates you?'

'Yes.'

'It infuriates me, too,' she admitted. 'But right this moment, I am glad to know that at least *someone* wants me. Really wants me. Enough to scandalise everyone else at the house party by taking me to bed in the afternoon.'

And then, because he still looked so torn between the wanting, and the resentment, she tugged her hand free. But only so she could reach up and loop both her arms round his neck. She pushed her fingers into the soft curls that caressed the nape of his neck, and did a little caressing of her own.

He smiled with his eyes. That was the only way to describe it. Because although his mouth hardly changed shape at all, she knew he was smiling at her as he put his arms about her waist and tugged her into his reassuringly hard body.

'This time,' he informed her sternly, 'we are going to take it slowly. Neither of us is angry with the other, so we should be able to savour the bedding, rather than just exploding into release like when a match touches powder.'

'S-s-savour?' He made it sound so decadent, when his voice went all soft and growly like that, with that slight lilt emphasising his Scottish heritage.

'Oh, yes,' he said, lifting her off her feet and carrying her to the prepared bed. 'I want to strip you naked, and gaze on all that perfect, porcelain skin. Stroke it, and taste it. And bring you to release several times before I even enter you.'

'B-before you…?' Her heart was hammering so hard as he laid her gently down on the mattress that she couldn't breathe the words out properly.

'Aye. Before. That is how a husband should bed his wife, I think.' He shook his head ruefully as he turned her to one side, so that he could undo the ties at the back of her dress. 'Not hard, and fast, as though her own pleasure is of no account.'

She'd had pleasure in their couplings so far, she wanted to tell him. But he'd slid his hand inside her gown and was easing it off her shoulders. Kneeling over her and kissing his way along the skin he bared. And she found that it was all she could do to breathe, never mind say anything.

So she just reached for him, and touched him

the way he was touching her, to show that she was, for once, willing to do *exactly* as he wished.

And soon discovered that obeying a man could bring the kind of reward she'd never dreamed possible.

She didn't argue the next day, either, when he forbade her to leave the room to go down for breakfast.

'You promised to obey me, woman,' he growled provocatively, rolling her into the centre of the bed and pinning her down. 'And I promised to cherish you. I cannot have you leaving this room until you look…' He ground into her with his hips. 'Sufficiently cherished.'

He spoke in a jocular fashion. But she had to admit that—in the bedroom at least—he was doing his level best to be a good husband, even though he hadn't wanted to be any such thing. The least she could do was reciprocate. Which she did with such enthusiasm it was noon before she thought of raising the topic of leaving the bedroom again.

'I really cannot stay in here all day.' She sighed, running one foot up and down his calf.

'Nobody else much emerges from their rooms before noon.'

'Yes, but not me. It is not the behaviour of a lady to neglect her guests.'

'Not even when she's only just got married?'

'Not even then. Going down a little late might just be forgiven, since we are newlyweds. But it really isn't fair on the staff. They have so much extra work to do this year.'

He'd nodded then. And, was she imagining it, or was there just a touch of approval in his expression when he answered?

'Wouldn't expect my crew to do all the work while I lounged about in my cabin, either.'

Good grief. She'd actually won a little grudging respect from him, at last.

They took turns to use the dressing room to get washed and dressed, and left the room arm in arm. In perfect amity with each other.

At least, she felt in perfect amity with him, when he gave her a peck on the cheek when their ways parted. There was a lightness to her step as she turned and began to make her way to Mrs Dawson's sitting room. And a smile came to her lips when she heard her husband start whistling on his way to the rehearsal room, where he planned to spend what was left of the afternoon with his sister.

Mrs Dawson had been coping magnificently without her input, she soon discovered.

'All that time you spent drawing up those charts of which rooms to use,' said the house-keeper, pouring her a cup of tea, 'in what order, and all the special likes and dislikes of those what would be using them have made things wonderfully easy. And it's not as if I couldn't have come to you if there was a real emergency now, is it?'

Julia's face flamed as she had a vision of Mrs Dawson bursting into her bedroom and catching Alec doing one of those delightful, yet totally shocking things he'd spent the morning doing to her.

And then her attention wandered as she relived one or two of them. When Mrs Dawson said she was glad they'd settled the matter, she had no idea what she'd just agreed to. She'd just been humming a yes, or a no, whenever the house-keeper had paused, in a sort of expectant way.

'Oh, dear,' she said, setting her tea cup down. 'Is that the time? I should be getting ready for dinner.'

'Before you go,' said Mrs Dawson, pursing her lips in an oddly disapproving way, 'we should discuss the wedding tomorrow.'

'Wedding?'

'Of that Miss Marianne and David Kettley.'

Goodness—she'd completely forgotten about the wedding.

But now she *had* been reminded of it, the distaste, and the hurt, and the sense of betrayal all came surging back.

'Ah. I see you do feel it,' said Mrs Dawson sagely.

'Feel what?' She bridled at the suggestion she might be betraying a single one of her feelings regarding Marianne's treachery.

'That if she wants to go and get married all in haste, like this, then she shouldn't expect any of us to run round helping. As if we haven't all got enough work to do with the house full of his Lordship's guests.'

None of them had seemed to mind the extra work her own wedding had caused. Unless they'd all just hidden it very well.

'Does she…expect any of you to…do anything?' Strange how loath she was to ask Mrs Dawson outright if her own hasty marriage had created so much resentment below stairs.

'She's just been playing her tricks, same as usual,' said Mrs Dawson with a sniff.

'Her…her tricks?' Julia reached for a scone, split it in two, and slathered one half with butter. Why was it she was only seeing now that people might have had reason for disliking Marianne so much? Was she such a poor judge of character?

'Giving orders, and pretending they were coming from you when we know very well she's not been within twenty yards of your room to obtain them.'

'What orders has she tried to give?' In her name? That really was going a bit far.

'Oh, wanting Cook to provide food for her wedding breakfast, trying to get Mabel to make alterations to one of her gowns for the ceremony. The usual sort of thing.'

'I must say, I'm surprised.' Marianne had always seemed so…humble. She couldn't imagine her trying to give any servants any orders. Indeed, she'd always seemed so timid, so reluctant to pass on the messages she really had given, insisting that the servants all terrified her.

And then she suddenly recalled Nellie, when she'd been mimicking Marianne saying *Oh, no, I couldn't possibly*, in an arch, false sort of way that had made Marianne look rather cross.

'Well, that's just like you, my lady,' said Mrs Dawson with a fond gleam in her eye. 'Always willing to see the best in everyone. And so kind as you have been to that girl.'

Why did everyone always refer to Marianne as *that girl*? And what else should she have been, but kind, when nobody else had ever spared a thought for Marianne's feelings? Her mind flew back to the very first day Marianne had come to live with them. She'd been in the schoolroom, poring over a grammar book, when Nick and Herbert had burst in, asking if she'd seen *'the little Froggy orphan'*.

'We haven't been able to catch her scent this past half-hour or more,' Herbert had said.

'Gone to ground,' Nick had said. And then, in spite of her governess's objections, had begun to wrench open all the cupboard doors, look behind the curtains and inside the window seat, even upsetting her desk before they were satisfied she wasn't hiding the fugitive. Only when they'd completely ransacked the room did they caper over to the door, blowing a reedy fanfare on a hunting horn they'd brought with them. It was with a cry of *Tally-ho!* they'd set off in renewed pursuit.

Later that day, she'd found Marianne, huddled behind the sofa in the morning room, weeping silent, bitter tears. And had naturally taken the poor little mite under her wing.

'She had nobody else,' said Julia firmly. 'I know that Marianne has never been popular in this house. But…once she came to live with me, at least I never felt so alone.' Instead of having to deal with Nick and Herbert alone, she had another girl to stand with her. 'She was my childhood playmate,' she said wistfully. And later, they'd started poring over fashion journals, and gone shopping together, and oh, all the hundred-and-one things that all girls did as they became young ladies. 'She was my companion when I went up to London for the Season.'

'Ah, well, yes. I suppose she was a comfort to you. Like a little wraith you were, for a time after your mama passed on. And only you to comfort the boys with your papa shutting himself away like that...'

Exactly. Just because they'd fallen out, over a man, could she really forget how close they'd been, for so many years?

Especially since she no longer wanted the man Marianne had won. In fact, if someone handed David to her on a silver plate, with a red ribbon round his neck, she wouldn't have him. Not now she knew how he'd toyed with her affections. What sort of man did that to an impressionable, lonely girl?

'Well then, would it not be possible to donate a little food to her wedding breakfast? I wouldn't ask Cook to provide the entire thing, but a cake or two, from his hands, would make such a difference to the kind of spread I should think David's parents capable of providing at such short notice.'

'Looked at in that light, I can see why you would wish to give her a good send-off. Very well, my lady,' said Mrs Dawson, setting down her teacup decisively. 'I shall see what I can do. Once everyone knows that it is you asking, I am sure Cook will make the effort.'

'Thank you, Mrs Dawson. It would mean so very much to me. I don't like to think of her feeling that we've all turned against her. Especially not at Christmas.'

At the mention of Christmas, Mrs Dawson wriggled a touch uncomfortably.

'If you don't have the time,' she offered, 'shall I have a word with Mabel, too?'

'Thank you. Tell her she may...she may have the lace I'd been planning to use for my own wedding gown.' It had been bought to adorn the dress of David's bride. Sending Marianne that particular length of lace would send her the clear message that she was welcome to David. And she was. Only think, if Marianne hadn't waylaid David, then she might have succeeded in luring him out to the orangery. She might have been obliged to marry *him*.

Her stomach turned over. She reached for the

buttered scone, and devoured it in two bites, in an attempt to settle it down.

She would have to attend the wedding, of course. She had to show Marianne that she forgave her. And if she hadn't completely forgiven her for everything, she had at least forgiven her for the mix-up at the Christmas masquerade.

Because that mix-up had freed her from David. The hold he'd had over her empty, lonely heart.

And she was married to a far better man.

She licked her lips on the last of the scone.

'Delicious,' she informed Mrs Dawson.

Who smiled back, with no idea Julia hadn't just been referring to the scone.

Chapter Ten

~~~

The next morning was one of those days when the rain felt like needles of ice. Snow would have been less unpleasant against his face.

'I ordered the coach to take us to the church,' said Julia, darting him an anxious, and apologetic, look as he stepped back up into the shelter of the porte-cochère. 'As soon as I knew you intended to come with me.'

'You didn't expect me to come with you?' So that explained the way her eyes had widened when he'd put on his own coat and reached for his hat when she'd told him where she was going. She'd really thought he would let her attend the wedding of the two people who'd so foully betrayed her, alone? Had nobody ever considered her feelings, or attempted to support her before?

At least that explained why she'd sent the little housemaid scurrying off—it must have been with a message to the stables to have a carriage prepared.

'I am sorry, it isn't the most comfortable carriage in the stables,' she said as an ancient vehicle rumbled through the arch. 'I do hope you don't mind the state it's in. Only I ordered the best chaise to take Marianne to church. A bride should have a little luxury on her wedding day, don't you think? And anyway, I'd planned to walk.'

'Walk?' Her maid clucked her tongue as she draped a sable cloak round her shoulders.

'I normally walk to church across the park,' Julia retorted as the maid handed her a matching muff. 'It's hardly any distance at all.'

'Not in this cold, my lady,' said the maid with a disapproving sniff.

'You certainly won't feel the cold today, my lady,' put in a towering footman as he opened the carriage door.

'That you won't,' said the maid. 'There's heated bricks for your feet and an extra lap robe, too.'

The coach into which they clambered might be past its prime, but when it had been new it must have been the last word in comfort and convenience. The seats were well padded, the doors let in hardly any draught at all and when they set off, the quality of the springs gave them a smooth, gliding sort of ride.

This was her idea of second-best?

'I would have walked with you,' he said testily. 'Had you decided to do so.'

'But I couldn't possibly expect you to trail all the way to St Andrew's in this weather…'

'Nonsense. Do you think I haven't been outside in worse weather than this in my time? What do you think it was like sailing with the Baltic Fleet?'

'I was just trying,' she said snippily, 'to show my appreciation. It was so good of you to come with me, that…'

He sighed, and clenched his fists on his lap.

'And now I have spoiled it by taking offence at your attempt to shield me from the weather.'

He'd done a similar thing when she'd offered the use of her family's town house. Perhaps it hadn't been so much a desire to remain a Whitney that had motivated her then, either. Perhaps it had been a generous, impulsive show of appreciation, as it had been today.

With great deliberation he uncurled his fists, reached out, and patted her hand—or at least where he guessed her hand would be inside the muff.

'It is…' He cleared his throat, and started

again. 'That is, I wish to commend your *sang-froid*. This must be a very painful occasion for you. I was not sure you would wish to attend.' But perhaps he should have seen that she wouldn't want the world to know how much it hurt to discover that her childhood sweetheart preferred another. Especially since she'd even pretended she was keen to marry *him*, just to save face. 'But, since you have chosen to do so, then you should have known you would have my support, and my company.'

'Should I?' She turned to look at him then, her brow creased in a frown. 'Not many men would...especially since we...' She floundered to a halt, her cheeks flushing.

'I am your husband,' he replied, with a shrug. 'We did not marry for conventional reasons, it is true, but that is no excuse for neglecting my duties. This is our life now.' He squeezed her hand inside the muff as tightly as he could. 'And it will be what we make of it.'

'What we make of it,' she repeated, searching his face intently. Then she gave a decisive nod, and sat up a touch straighter.

God, but she was a proud piece. Though today, her pride didn't seem such a terrible thing. She reminded him of the figurehead of a ship. Carved of oak. Bravely holding up her face in the teeth of a gale.

No matter what life threw at Lady Julia, she would just lift her chin, and weather it. The way she was weathering being married to him. To look at her now, nobody would guess at the turmoil that must be raging inside her.

She was the kind of woman he'd have been proud to have as his wife—if she'd actually chosen him, that was.

His heart gave a funny kind of tremor when she smiled into his eyes as he handed her out of the carriage when they arrived.

'Oh, goodness,' she murmured a few seconds later. 'I am glad we came. We are the only ones sitting on the bride's side of the church. Nobody else from the house has come.'

Though plenty of people were sitting on the groom's side. He had to suppose they were his friends and family.

He felt a strange shifting inside him as she bowed her head in prayer. How could she still wish to show friendship to a girl who'd so thoroughly deceived her? He would have thought most women would want to scratch out a rival's eyes. She didn't even seem to care that the stoutly built medical student was waiting at the altar for the arrival of a bride who wasn't her, even after all the effort she'd gone to, to try and trap him.

Though the moment the poor relation took her place at the groom's side, Julia's hold on her emotions wavered. She had to delve into her reticule and pull out a tiny lace-edged square of linen, with which she had to repeatedly dab her eyes.

He braced himself for a flood of tears.

But it never came. Indeed, Julia made no more use of her handkerchief than any of the other females present.

There had been a good deal of sniffing and nose-blowing during his own wedding, he recalled now. It must just be one of those unfathomable things that women did at weddings. All of them.

She attempted a watery sort of smile for the bride as the newly married couple went back down the aisle, arm in arm, though the girl gave no sign she'd noticed.

He looked at the crown of Julia's downbent head as she stuffed her sodden hanky back in her reticule. No, she wasn't as unaffected as she was attempting to make out. The way the bride had cut her had hurt. It must have done.

He wasn't a man who was used to making gestures of affection, but he couldn't help taking her hand, then, and raising it to his lips.

She looked up at him, wide-eyed with surprise, for the second time that day.

'What was that for?'

'For being you.'

'Me? But…' Her forehead creased into a perplexed frown.

She ducked her head and blushed fiery red as he tucked her little hand into the crook of his arm to follow the bride and groom to the door of the church.

'I must just wish Marianne well,' she said the moment they emerged into the churchyard. 'I don't think it would be appropriate to actually attend the wedding breakfast, but I do want to let her know that…' She floundered to a halt, a world of regret and trepidation in her face. 'I cannot let her go into her new life with this…hanging between us.'

Marianne had deliberately ignored her. She must have done. For she and Alec had been the only two people on her side of the church. She couldn't have not noticed they were there.

Thankfully, Alec didn't raise any objection, though most men would have had plenty. He really was being terrifically supportive today. And…gallant, the way he'd kissed her hand for no reason at all. Suddenly it felt rather silly to be rushing away from him towards the groom who'd been the object of her girlish infatuation. For that was all it had been, she saw now. But then, David had *seemed* to have more substance, more worth than the titled, wealthy men who considered themselves eligible suitors for her hand. And he was clever, and hard-working, and determined to do good with his life, not fritter it away in clubs or at the races.

Her steps faltered as she neared the lychgate, where the newly married couple were sheltering from the freezing rain. But she'd come this far...

'Congratulations, David,' she said, thinking it might be easier to deal with him first. He granted her a slight nod of the head, and a frosty look. Oh, well, it was all she could expect, she supposed.

'Marianne,' she then said, stepping closer and holding out her hand. 'I do wish you well. I do not want to part on bad terms. And you seem...'

Marianne let go of David's arm and stepped close, so they could hug rather than just shake hands. Heartily relieved by the show of friendship, Julia hugged her back, hard.

'I'm angry,' Marianne hissed into her ear. 'Can't you see that? You never pay for anything you do, do you? If it had been me caught with my legs spread like that, I would have been cast out in disgrace. But since you are your father's pampered pet, you get a lavish wedding, and a ball thrown in your honour, and a groom who can't keep his hands off you.'

Julia flinched away, wounded. But Marianne hadn't finished.

'But I got David,' she said quietly, so nobody could overhear. 'There's something you couldn't get your hands on, no matter how you tried. He's mine. Has always been mine. The only thing I've had that wasn't yours first.'

Julia was dumbfounded. She hadn't expected the venom in the words, or the hatred sparking from Marianne's eyes.

She stepped smartly back, pinned a smile to lips that felt strangely stiff, and walked away with her head held high.

Alec held out his arm, then handed her into the carriage without saying a word.

'You look,' he said once the door was shut and they were under way. 'As though you regret lending them the best chaise now.'

Lady Julia's eyes filled with tears. For the first time that day, she really did look as though she was struggling to contain her emotions. Perhaps he shouldn't have said anything at all.

But then she pulled her mouth into the semblance of a smile. 'As a matter of fact,' she said, 'I do. Because she said…she seemed to think…' She shook her head and squeezed her eyes shut.

'What is it? Tell me.'

After only the briefest of hesitations, Julia looked up at him, her face working with indignation.

'She said she was sick of only ever having things that had been mine first.'

'Ah.'

'And that she was glad that for once she'd walked off with something I wanted but could never have. Oh, lord,' she said, her gaze turning anxious. 'Do you think she's only married David because she thought I wanted him?'

'If she has, then she's a very stupid girl.'

'I don't understand.' Lady Julia searched his face as though he might possibly have the answer. 'Why does she resent me so much? I stood up for her. I shared everything with her. Why, the very first day she came to Ness Hall, and I saw her weeping for her parents, and from fright at what Nick and Herbert were trying to do, I gave her my favourite doll. I loved that doll.' She looked the very picture of bewilderment.

'You have never been on the receiving end of charity, have you?'

She shook her head.

'It isn't a pleasant feeling.'

'Are you saying that I made her feel uncomfortable?'

'You made me feel uncomfortable,' he pointed out. 'When you offered me the use of your father's town house.'

'But I—'

'I know you didn't mean to. But you see, I have a particular aversion to becoming the kind of man who lives off a woman's money. It was what my father did. He squandered my mother's fortune on his own pleasures, leaving us all nothing but debts upon his demise. I have always sworn I would do better.'

'But I offered it freely. And, yes, it was to help you achieve your goals, but…well, I am your wife.'

'But only by accident. And I'm a proud man, besides.'

She looked as hurt as though he was rejecting her, not just her offer of help.

'How would you feel if you suddenly became penniless, and dependant upon the goodwill of others? And people suspected you of marrying someone only to get your greedy, grasping hands on his money?'

Her face cleared.

'Just like you, I suspect. I'd throw the money back in your face.'

'Exactly.'

'But…' She frowned. 'Marianne never did. She always seemed…grateful. I never dreamed she…'

'Ah, but perhaps she was frightened as well. Perhaps she felt she had no choice but to appear grateful to you, since it sounds as though you were the only person to show her any sympathy.'

'Which…might have made her resent me all the more,' she said slowly. 'I had everything she'd lost. Wealth. A secure home. Family. Oh, why did I never see it? I couldn't understand why others thought she was sly, and spoke of her with such dislike.'

He plucked her hand out of the muff. Patted it.

'Well, she's out of your life now. And it sounds as if you are well rid of her.'

'But…David. Poor David. Can he know? Does he have any idea how…how two-faced she is?'

Poor David? The blasted man had been as underhanded as the girl, from what he'd heard.

'What is it about that man?' He'd meant to remain sympathetic and understanding. He'd come to this benighted wedding to show his support. He'd even let her go and speak to the podgy groom alone, to show that he trusted her. But as that man's name fell from her lips with such obvious emotion, something very far removed from sympathy and understanding swept his good resolutions aside.

'He isn't handsome. He isn't wealthy. He has no title. And yet the two of you appear to have been fighting over him like two dogs over a string of sausages.'

'He was…different,' she said, turning her head to look out of the window. Probably just as well. He was so angry at her persistent refusal to see any wrong in that man that it must, by now, be showing on his face. And he didn't want her to see how angry he was growing—not while she was still so hurt. She'd had enough hurt for one day without him adding to it with a display of… petty jealousy, or whatever black humour it was that David stirred up.

'Most of the village boys, you see,' she resumed, without turning back to him, 'were horribly rough. And followed Nick and Herbert's lead in bullying and tormenting Marianne. David was the only one who didn't. He was quiet, and studious. Eventually, Papa learned that he had a very quick mind, and granted him permission to borrow books from his library, so that he became a frequent visitor to the house. And we— the three of us—became friends.' She heaved a sigh. 'And then there was the spaniel, Silky. Papa let Marianne and I have her for a pet, because she was gun shy. One day there was an accident in the stables. Silky got trampled. Nick was going to break her neck, to put her out of her suffering, he said. But when Marianne burst into tears, David stopped him. Promised to heal her. Even then, he was interested in medicine.'

Good grief. The way she was talking made it sound as if she regarded him as a cross between Sir Gawain and St Francis of Assisi. He was still trying to school his expression into its usual wooden immobility when she finally turned her head and looked up at him.

'He will be a good doctor,' she insisted.

Maybe. But with that stocky build and scholarly disposition he'd run to fat before he turned thirty.

'And I can see that marrying Marianne will be a good match for him, in many ways.' She sighed. 'For one thing, Papa has told me he arranged a very generous dowry when she told him of their intention. Which will ensure they can set up house, and David can start up a practice somewhere, in some comfort when he qualifies.'

'Wise man, your father. He has rid you of them both at a stroke.'

'Oh.' Her eyes widened.

He braced himself for a flurry of feminine fury. Instead, after only a moment's reflection, she slumped into the squabs in an attitude of defeat.

'Yes,' she admitted glumly. 'You are probably correct. He never appeared to dislike Marianne more than he disliked anyone else. But then neither does he appear to understand how...lonely I will be without her.'

You have me, now, he almost blurted. But what sort of a damn fool thing was it to say? He was no substitute for a lifelong companion, or the chivalrous knight she'd created out of her girlish imagination. He was just a man. A man, moreover, who wasn't used to dealing with women.

'We are here now,' she said despondently as the carriage drew to a halt. But she made no move to get out. And her face was working, as though she was really, really struggling to compose herself.

Well, here was his chance to prove that he was worth a dozen of that weasel Gawain of Assisi. Taking her in his arms, he planted a ruthless kiss on her mouth.

She stiffened in surprise. But only for as long as it took to gasp. With her second breath she was melting into his embrace like butter in a hot skillet.

When a footman opened the carriage door, she yelped in surprise. The footman withdrew in haste, though he remained standing in his position, holding the door open for them to alight.

Julia's face was beet red as he handed her out of the coach. She looked anywhere but at the footman. Though he'd already averted his eyes and adopted the wooden expression of an underling who was pretending he hadn't seen what he'd just seen.

Before she had a chance to do or say anything to ruin his plan, he hefted her into his arms and carried her into the house.

'What are you doing?,' she hissed into his ear. 'How could you embarrass me like that? Like this?'

'Easily,' he replied as he swept past the butler, and up the stairs.

He set her on her feet only when they'd reached her room and he'd kicked the door closed behind them.

'You are too fragile to face anyone just yet,' he explained, stepping back from her, just a touch.

'Fragile?' She looked affronted.

'And too proud to admit it. I have just given you the perfect excuse to stay out of sight until you do feel ready to resume your duties for the day.'

'I… You…oh!' Her face worked as she fought for composure. 'You are right,' she admitted, her shoulders slumping.

'Damn you, you want to add, I dare say.'

She lifted her chin, a mutinous glint in her eye. 'I would never descend to using such language.'

'But you wish you could. You'd feel better for it.' He placed his hat on the table by the door, removed his gloves and dropped them inside it, then crossed the room to make use of the bell pull.

'We will need supplies,' he explained, when she looked at him in a mixture of exasperation and confusion. 'Enough to last us until you are fit to return to active duty.' He went to her side and removed the furs from her shoulders.

'Mabel can do that,' she snapped, taking a step back.

'Ah, but it will look much more the thing if you are a bit less…dressed,' he said, tugging the ribbons of her bonnet undone, 'by the time the maid gets up here. A bit more…' he tossed the bonnet aside, and set to work on the buttons of her coat '…ruffled.'

When she opened her mouth to make another protest, he silenced her with a kiss. A long kiss. A kiss in which their tongues duelled for mastery. A kiss which left them both heated and shaking with desire.

When the maid eventually did arrive, Julia looked delightfully ruffled. As well as bemused, and a bit cross. Like a kitten who'd just had her fur stroked the wrong way.

'We need hot drinks,' he informed the smiling maid. 'And a loaf of bread, butter, preserves, and a toasting fork.'

The maid bobbed a curtsy and left.

'A toasting fork?' Julia eyed him with confusion.

'I'm hungry,' he said with a shrug. 'Aren't you?'

One of her hands went to her stomach. 'Yes. I could eat something. But...'

'Come,' he said, taking hold of her other hand. 'Let's sit by the fire.'

She eyed him warily as he pulled her down onto the hearthrug.

'Don't worry. I'm not going to pounce.' Did just the tiniest hint of disappointment flicker across her face? 'Yes, we would enjoy it. Both of us. But we will enjoy making...toast together, too.'

Her face flushed. But the tense set of her mouth relaxed. Which was a start. He couldn't resort to kissing her crotchets away every time they hit a snag. He wanted their marriage to be about more than just physical pleasure. So they were going to have to learn to get along with each other out of bed, as well as in it. And right now, while she was unwilling to leave the shelter he was providing for her, was as good a time as any to start creating new connections. To do something as harmless, and as pleasant, as kneeling on the hearthrug, toasting bread. To show her that she had a new companion now, rather than just telling her.

A companion who was worth ten of either of her childhood playmates.

'I...I do like toast,' she admitted shyly. Then gave him a smile that rocked him on his heels. For she'd never looked at him like that before. As though he'd just done something utterly wonderful. As though he'd provided the answer to how she was going to get through the day.

As though he could be her answer to anything.

Who would have thought being married to Alec could be so...pleasant? Julia raised her arms above her head, stretching her whole body like a cat. She felt like a cat. A cat who'd got at the cream, she smiled. Beside her lay the man she'd only met a handful of days ago. The man she'd accidentally coerced into marriage. The man who hadn't cavilled at his fate, but simply decided to make the best of it.

And what a best it was turning out to be. Not only could he drive her wild with pleasure in bed, but she was starting to enjoy just...just talking to him. Or doing something as silly as kneeling on the hearth toasting bread. Or walking briskly round the gardens first thing, before the day began to make demands upon them which invariably separated them until mealtimes.

He'd even made mealtimes more enjoyable. He only had to meet her eye across the table, with a certain slight lift to one eyebrow, to let her know that he was completely in tune with the way she was feeling. And afterwards, he'd confirm it by saying exactly the kind of thing she'd thought about various of her relatives for years, but had never had the freedom to say openly.

Not even with Marianne.

She'd never had real discussions with Marianne. Whereas Alec—and oh, how she was starting to relish the way his name rolled off her tongue—Alec spoke his mind. Behind closed doors, that was. And the more he spoke, the more she was beginning to think they might be able to forge the kind of marriage she'd always hoped to have. A meeting of minds. A sort of close and loving friendship.

A better, truer sort of friendship than she'd shared with David, or Marianne, who, actually, she realised, had never been true friends at all. Now that she knew Marianne had always been jealous of her, and resentful of her lot in life, she'd started looking on their time together in a new light. And what that light shone on their relationship threw up a lot of ugly, dark shadows.

What stood out the most, though, was the way that Marianne always managed to make her feel big and fat and ungainly. She'd always thought it was just because Marianne was so slight, and dark, and elegant. But now she recalled dozens of innocuous little remarks that had gradually built up into a mountain of insecurity. The masquerade, for instance. Marianne had made such a production of getting the dress done up, but if she'd really been putting such a strain on the fastenings, at least one of them would have given way during the course of the evening, considering the activities she'd performed in it. It was, without question, a snugger fit than any other gown she'd ever worn, but not a button had popped, not a seam had split. In fact, Nellie herself had said that the dress looked better on her. Every single man she'd met had positively drooled at the sight of her in it.

She was going to have all her gowns made to

fit better, rather than having them all cut loose to disguise what she'd previously thought of as a lumpish body.

Alec didn't think her body was lumpish at all. He adored it. He thought her breasts magnificent, and her bottom, lush. And if he said that, then he meant it. He'd always been honest with her. Had been brutally honest, to begin with. Though even then, it had never been with intent to wound. Which, she found, made all the difference.

For the first time in her life, he'd made her feel as if there was nothing wrong with her after all. Her older brothers had always despised her for being Papa's pet. The younger ones naturally preferred each other's company. And even Papa only praised her for the attributes he decided came from her mother, rather than all of her, exactly as she was.

'Are you staring at me again, woman?'

She came out of her reverie to note that Alec's eyes were half-open, and a slow, rather arrogant smile was spreading across his wickedly clever mouth.

She shut her eyes swiftly, but not swiftly enough. He chuckled.

'You don't need to pretend you don't like looking at me,' he growled.

She screwed her eyes tighter shut as her cheeks

flamed. She *did* need to pretend she didn't like looking at him. Because it was highly improper. Ladies didn't ogle men when they were shaving, or lick their lips at the sight of a bare, hairroughened chest. Or lay and gaze at the curve of a shoulder in the firelight, marvelling at the beauty of masculine musculature.

'I like looking at you, when you are unclothed, too,' he said.

His admission pulled her in two opposing directions at once. She knew he liked the sight of her body. She'd just been lying there reflecting on how wonderful it made her feel when he told her. What a thrill she'd get when he buried his face between her breasts and sigh, as though he'd found a sort of heaven.

And yet she still couldn't get used to this sort of licentious talking. It was highly improper to hear a man talking about parts of her body she'd been brought up to believe weren't polite to mention. Especially when he'd had his hands on them. Or his mouth. Or other, unmentionable parts of his body.

And, oh, heavens, just letting her mind drift in that direction was making her go all heated inside.

'I should be getting up,' she said, darting free

of the covers just before his hand could close over its target. 'I have so much to do today.'

'Another ball?'

His mouth tightened as she thrust her arms into her wrapper, her feet into fleece-lined slippers.

'I know it must look to you as though my life is just one long round of parties,' she explained as she crossed the room to ring for hot water. 'But, you see, at Christmas, Papa fulfils a great many of his obligations to his people. While he is in residence at Ness, he always extends invitations to everyone in the county that matters. As well as the locals, and the extended family. Some days he takes parties of local worthies out shooting, and then he relies on me to make sure their wives and daughters are looked after within doors. And there isn't anyone else to do it. Nick's wife…' She pulled a face.

'I get the distinct impression that when your brother comes into the title, all the hospitality will cease.'

'I wouldn't be a bit surprised.' She sighed. 'He doesn't seem to think that he owes anybody anything. The tenants, as far as he is concerned, are only there to provide him with the means to live in luxury. I worry,' she said, settling her hip on the edge of the bed when he held out his hand to her. 'About what will happen to the estate once Papa…goes.'

'I can understand that particular mix of interest and impotence,' he said, surprising her because she'd half-expected him to say it wasn't her concern.

'You know my own lands are mortgaged. That there is nothing much I can do for my tenants, but it doesn't stop me wishing…'

'But you could redeem those mortgages now, couldn't you?' She'd blurted it before she had time to consider how prickly he was about spending her money on himself. When he started to scowl, she hurried on. 'I know you have scruples about what you call squandering my money, but you wouldn't be squandering it, as far as I'm concerned. You would be investing it for our children. For your estates, your heritage, will be their inheritance, won't it?'

Oh, heavens, if he did decide to redeem the mortgages, and put his estates to rights, it would mean going to live in Scotland. All the way up there in Scotland. She swallowed. Julia had never visited Scotland. It was supposed to be very rugged, but in a way that many people found beautiful.

Well, if he did decide to go there, she would

just have to find it beautiful as well. And if she didn't…

Oh, why was she even thinking about it? He was just as likely to go back to sea and leave her behind. And until he'd made up his mind what to do, there was no point in worrying about it.

'Well, anyway,' she continued with forced brightness as he continued to glower down at their joined hands, 'there are only really two more significant events before the house party breaks up. Tonight's New Year Ball, and then the Twelfth Night festivities. Tonight's ball is one that all the local worthies will attend. And many of them who come from further away will need rooms, which is why I will be so busy today, making sure everything is ready for their arrival.

'But the Twelfth Night celebration is mainly for the household. The family, and any guests who wish to take part, put on an entertainment for the staff, by way of thanks. And the day after that, all our guests will leave. So…' She played with his fingers, looking at them rather than at the expression on his face. Or rather, the lack of expression she would find should she look into his eyes. It was as if he didn't want her to know what he was thinking. Which was extremely annoying. How was she to know what he wanted if he would neither tell her, nor give her a clue?

Clearly, the only way to find out would be to ask him outright.

'I was just wondering, what we shall be doing? You mentioned going to London, to lay siege to the Admiralty. Will you still wish to do that? Or…I mean, I understand why you became angry with me last time I suggested using our family house. It was tactless of me. It is just that I am in the habit of getting it opened up for the Season. It was more of a habit, and I spoke without thinking…'

'Julia,' he said, squeezing her hand. 'You don't need to keep on apologising. You meant no harm. I can see that now.'

'Well, do you think you might consider it then? As a form of…compensation for having to marry me? I know you didn't want to. And I know you don't want people to think you are… sponging off my family either. But, Alec, everyone makes use of family connections. And only think what an advantage it will be to launch Lizzie from the house in Belgrave Square. You want her to have the best start in life you can provide, don't you?'

He shook his head, though his mouth was curving into a rueful smile.

'I'm not going to be able to stop you flinging yourself into my affairs, am I?'

'Well, but—'

'I know, I know. And you will say it is for my own good.'

'But—'

'No. Just listen to me,' he said sternly. 'Lizzie won't be ready for a Season this year. And when she is…'

'When she is, she will need every advantage she can get. The Season is a cut-throat business, Alec. Girls get…mown down.'

'I can see,' he said, 'that you are determined to help me, whether I want you to or not.'

'Well, I'm your wife. That is what wives do.'

'Is it?' He searched her face as though he really hadn't a clue what wives were for.

But then, he hadn't been looking for one when he came to Ness Hall, had he?

Chapter Eleven

She was heartily relieved to hear the knock on the door heralding the arrival of her hot water and drinking chocolate. Because it had hurt to realise that Alec didn't want to receive anything from her.

'I shall go and get dressed now,' she informed him with a tight smile.

She went to the dressing room in Betty's wake. Usually she let him go first so that she could lie on her side, watching through the door he'd leave half-open as he washed and shaved. There was something so appealing about the way he dressed himself. So casually assured in his masculinity.

But she didn't want to this morning. Their discussion had left her feeling all on edge. She was trying her hardest to be a good wife to him, and he just kept on…putting her in her place.

Which confused her. Because every so often

he seemed to be growing almost fond of her. Look at the way he'd kissed her hand at Marianne's wedding, for no apparent reason. Or the way he'd smiled at her, just now, when he'd said he could see she would always be flinging herself into his business.

She'd known that marrying a stranger was going to require a great many compromises if they weren't to make each other miserable. And she could have taken them all in her stride if only she wasn't starting to have such strong feelings for him. If she wasn't starting to wonder how he felt about her. But as it was…

She drew in a sharp, painful breath as she worked the soap into a lather.

She was no good at working out what people truly felt for her, that was the trouble. She'd believed David and Marianne loved her as much as she loved them, but they hadn't even liked her.

She couldn't, she simply couldn't tell Alec that she was glad they were married, and that she was starting to look forward to spending the rest of her life with him. He might…laugh at her. Or say she was fickle for transferring her feelings from one man to another so swiftly. Or fire up in annoyance, and tell her that he was making the best of a bad job, but that the last thing he wanted to be was married.

Or even worse, look at her with pity. Which he might actually feel if he couldn't return her affection, because he was a kind man, beneath that gruff exterior.

But as for what he really thought—how could she tell? How could anyone tell what went on behind those cool grey eyes? He could say he loved her breasts one minute, and the next, flare up with irritation over a perfectly innocuous remark.

She'd been pleased as anything when he'd said she was generous. Yet he'd criticised that very generosity later, telling her it wasn't pleasant being on the receiving end of charity. Which had made her feel the way David had so often made her feel. When he'd given a compliment with one hand then taken it away with the other.

She couldn't even place any reliance on the fact that so far, Alec was enthusiastic in bed. Enthusiasm in bed was no indication of deep feelings. Men could even be enthusiastic in bed with women they despised. She'd overheard Nick mock his own conquests often enough to know that much.

Besides, Alec had told her, with that brutal frankness of his, that he'd been without a woman for so long that he'd have been grateful to get into bed with just about anyone.

So, no, she wasn't going to blurt out how she felt—how she was starting to feel about him.

But she could show him.

A rather naughty smile came to her mouth as she dried her face on her towel. She hung her wrapper loosely from her shoulders, rather than tying it tightly, and sashayed back to the bed, the way Nellie had taught her. She bent over to kiss him on the forehead.

'I changed my mind…about getting dressed,' she said.

'I can see that,' he replied, cupping the nape of her neck and kissing her mouth.

So—he didn't mind her making the first move sometimes. First thing in the morning. He was always keen on having marital relations first thing in the morning.

'And I'm glad. I rather thought I'd offended you, the way I snapped when you mentioned the town house, and Lizzie's come-out.'

Well he had. So why hadn't he been the one to try to make amends?

The answer came back quicker than blinking. It was because he was a man. Men didn't patch up quarrels. Lest it made them look weak.

'It takes a bit of getting used to,' she conceded. 'Being married, doesn't it?'

'I could easily get used to this,' he growled,

sliding the wrapper from her shoulder, and nuzzling where her shoulder joined her neck.

'Mmmhh...' she agreed.

They didn't make it down to breakfast.

And so Julia had to spend the rest of the day making up for lost time. There were always a dozen last-minute hitches whenever there was a further influx of guests into a house that was already fairly full. Always a series of crises whenever a ball was being arranged. Besides the mundane lists she had to go through with Mrs Dawson, discussions with the cook and Gatley, as well as handling the friction that arose between the staff of Ness Hall and visiting servants.

But at last it was time to return to her room to prepare for dinner. She was looking forward to a wash and a change of clothes. Her gown bore testament to everything she'd done that day, from emptying stale vases to inspecting and tasting Cook's latest sauce. Hoping to avoid the eagle-eyed scrutiny of any of her aunts, she made for the back stairs, just as Nellie came running down them, almost colliding with her.

'Nellie! How lovely to—' She broke off her greeting when she saw that the opera singer's face was white, her eyes wide with alarm. 'What is it? What has happened?'

'It's that bugger Eduardo, pardon my language, my lady. I've got to stop him.' She darted past Julia, then whirled round. 'Actually, it might be a good idea if you was to come with me. I've a feeling the young lady will want you. Or someone like you.'

Julia's stomach contracted with a cold, twisting sensation. She'd noticed the way all her young cousins batted their eyelids at the handsome young actor. The way he'd played up to their adulation, flirting impartially with each and every one of them in turn.

'I saw 'em out the winder,' panted Nellie as she dashed down the corridor to one of the doors that led from the servant's hall to the grounds at the rear of the house.

'He's taking her into that *orangey*. Which can only mean one thing.'

Oh, dear me, yes. A young man could only have one purpose for taking a young lady out to the orangery. And it wasn't to study botany.

'He can't have been in there with her very long, though,' Nellie said over her shoulder. 'I come running down the stairs as fast as me legs would carry me. So he can't have got very far.'

Though it didn't take as long to become thoroughly compromised as one might suppose.

Julia should know. She'd never have believed how quickly Alec could get her onto her back, had she not been there.

It was hard to make out anything very clearly through the windows of the orangery, since they were streaming with condensation. Though she could perceive the shapes of a man in a dark coat, and a female in the regulation white of a young girl. And that they were in each other's arms.

Nellie tried the door, which was of course locked. The pair inside sprang apart guiltily as it rattled.

'We'll have to use the window,' Julia told her, going to the one with the broken latch.

She heaved up the sash and stepped over the sill. And gasped in shock when she saw that the girl Eduardo had persuaded into the orangery was none other than Alec's sister.

'Lizzie!'

As she came to a shocked halt, Nellie cannoned into her back, having tripped over the sill as she climbed inside.

'It's not what you think,' said Lizzie. 'Eduardo said he knew where to find some blooms to take the plainness off my costume for the play.'

'I'm sure he did,' said Nellie with sarcasm.

'And just as sure that ain't what he showed you when he got you in here.'

While Lizzie flushed and fidgeted, Eduardo sidled closer to her and put his arm round her waist. And then smiled. A not-very-nice smile.

'I am sure you don't want anybody to know what a very forward young lady your sister-in-law is, do you, Lady Julia?'

Lizzie turned a stunned face to him, her face turning sickly pale when she saw that shark-like smile.

'What do you want?' Julia asked scornfully. 'Money, I suppose.'

'Money?' Lizzie looked from Julia to Eduardo in bewilderment.

'Five hundred pounds,' Eduardo continued smoothly. 'To ensure I never speak of how easy it was to entice Captain Lord Dunbar's sister into a secluded spot, where we proceeded to make passionate love.'

'Oh,' cried Lizzie, stepping smartly away from him. 'We never did any such thing! Honestly, Lady Julia,' she pleaded. 'He just kissed me, that was all. And people have been doing lots of kissing all over the house.'

'No mistletoe in here, though, is there,' said Eduardo mockingly. 'So of course, you slapped my face.' Which statement made Lizzie blush, because she'd done no such thing. 'Well?'

'I don't have five hundred pounds just lying about the place,' said Julia.

'Lady Julia! You cannot give him money. I didn't do anything. We didn't do anything, not really!'

'But she knows that I can make it sound bad, very bad. Particularly to your brother. Who knows all about the kind of things that go on when a man gets a woman alone amongst all this tropical foliage.'

Now Julia felt sick, too. Sick with outrage. 'Who told you?' She whirled on Nellie. It felt as if everyone she'd ever liked, ever trusted, had betrayed her over this Christmas season.

'It weren't me,' Nellie vowed. 'I know it looks bad, what with me bringing you out here, as if we was in it together. But I swear I'd never do anything to hurt a young lady's reputation. Not after the way I started out in this business. Wouldn't wish that fate on anyone.'

Though she knew Nellie was a brilliant actress, she couldn't see any reason why the woman would lie about this. Besides, from other veiled remarks Nellie had made, it now seemed clear that her career on the stage had only begun after some man had stolen her virtue.

'Then who?'

Eduardo smirked. 'Can you not guess who would leap at the chance to have her revenge upon you? Not very wise in your choice of friends, are you? Or very tactful in the way you bestow largesse, like some kind of Lady Bountiful, putting everyone's backs up?'

'Marianne,' Julia whispered. Only she and David had known what had happened to her in this very spot—apart from Nellie. Only she had anything to gain from repeating the tale. Besides, David hadn't had the run of the house of late. He wouldn't have had the chance to strike up that kind of conversation with any of the actors, let alone Eduardo.

'Nellie,' she said, turning to the opera dancer, who was quivering with as much rage as Julia was feeling. 'Could you please take Lizzie back to the house, while I deal with this…this…?'

'Yes. Of course.' Nellie drew Lizzie away from Eduardo, and over to the window. Where she muttered a blistering oath.

'Someone's coming!'

'Hide!' Julia pointed to a row of large urns at the far end of the orangery. 'Get down behind them. You can get in at the end of the row.'

Eduardo frowned, and looked towards the window nervously. And it hit Julia, in a burst of clarity, that he really didn't want anyone else to know what he'd been up to with Lizzie. When the theatre was closed his company made a lot of money by performing at private house parties like this one. If word got out that he couldn't be trusted with young, innocent female guests, the work would dry up. Or more likely, he would be expelled from the company.

'You've as much at stake as Lizzie, haven't you?'

'What? No.'

'Oh, yes, you have.' Julia shook her finger at him. 'So this is the deal I'll make with you. I won't say anything about your behaviour, and nor will you. You will not damage Lizzie's reputation, and I will not damage yours.'

He stared at her for a second, his face registering shock, then defeat, then pure unadulterated fury.

'You think you're so clever,' he hissed. His words were almost drowned by the grate of a boot heel at the window.

Julia saw the swirl of a man's coat out of the corner of her eye, in the same instant that Eduardo grabbed hold of her. And ground out one final threat.

'If you don't want her ruined, then you won't

struggle. Or I'll point out exactly where she's hiding, to whoever comes in through that window.'

Then he placed his mouth over hers and kissed her.

It was a loathsome kiss. Every nerve in her body screamed to break free, but she didn't struggle and she didn't slap him. She just stood slack in his arms and let him run his tongue over her lips. Allowed him to exact his paltry revenge. Because she knew that whoever had just poked his head through the window would only see a married woman committing an indiscretion, and wander away again, chortling to himself over the latest scandal created by one of the notoriously unfaithful Whitney family. And the whole incident would soon be forgotten.

Nobody could have been more surprised when instead of doing any such thing, the man came marching over to where she stood, frozen in Eduardo's vile grasp.

'Get your hands off my wife!'

It was Alec! He seized the actor by the scruff of the neck and tore him off her. Eduardo's heels skittered across the tiled floor as Alec lifted the slender young man almost off his feet.

'Bastard!' Alec let go of Eduardo's collar, but only so that he could punch him in the face. The actor reeled back, blood pouring from his nose.

But Alec wasn't finished with him. He gripped
him by the collar and the seat of his breeches, and
heaved him in the general direction of the window. She wasn't sure if it was by luck or judge-
ment that Eduardo went sailing straight through
the open part. Even so, his flailing arms caught
the frame, showering splintered wood and broken glass onto the gravel path.

Eduardo got shakily to his feet. Opened his
mouth as if to make a protest. Alec gave a low
growl and stalked in his direction. The actor
changed his mind about whatever he'd been
about to say, and took to his heels instead.

Only then did Alec round on her, his face a
mask of fury.

'You trollop.'

She flinched. And was about to protest that
Eduardo had forced the kiss upon her. That she
was only covering for Lizzie. But Lizzie clearly
didn't want even Alec to know what she'd been
up to, or she would have come straight out of her
hiding place the moment she'd realised the new-
comer was her own brother, who could be trusted
not to spread malicious gossip.

Her hesitation was all it took to fuel Alec's
fury to new heights.

'I thought what happened in here at Christmas
was a terrible accident,' he ground out. 'The cul-

mination of a series of blunders. I was prepared
to overlook your behaviour because I thought you
were just a naïve, foolish girl with a head stuffed
full of nonsense. But now I see that this is a reg-
ular trysting spot for you. Good God! You must
be insatiable. You kept me in bed all morning,
and then arranged to meet another man out here!'

How could he think that? Didn't he know her
at all?

No. Come to think of it, he was *always* jump-
ing to the worst conclusion whenever she made
the slightest blunder. And she was sick of having
to…to *crawl* to earn every scrap of affection. It
was the story of her life. She only had to put one
foot out of place and all affection was instantly
withdrawn.

She lifted her chin and glared at him. If he
could come to such a horrid conclusion, simply
because she'd been reluctant to instantly provide
a plausible excuse, then he didn't deserve *any*
kind of explanation!

'You're nothing but a spoiled, wanton trollop!'

He had clearly only just managed to prevent
himself from plunging to even deeper depths,
but the hurt remained the same. She wasn't any
of those things! But he'd taken one look at the
situation and decided she must be guilty of the
worst sort of conduct. He hadn't even asked her

for an explanation. Not that she would have given him one.

'You pick up men like pretty toys and toss them aside when you're bored.'

She sucked in a sharp, shocked breath. She'd never treated anyone like a toy. She'd had her own feelings trampled often enough to ever contemplate treating anyone else so shabbily.

'I thought you were struggling to control your hurt,' he bellowed. 'I thought you were brave. God, I actually admired you for your fortitude. But it was no such thing, was it? You just didn't care. You swapped me for David the way most women change their shoes!'

He might as well have slapped her, that last comment hurt so much.

She lifted her chin another notch. Fine then! If this was what he really thought of her it was as well to know now, before she…before she began to really care what he thought. Because she didn't. She didn't.

In fact she hated him. In that moment she really hated him for speaking to her that way.

'Nothing to say?'

'No.' She gave him a hard smile. 'You've clearly seen through me, so what is the point? I won't beg for your forgiveness, if that is what you're hoping for. Nor offer you an explanation. You don't deserve one.'

She made as if to get past him. His hand shot out and gripped her arm.

'Where do you think you're going?'

'Back to my room.' She pulled her arm out of his grasp with all the disdain she could muster. 'There is a ball tonight, in case you have forgotten. For which I need to prepare.'

'You mean to dance, and smile for your father's guests as if nothing has happened?'

She looked over her shoulder as she stepped over the shattered window frame. 'Nothing has happened,' she said. But it might at any moment. For the fronds of the potted palms at the end of the orangery were quivering, as though someone was trying to get out from behind the pots.

Now that she'd been treated to a dose of Alec's temper she wasn't surprised Lizzie had chosen to hide from him when he'd first come in. And now there was no point in Lizzie confessing to the truth. If Alec really thought so poorly of her, then what was the point of trying to salvage anything? She should have known their marriage was never going to work. Should have realised that it was too good to be true. No man could possibly be as decent, and kind as she'd begun to think Alec was.

'Apart from you behaving like a brute, and breaking the window, that is. Gatley is going to be furious. As am I. Honestly…' she sent him a withering look '…anyone would think you expected me to behave like a nun. A little kissing is nothing.' She tossed her head airily as she set off towards the house. Just as she hoped after making such an inflammatory remark, Alec surged through the shattered window frame to give her a piece of his mind.

'To think I was trying my damnedest to make a go of this accursed marriage,' he shouted at her back as she strode across the terrace. 'Now I see that I was the one who did all the trying. I put in all the effort. You did nothing!'

That remark was so unjust that it was all she could do not to turn round and slap his self-righteous face. But she refused to lower herself to his level.

Instead, she held her head high and remained mute, hoping it would look as though the torrent of abuse and foul accusations was washing right over her. Because while she stalked away from the orangery, he followed. Which was, at least, giving Lizzie and Nellie the chance to escape undetected.

'All you have done is moan about your bloody

so-called friend, and complain I'm nothing like that saintly David!'

Which was completely untrue. She'd never complained of *that*. On the contrary, she'd been glad he was so different from David.

Well, all that was at an end.

He made sure of it by continuing to say unfair things, all the way up the stairs. And every insulting thing he'd thought about her, and was now actually saying to her, felt as if it was flaying a little more flesh from her bones.

She marched into her room, and right through to the dressing room. Because there was only so much she would tolerate.

'Well, since you are so obviously finished with any pretence you can stand me,' she said, seizing his valise, 'there is no further need to play at being husband and wife, is there?'

'What are you doing with that?' He pulled the valise out of her hands.

'What do you think I'm doing?' She tried to take it back. The clasp snapped open as they tussled over the case. 'I'm throwing you out of my room.'

'Fine,' he said. Which made her let go of the case. 'Do you think I want any more to do with you?' He went to the washstand and began shoving toiletries haphazardly into the valise which hung open over his arm.

He was just going to walk out on her, after only a handful of days, because he'd seen another man kissing her, was he? And thought he could get away with shouting abuse at her all the way through the house? So that everyone—from the footman who'd been lighting the hall candles, to the mayor's wife who'd opened the door of her bedroom to see what was going on—knew exactly what he suspected her of doing?

Well, she'd see about that!

She grabbed everything she could see that belonged to him—which comprised his evening shirt, which a maid had laid out over the back of a chair, a pile of freshly starched cravats, and his telescope—marched over to the main door to her suite, and threw them all out into the hall.

A couple of his neckcloths sailed over the banister and fluttered down to the hall several floors below. His telescope rolled to the top of the stair and went rattling down to the next landing.

'Bloody hell!' He pushed past her, running down the stairs to recover his telescope. 'You've broken it!'

'Good!' She was glad she'd managed to break something of his. The way he'd broken her...

No. He hadn't broken her heart. That was just

an expression. She did feel shattered, but having such a violent argument with anyone would have made her feel this bad.

The feeling would pass.

It would.

But, since he was one flight down, kneeling on the carpet, cradling the dented brass instrument to his chest, she took the opportunity to slam the door shut on him. Shutting him out. Ooh, how she hated him. Almost as much as she hated that telescope. If he hadn't been carrying it around on the night of the masquerade she'd never have mistaken him for David. She was glad she'd broken it. Glad!

She whirled from the door, her hand to her mouth as just one sob tore free. She couldn't break down and weep. She didn't have time. Besides, going about her normal duties, as though nothing mattered, would help her keep herself together. She would smile, and pretend nothing was amiss. The way so many society brides had to do.

The way Ellen always did. Oh, Lord, now she was feeling just the way her poor sister-in-law must have felt every time Nick had been unfaithful, and then abused her for daring to complain. No wonder she just drifted about the place, looking as though her mind was somewhere else. No wonder she took no interest in the running of a household and estate that would one day belong to her husband. She must wish she was anyone else's wife. That she could live anywhere else.

Well, Julia wasn't going to behave like Ellen and have everyone feel sorry for her. She was going to behave with dignity. So, she'd ended up in exactly the kind of marriage she'd never wanted. Did that mean she had to let everyone see she was miserable? No. All her married aunts managed to pretend they were fine with the boors whose children they were obliged to produce. She could do no less. In fact she'd had good training for the position. She'd been pretending she was fine, when inside she'd been cold and lonely, ever since her mother had died.

She yanked at the bell pull viciously. She was going to wash off the feel of Eduardo's mouth on hers, instruct Mabel to burn the dress he'd had the cheek to put his hands on, and deck herself out in her finest clothes and jewellery. And to-night she would dance with anyone who asked her. And laugh at their witticisms. And show the world she didn't care *what* Alec thought.

And then she'd come back up here and sleep alone.

'Mabel,' she said, the moment her maid arrived. 'When you've finished here I want you to take a message to Mrs Dawson. I would have her make sure there is a fire up in Captain Dunbar's room.'

'Captain Dunbar's...?'

'The one he had when he first arrived.' It was still vacant, since it was only large enough to contain one person, and the other guests who'd been invited for tonight's ball were all couples or families. 'I want you to make sure that not one item belonging to him remains in my room, too. And just one more thing. Have Stephens keep an eye on him.' She'd been amazed—though perhaps she shouldn't have been, given she'd seen the muscularity of her husband's body—at the ease with which he'd dealt with Eduardo. There was only one footman on the staff who was likely to be able to match him. Stephens. Well over six feet tall and as broad as a barn door.

'On no account is Captain Dunbar to be permitted access to my room. If he attempts to come in here...well,' she said with a toss of her head, 'Stephens will know what to do.'

'Alec?'

'Yes, Lizzie?' He looked up and pulled his mouth into a smile for his sister. She'd been creeping about him for the last couple of days as though she was half-afraid of him. He sighed. He supposed it wasn't so surprising. Rumours of how he'd broken the actor's nose, his arm, and the greenhouse window were running rife. And Lizzie had been rather fond of the actor. Well, all the girls had. He'd watched them at rehearsals. Fluttering and blushing whenever he singled one of them out for any reason whatever. He rather thought a couple of them deliberately fluffed their lines in an attempt to get him to give them individual tuition. Not that he'd succumbed to their machinations. No—Eduardo was clever enough to keep them all dancing to his tune, while he kept his eye on the bigger prize. A married woman. A woman he could dally with in safety.

Or so he'd thought.

Well, hadn't he fallen into the same trap? Alec had managed to fend off all the eligible young girls, only to succumb to the advances of a woman who was more experienced.

Or so he'd thought.

The hell of it was, they'd both fallen prey to the same woman. The same deceitful, conniving…

'Alec, I was just wondering…'

'Hmm?' He set aside the block and tackle he was mending. Since he'd had the fight with Julia, he'd actually found some solace in spending his days with Lizzie. His marriage might be over before it had properly begun, but Lizzie would always be his sister.

During the first night he'd spent curled up in the freezing attic to which his wife had banished him, he'd reminded himself that she was only a detour anyway. Lizzie was the reason he'd come to Ness Hall. And he was damned well going to stay here as long as Lizzie did. For her sake. And take part in the activities that amused her. And since she was so heavily involved in the theatrical production, that meant lending his skills to the carpentry, and other backstage work that required a man who was handy.

Besides which, the amateur dramatics were now one man down. Eduardo had been sent back to London, his future with the company in question.

'That is…when are you going to make it up with Julia?'

He scowled at her. 'I don't think that's any of your business.'

'Oh, but it is. I want you to be happy. And you aren't happy, are you?'

He bent his head to the task in hand. No, he wasn't happy. He was damned miserable. But he'd have to make more of an effort to appear content, if even his sister could see through his attempt at nonchalance. It was just that whenever he saw Julia, striding about the place with that little smile on her lips, busily tending to all her father's guests, he wanted to…shake her till her bones rattled. Kiss that treacherous mouth until she melted in a puddle at his feet.

And then step over her as though she was nothing. Nothing!

'Alec,' Lizzie said again, clasping her hands together at her breast. 'It…it wasn't fair, what you said to her.'

He lifted his head and stared at her in disbelief. This chit had no right to correct him. No right at all. Besides which, how the hell could she know what he'd said to his own wife? Such things were private.

Although he hadn't exactly been discreet, had he? He'd shouted at her proud back all the way to their room. Then got into a tug-of-war over his valise. Which ended only when she threw his telescope down the stairs, denting the tube and shattering one of the lenses.

It had pretty near shattered him. He couldn't put into words what that telescope meant to him. His captain, and the ratings, had bought it for him when he'd passed the exam to be made up to lieutenant. It not only marked his transition from boyhood to manhood, but was also proof that he'd left his past behind. That he wasn't the kind of man his father had been, but the kind that other men approved of, and could even look up to. It had become a sort of…talisman. A reminder that he'd escaped from under his father's ignominious shadow, and was making his own reputation.

And she'd ruined it.

He'd started to think that he might have a future with her. That with Julia at his side, he could undo the damage done by his own father, and build up something of value to leave his own sons. But as he'd knelt over the dented remains of the one symbol of hope he'd ever been given, freely, by his peers, it was as if she'd destroyed that hope.

It would have been better had she never given him that hope, only to wrest it from him and toss it away.

'The only thing I regret,' he growled, 'is marrying her in the first place.'

'Oh, Alec, no! You were happy with her, delighted with her, in fact, at first. Until Eduardo ruined everything.'

He gritted his teeth. That his own sister, an innocent girl, should have to learn that married women could be so faithless…

'It is better I learn what she's like now, than later.'

'But you haven't! That is…' Lizzie wrung her hands. Which were shaking. 'Oh, Alec, I can't bear it. I have to tell you the truth. It was me.'

'What do you mean? What was you?'

She looked over her shoulder. Then the other. Leaned forward. Lowered her voice to a tortured whisper.

'It was me out there with Eduardo.'

He set down the block and tackle. Drew in a deep breath. 'I don't know what game you're playing this time, Lizzie, but I have to say I don't appreciate it. Julia was…'

'Julia was protecting me!' Tears sprang to Lizzie's eyes. She sniffed them back. 'Eduardo took me out there, to get me some flowers for my hair, he said. He said we had to do it in secret because some old gardener guarded them like a dragon does its hoard of gold. I thought it was just going to be a bit of a lark. And that I could laugh over it after, with Winny and Electra. But when he got me out there, he…' She dashed a tear away swiftly with the back of one hand. 'He…'

'I think you'd better sit down.' He sighed, bracing himself for a full melodrama. God alone knew why she felt the need to keep on interfering in his life. But he supposed it showed she cared. And he'd be a fool to dismiss her, when she was all the family he had left.

She sank onto the chair beside him, and turned a tragic little face up to his.

'He didn't do anything much to me. But when Julia came in, and Nellie, he made out that we'd been doing something wicked. And told Julia that she'd have to pay him to keep my name out of it. She refused. Said he had as much at stake as I did. And then Nellie saw you coming, and we hid behind the potted palms. And that is when he grabbed her, and kissed her...'

'That's enough, Lizzie,' he snapped. 'I don't know why you're making up this ridiculous story. I was there, remember? I saw her. If it was as you claim, that he grabbed her and she was just an innocent victim, then she would have slapped his face. But she didn't, did she?'

'No. Because he said he'd expose me if she struggled—show them where I was hiding, and it would all come out and I'd be ruined.'

His fingers froze over the pulley assembly. Could that be true? Was it possible that Julia *hadn't* gone out there to tryst with the actor? That it had been Lizzie all along?

'Why didn't she say anything? After I'd disposed of him? Why didn't she defend herself?'

'Alec, you didn't exactly give her a chance, did you? You were so angry you hardly stopped to draw breath.'

And she'd just stood there, as he'd shouted at her. Going whiter and whiter. Trembling. Clenching her fists. And finally, tossing her head and stalking off.

The block and tackle fell from his suddenly clumsy fingers.

What had he done? Dear God, what had he done?

Chapter Twelve

Alec turned to look at Lizzie, a strange, cold shakiness stealing through his limbs.

'Why didn't you say anything at the time?' He drove his fingers through his hair, leaving it standing all on end. 'Why didn't you come out when you saw it was me? I could have understood you hiding if it had been anyone else. But not me, surely?'

'I wanted to. I tried to,' she wailed. 'But Nellie pulled me down and held her hand over my mouth. And whispered it was best to let you get it out of your system. That Julia knew what she was doing. I should let her take the force of your first fury. That you'd calm down, and make up after a day or so, the way all married couples did. Because it had been nothing more than a kiss. And what was a kiss, after all? All the gentry go about kissing indiscriminately at Christmas, she said, once they've had a drink or two, and if there's any mistletoe about. And that you'd get over it. But you haven't, have you? And you haven't made up with Julia. Anyone can see that you're both still really cross with each other. And I can't bear it any longer. Not when it was all my fault.'

He shut his eyes. Shook his head. 'No,' he said grimly. 'It wasn't all your fault. It was that… actor's fault, for using the threat of a scandal to try to extort money from Julia.' And his own, for being so hasty to judge her.

He couldn't think what had come over him. He was renowned for being level-headed. He never condemned anyone without a fair hearing, no matter how bad the circumstantial evidence might be.

Yet he'd taken one look at Julia, in another man's arms, and was overcome with fury. If the actor hadn't taken to his heels he'd have beaten the blackguard to a pulp. And as for the things he'd said to Julia…

'Well, now you know the truth,' said Lizzie firmly. 'So you can make it up with Julia, can't you?'

'Make it up with Julia?' He turned slowly to look at Lizzie. Her bright, hopeful eyes. And shook his head again. There was no way he could

ever make it up to Julia. No way she would forgive him.

He'd called her a trollop .

Twice.

His stomach lurched and cramped, as it would
had he fallen from the crow's nest to the heav-
ing deck below.

'All you have to do is say you're sorry,' Lizzie
persisted. 'Tell her that I owned up. That now you
know the truth. And then...' A troubled frown
pleated her brow. 'Oh. I suppose it would be better if you didn't admit that I'd told you everything. Tell her,' she went on, a bit more brightly,
'that you know she couldn't have played you
false. That now you've calmed down, you know
there must have been a good explanation for what
she was doing in his arms. And ask her to tell
you what it was.'

It was too late for that. She'd told him on the
spot that he didn't deserve an explanation. If he
hadn't deserved one then, how much less did he
deserve one after an interval of two more days?

'Let her tell you what really happened. That
should do the trick. Especially if you admit that
the sight of her in another man's arms drove you
to such heights of jealousy that you couldn't think
straight.'

'That much, at least, is true,' he mused. Jealousy. That was what had made him behave so abominably. Not that it excused him. Nothing did. Nothing could. Which meant he couldn't compound his error by spinning her a pack of lies. There had been enough lies and deceit already in this marriage. It was practically founded on them, which was what made it so shaky.

'And then just tell her you love her. You haven't said it to her yet, have you?'

'No,' he said bleakly. Because it hadn't occurred to him that he did. Only now did he see that it was the only thing to account for the way he'd reacted. Why his fury had been so completely out of proportion to the offence.

'Well, then tell her. And convince her that you do.'

'It won't do any good.'

'Of course it will. Once she knows that you love her, too, she will forgive you anything.'

Love her...too? That implied that Julia loved him.

Oh, dear God—of course! Lizzie believed they had fallen for each other on sight. That it was a love match between them. She had no idea that they'd only married because of the terrible indiscretion they'd committed.

But Julia had *never* loved him. She'd only agreed to marry him because he'd insisted. And because it was better than facing the possibility of having a child out of wedlock. And now that he'd given her a taste of his bitter jealousy, his violent temper, and his hasty condemnation of her when she'd been completely innocent of any wrongdoing—had in fact been selflessly shielding a vulnerable younger girl from a situation that had gotten out of hand—she never would.

Twelfth Night couldn't come fast enough as far as Julia was concerned. Because then everyone would go home. She was sick of them all whispering about her behind their fans, stealing glances at her whenever Alec walked into the room, to see how she would react. Or he would react.

He'd taken to being scrupulously polite the last couple of days. As if, now his first flush of anger had died down, he was resigned to having the kind of wife no man could want, but no gentleman would complain openly about.

Those few days they'd shared such passion, which had given her such hope, might as well never have happened.

'I must say,' said Aunt Constance, strolling into the breakfast room, and up to the buffet table, which was kept stocked with a selection of fresh cakes and cold meats all day long, 'that

I'm really enjoying this house party. I haven't had so much fun for years. To think I expected the usual dull round of family sniping, behind masks of polite, restrained behaviour. Instead of which there's been a delicious undercurrent of torrential passion.' She sighed, and lowered her eyelids. 'Two indecently hasty marriages and a defenestration.'

'I'm so glad,' said Julia with a tight smile, 'that we have provided you with so much entertainment.'

'Oh, don't poker up so,' said her aunt, knocking back a glass of Madeira in a most unladylike fashion, and holding out her empty glass to the footman whose turn it was to make sure guests could have whatever reviving cordial they fancied, no matter the time of day. 'I think the better of you for acting like a real woman instead of a plaster-cast saint. I used to think you so deadly dull, but now...' She cast a speculative eye over Julia's tense posture.

'There is just one teeny little thing I feel I should tell you.' She waited until the footman had retreated to a safe distance, having replenished her glass. 'If your mama had lived to see you reach marriageable age she would have done so, but since you have no mama, and your other female relatives don't appear to have the backbone to approach you,' she said with a wry twist to her mouth, 'it falls to me. Julia, my dear...' she leaned in closer and lowered her voice '...you should never, ever dally with the help. Not until you've presented your husband with an heir, anyway. After that, nobody will bat an eyelid if you want to have a few adventures.'

Julia didn't think that was the kind of advice her mother would have given her at all. But she didn't like to say so. Aunt Constance was trying, in her own inimitable style, to be helpful, which was more than any of her other relatives had done.

'I don't suppose, after your little *contretemps* with your husband, there is any need for me to tell you to be a little more...circumspect in future. Men of our class don't expect their wives to be wholly faithful. But they do expect discretion. They don't want everyone to know they cannot keep their wives satisfied, d'you see? Reflects poorly upon their masculinity.'

If they didn't want people to know they couldn't keep their wives satisfied, they wouldn't throw their wives' lovers through windows, Julia wanted to say. Not that she'd had a lover. The very thought of Eduardo's kiss made her stomach curdle all over again. To cover her revulsion, she turned slightly away from Aunt Constance on the pretext of picking up a plate.

'When you next come up to town,' Aunt Constance continued, blithely unaware she was talking arrant nonsense, 'you must come and call upon me. I have a little group of friends, all married ladies, who meet together to study...*literature*.' Her tongue flicked over her lower lip as she said the word, which made it come out sounding like a most lascivious, and improper pastime. 'You would enjoy it.'

'Thank you, Aunt Constance,' said Julia politely.

Aunt Constance went off into a peal of laughter.

'I do declare you look as if butter wouldn't melt in your mouth! You are priceless!'

'Thank you. Now, if you will excuse me?' She stepped towards the selection of Cook's fancy cakes. The little treats were about the only things keeping her going through the day. Her stomach churned so much when she sat down to any table at which her husband was also seated, that she could do little more than push the food round her plate. Consequently, she'd wake up starving in the middle of the night and wish she could ring for a pot of chocolate and a plate of toast. But she didn't have the heart to wake any of the servants.

They needed their rest. So she lay there, wishing there was something she could do to fill up the hollowness. Wishing she'd had the foresight to order someone to bring her a loaf and a toasting fork before she'd climbed into bed. Which inevitably led to her recalling the interlude by the fireplace, during which she'd come to think of Alec as someone with whom she could be friends.

But he'd gone, now, that friendly, affable man. The man who'd held her through the night, keeping her warm. She'd huddle further down under the covers, but nothing could dispel the chill that seemed to emanate from her very core. She was starting to think she would never feel warm again.

She finished her first slice of plum cake, and helped herself to another. Though it didn't make any difference. She was going to feel hollow, she suspected, for a very, very long time. Until she grew accustomed to losing the respect of her husband. Which wasn't going to be easy. Because, deny it as strenuously as she might through the hours of daylight, during the empty, lonely nights she couldn't hide from the truth. Which was that she'd started to fall in love with him. Every time she dozed off, she would jerk awake, reaching for him, then recoiling in anguish when all her questing hand found was emptiness. She hadn't felt so alone since her mama had died. No—even then she'd had her doll to clutch to her chest. But grown women couldn't have dolls. Instead, they took lovers. Men who'd make them feel desirable at least, if not actually loved, for a few short hours.

But she didn't want a lover. She wanted her husband. She wanted Alec.

They could have had a good life together if only Eduardo hadn't…or if Lizzie hadn't…or she had…aargh!

What she'd felt when she'd discovered David had betrayed her had been nothing like this. She'd been angry, yes. Insulted. But not…shattered. What she'd thought had been love was a feeble imitation of the feelings she had for Alec.

She moved away from the table lest people started accusing her of gluttony. And paused. Hadn't she only just sloughed off the horrible feelings Marianne had induced, about her being greedy in contrast with the French girl's bird-like appetite? Hadn't she decided that comparing her fuller figure to Marianne's delicate little frame all the time had been a serious mistake? Anyway, what did it matter if she was overweight? What did she care what anyone thought of her looks? Since her own husband couldn't bear to look at her any more, and she was *never* going to go looking for a substitute, like a pitiful child running round begging someone to love her, then it didn't matter what she looked like.

She turned, mutinously, went back to the table, picked up a mince pie and crammed it, whole, into her mouth.

If only Alec still looked upset, she could have deluded herself that she'd started to matter to him, too. But after an initial spell of glowering whenever she walked into the room, he'd made a remarkable recovery. Though he never spoke to her, he'd gone out of his way to have conversations with every single other member of her family. Even her older brothers. After an initial reticence they appeared to have accepted him as one of their own.

She might have known Nick and Herbert would bond with the man who'd hurt her so badly. So publicly. They'd probably congratulated him for *taking her down a peg.*

Perhaps the most telling thing of all was the fact that he'd made no attempt to regain admission to her room. Not even once.

Sometimes she saw him pacing the length of the terrace, head down, hands clasped behind his back—as though he was pondering some deeply perplexing problem. But for the rest of the day—when he wasn't charming his way through her family, that was—he disappeared into the east drawing room with the young people, specifically his sister, she supposed.

And when she pressed her ear to the door, she'd hear gales of laughter above industrious noises of hammering and sawing. And flinch away, knowing that he was in there with all those others, enjoying himself immensely, while she…

She sighed, and absently picked up a Spanish biscuit. One good thing about the stand she'd taken in the orangery—at least he wasn't angry with Lizzie. In fact, by all accounts, Alec and Lizzie were getting on like a house on fire. There hadn't been a single murmur about Lizzie in connection with Eduardo, either. Which there was bound to have been if anyone had even the tiniest suspicion anything untoward had happened. So this estrangement from her husband wasn't utterly in vain.

It was small consolation, but all she had.

At last, it was Twelfth Night. She was eating the last family dinner of the season. And later, she would attend the last theatrical production. And then it would be over. Everyone would leave.

Everyone.

She pasted a bland smile on her face as her Uncle Maurice droned on about some horse he'd backed last race meeting. But her mind was completely taken up with what Alec intended to do once this house party broke up. She'd begun to think that wherever he intended going, he would be taking her with him. That they'd be starting a new life together. But now...?

A sick, roiling panic had her reaching for her wine glass and taking a large gulp. What would she do if Alec just walked away without her? Which was beginning to look increasingly likely. And she couldn't even blame him. When she looked back at the things he'd said, when he'd caught her in Eduardo's arms, the things which she'd found so insulting at the time, they were all looking more and more reasonable. She *had* seduced him in that very place, in mistake for another man. So she could see why he might think she had no discernment. And then she *had* leapt into the marriage bed with a sort of wild abandon that she couldn't quite explain. Considering the reputation the Whitneys had for infidelity—which he must have learned of by now even if he hadn't known before he arrived—coupled with the lack of regret she'd displayed over the loss of David—who was supposed to have been the love of her life—what was Alec to think except that she was a...well, she didn't know what the word was to describe the female equivalent of a rake, but she had no doubt acted like one. Her behaviour *must* have looked fickle and heartless.

If only he'd come anywhere near her, once she'd calmed down and started to look at things from his point of view, she could have explained that it was impossible to pine for a man like David, once she'd seen through all his lies.

She could have told Alec that the feelings he evoked had swiftly eclipsed anything she'd felt for the disappointingly devious David. That even before they were married, it had been thoughts of Alec that filled her head, Alec to whom she reacted whenever he was near. Because Alec had been the man to awaken her passion. Not David. Who now held about as much appeal as a plate of congealing lard.

'And so I told her,' Uncle Maurice was saying. 'Wonderful idea, don't you think?'

'Absolutely,' she said politely, having no idea what the idea was, or why Uncle Maurice should think it so wonderful.

'Capital, capital. Christmas is all about family. Nothing more important than that. I knew you'd see it the same way. Nobody more dedicated to the family than you. I'll tell her you're agreeable then, shall I? She had some silly notion that you might cut up stiff, but I told her you wouldn't. That you are a good sort.'

She placed her wine glass carefully next to her plate, wondering what she'd just agreed to, while her mind had been wandering.

'What, exactly, will it entail?' she asked, feeling pretty sure that such a vague question wouldn't alert her uncle to the fact she had no idea what he'd been talking about.

'Oh, nothing much. Dressing up in a costume the girls have made. Reading your lines from a script. Not a taxing part, she said.'

Oh, so that was it. She appeared to have agreed to take part in the theatrical production the young people had been working on with such enthusiasm for the past few days. Under the supervision of the actors. And with Alec's determined help. She wondered what he was trying to prove, with her family. He had the younger boys running around, saluting him, crying out 'Aye-aye, Cap'n!' He'd commandeered the estate carpenters and barred everyone not involved with the play from the ballroom, so that they'd all been intrigued by the renewed sounds of hammering and sawing filtering out from behind the locked doors. Anticipation was running rife. This year's production, everyone was saying, was going to be something they'd all remember for years to come.

'Only she was insistent,' Uncle Maurice continued, 'that all the family have a part, no matter how small. And that the servants should be the audience. Said something about the Lord of Misrule, and turning everything upside down for one night. And I said that should have been Christmas Day but she's got such a persuasive manner of speaking, and anyway your father has agreed so what could I say?'

'She?' Who was it that was organising things behind her back? Had she been so distracted these last few days that somebody else had taken over the organisation of this house party?

'The Neapolitan Nightingale.' Uncle Maurice sighed, a faraway look coming to his eyes. 'That woman could turn a saint into a sinner.'

And didn't she just know it! Where her Uncle Maurice was concerned, anyway.

'I mean...' He flushed guiltily. 'Begging your pardon. But she very nearly has. I mean, your Uncle Algernon. Bishop and all that—' He broke off, reached for his wine glass and took a hefty swallow.

Ah.

Somehow she didn't mind if it was Nellie who'd taken charge of the Twelfth Night production. Nellie had probably noticed how distracted she was, how unhappy, and was trying to help by taking everyone's eyes off Julia, and the way she was drooping round the place. She straightened up in her chair. She might be drooping in spirit, but she had no intention of letting anyone discern as much with poor posture. Nellie would know, of course, because the actress had been in the orangery both times Julia had got into hot water. She knew all Julia's secrets.

Including the fact that she'd fallen in love with the husband who'd only married her under duress? The man who'd spoken of the relationship in terms of being press-ganged? And who now, after giving it his best shot to begin with, had decided there was nothing worth salvaging?

She wouldn't be a bit surprised.

At last, the interminable meal came to a close, and she got to her feet to indicate the ladies could withdraw.

When they reached the drawing room, she was astonished to see a couple of wicker hampers set down under the windows, and various costumes strewn about over the backs of chairs.

Most of her aunts looked as bewildered as she felt. But her cousins looked as though they were going to burst with excitement.

Winifred went to the fireplace and clapped her hands to get everyone's attention.

'In honour of Twelfth Night, we have arranged a very special pantomime,' she said. 'All of the family are to take part. Well, nearly all,' she amended. 'We've made costumes for everyone.'

'How can we take part,' grumbled her Aunt Frances, 'when we haven't been to any of your rehearsals? Really, Winifred, this is too tiresome of you.'

'Oh, don't be such a spoilsport,' said Aunt Constance. 'The girls have clearly gone to a lot of trouble to put on some entertainment for tonight. It will be no worse than charades, I shouldn't think. What do we have to do?'

Winifred looked at Aunt Constance with gratitude. 'Just put on your costumes—each one has the name of the part and who is to play it, pinned on. And a copy of the lines you will need to say.'

'This is going to be dreadful.' Aunt Frances sighed. 'You cannot expect us to perform a play without any idea what it's about, or having a rehearsal.'

'Trust me,' said Nellie, striding to the hearth beside Winifred. 'It will be a lot of fun. It may not be the kind of thing I'd ever want to put on at Drury Lane, but it is just right for a family party. The young people have worked very hard to make sure of it.'

'Oh, very well,' said Aunt Frances. 'What am I to wear?'

For a few moments, everyone milled about,

discovering their costumes, the names of their characters, and reading over the lines they had to say.

'Thank you, Nellie,' said Julia, as the actress came up to her. 'For organising a sort of grand finale to this house party. I really should have done something. Something to include the young ones. And to thank the staff for all the work they've put in this year. More than usual, what with the weddings.' Not to mention boarding up broken windows. Gatley had been furious to discover his precious plants had been put at risk of cold draughts. She'd feared there would be an end to citrus fruit for the dining table. But he'd simply tucked extra layers of fleece round all the delicate plants, and got the estate carpenter to board up the broken windows before night fell.

'This will be wonderful, I'm sure.'

'I certainly hope so,' said Nellie, giving her hand a squeeze. 'Your husband has put a lot of effort into it. He's got all the cast fired up to play their parts. Even turned the younger boys into a sort of crew to work the scenery and such.'

'Lovely,' she said through gritted teeth. While she'd been mourning the stillbirth of their marriage, he'd been having what sounded like a perfectly splendid time. But there was no point in dwelling on her unhappiness. Best to keep busy.

With that in mind, she followed Nellie to a table on which were strewn various scraps of material and props. 'Well, what part have you decreed I should play?' She was already playing a part for her family. The part of unrepentant adulteress. How hard could it be to adopt one more role?

'You are to be the princess,' said Nellie, picking up what looked like a genuine diamond tiara, and setting it on her head. 'You will have a little pageboy—played by your cousin Freddie. Whenever you have a line to say, he will hand it to you on a card.'

'Isn't it past his bedtime?'

'It is already past most of their bedtimes, I should think.' Nellie chortled. 'That is part of the fun for them. That and feeling that for once they are in charge of the adults.'

'I see. All part of the spirit of misrule you seem determined to foster tonight,' she said, as Nellie settled a bright-red cloak, trimmed with what looked like ermine, but couldn't possibly be, round her shoulders. As Julia looked around the room she could see the other costumes were of a similar sort. Hats or headgear, coupled with a cloak, or some kind of prop to carry. Gradually, all her aunts were being transformed into clearly recognisable pantomime characters. Aunt

Constance had become a tavern wench with the simple addition of a stained apron, a mobcap, and a pair of pewter tankards. Aunt Frances was a peasant woman with a cloak of sacking and a hoe. And as for Aunt Joan—well, with the plain collar and steeple hat, she looked nothing so much as a Quaker woman.

'What is the pantomime we are to perform?'

It was what everyone wanted to know.

'All in good time,' said Nellie, who'd donned a very ugly false nose, glued on a wart and some hair to her chin, and clapped a large-brimmed, pointy hat on her head. To denote a witch, Julia would guess.

'Can you hear that?' Winifred was practically bouncing up and down on the hearth in excitement as the strains of a boisterous folk tune, played on fiddle and flute, sounded from just beyond the door. 'It's the band!'

Somebody banged three times on the door, then flung it open.

Benjamin, who was all dressed up to look like a town crier, stepped inside, and unrolled a scroll with a flourish.

'Come all you fair ladies who stay at Ness Hall. You've feasted, you've drunk and you've danced at a ball. Once more don your costumes—this time for the play. In which magic

abounds and true love…' at this point his face
went bright red '…wins the day.'

True love? Julia clenched her teeth. If the play
was to be a sickly love story, she didn't know
how she would bear it.

Aunt Frances rolled her eyes. 'Amateur theatricals,' she said waspishly. 'We shall all end up
looking ridiculous.'

Julia was rather horrified to realise she'd
started to think like her Aunt Frances. And wondered if it was Aunt Frances's natural disposition
to be waspish, or whether a series of disappoint-
ments in her youth had made her that way.

'This evening is about the young people,' said
Julia, with renewed determination to nip the slide
into Aunt Francesism in the bud. 'They've been
remarkably well behaved this year. They deserve
that we play along with them. After all, it is our
last night all together.'

'Oh, yes, of course, for the sake of family har-
mony,' Aunt Frances grumbled. Then twitched
her sacking cloak so that somehow it fell into
positively elegant folds, before wafting across
the room to the doorway.

In the corridor, the flautist and fiddler struck
up a new tune, and Nellie beckoned them to follow in procession to the ballroom. As they passed
the dining room, they were joined by the gen-

tlemen—got up in equally quaint costumes—
as well as a second fiddler, and the percussion
player from their hired orchestra, who was beating a little drum.

She tried not to look at Alec, the way she always tried not to look at him whenever he was
in the vicinity. But she couldn't help darting him
little glances. He was got up like a sailor. Not
an officer with gold braid and a cocked hat, either, but a common sailor in a stocking cap and
calico trousers. He was carrying his battered telescope tucked under one arm. And looking as if
he hadn't a care in the world. Which was why
she tried not to look at him again. Because it
hurt so much to see him carrying on as though
nothing was amiss, when she felt as if she was
dying inside.

As the family entered the ballroom, the servants who'd gathered there to watch the play
burst into a round of applause. Julia blinked
at the transformation the room had undergone
yet again. Since she'd last been in here, the actors—or perhaps it would be more accurate to
say Alec's crew—had transformed it into a series
of theatrical sets. There was a woodland on what
had been the raised dais used by the orchestra.
The dais was covered with some kind of green
floor covering, a painted backdrop had been sus-

pended somehow from the ceiling, and even half-a-dozen lemon trees had been brought in from the orangery. Who on earth had approached Gatley and persuaded him to have them brought indoors? It must have been someone with nerves of steel. Or perhaps Nellie had worked her usual mixture of feminine charm and ruthless determination on him. Uncle Maurice was of the opinion she could coax any male to do whatever she wanted.

Perhaps she should consult Nellie on the best way to win her husband back. It would certainly be worth a try. Perhaps she could approach him after the play. If it went well, and he was in a good mood, she could…but there her mind went blank. She couldn't begin to think how to persuade him to relent towards her, not without betraying Lizzie. Which she simply couldn't do.

Over where she usually had the buffet tables set out was an area done up to look like the outside of a village tavern. And by the chaperons' benches was the throne room of a palace. She recognised the handiwork of her younger cousins in the backdrops, though she could tell the outlines had been sketched by a professional.

The junior members of the acting troupe, all with little stocking caps the same as Alec's, which marked them out as members of his 'crew', guided the somewhat bewildered family to their places.

As she sat down on one of the thrones, and her father—who had a cardboard crown on his head—took the other, her little cousin Freddie trotted over and knelt at her side. He looked very solemn. He was also shaking a little with nerves. Once again, Julia squashed her own feelings. Though it was hard to be in the same room as Alec, though it made her want to weep to see him enjoying himself, and not caring whether she was hurt, or angry, or upset, she couldn't spoil the evening for the children by letting anyone know.

She sat up straight, lifted her chin, and watched Benjamin, who was taking up a position to one side of the audience, tugging at the lace collar round his neck, and clearing his throat.

The little band struck up a chord, the audience hushed, and Benjamin held up his script.

'Tonight, my lords, ladies and gentlemen,' he declaimed. 'The Ness Hall Players bring you the tale of the Golden Goose.'

The Golden Goose? Well that explained why Winifred had been painting the stuffed duck yellow.

Hurt stabbed a chill blade to her midriff as she saw why they'd picked her to play the part of the princess, too. For in the story of the Golden

Goose, the king promised to give her hand in marriage to anyone who could make her laugh.

No wonder Nick and Herbert had taken to slapping Alec on the back and going into huddles with him in corners. They'd been planning the ultimate way to hurt and humiliate her. Making her perform the part of a princess who was cold and humourless, who ended up married to a peasant simply because he made her laugh, was just typical of them. Just the nasty kind of thing they would do.

But—and her breath stuck in her throat, which felt as if it was closing over—how could Alec be a party to this? How could he deliberately hold her up to the world as a pathetic, miserable, stiff and starchy pampered princess with no fellow feeling for other people? Yet who was so shallow, she needed only the performance of a farce to make her laugh?

The answer was obvious.

He despised her.

And tonight was only the start. If she knew men, this would be just the first of many humiliations he would inflict on her.

He was clearly planning to make the rest of her life as miserable as he could.

The coldness at her core shimmered for a moment. And then, like a blizzard, swept to every last bit of her being. Turning her blood to ice in her veins.

So—this was how it was going to be? Fine! She shrugged one shoulder as she pouted her displeasure. She'd show him stiff and haughty. She'd show him cold and humourless.

Let the performance begin.

Chapter Thirteen

'Once upon a time,' said Benjamin. 'A young nobleman was riding through the woods...'

A young nobleman? That wasn't how the story started. But then Nick—of all people—strode onto the woodland area. Which explained why they'd had to change it. There was no way Nick would demean himself by dressing up—or rather down—as a peasant. The same thing must have occurred to one or two of the servants, to judge from the odd faces they were pulling—just as though they were trying their hardest not to laugh out loud at the sight of him walking onto a stage, carrying one of the children's hobbyhorses.

'Good sir, have pity on a poor old beggar woman,' cried Nellie, who had perched on a stool disguised as a tree stump, and was holding out a begging bowl in Nick's direction.

'Take yourself off.' Nick scowled. 'Trespassers will be prosecuted.'

'Trespassers against the laws of humanity,' cried Nellie, rising to her feet, 'shall be punished by a higher power.'

There was a bright flash and a clash of cymbals that made everyone jump, and half the maids scream. You had to hand it to Nellie's colleagues. They'd certainly got everyone's attention with that display of pyrotechnics. She just hoped they hadn't inadvertently set fire to anything.

When the smoke cleared, Nick had disappeared. From the spot where she was sitting, Julia had seen him use the distraction to nip behind the woodland backdrop. But to everyone else, it must look as though all that was left of him was a little pile of ash—no doubt plundered from one of the grates—which Nellie had dropped on the floor where he'd been standing. It had certainly convinced the housemaids, who were all clinging to one another in a state of delighted terror.

'Not so amateurish after all,' she heard Aunt Frances observe, through the background noise of gibbering housemaids. Though what she had expected, when Papa had paid a small fortune to have Nellie's company provide support to any entertainment that was got up over Christmas, Julia couldn't think.

Nellie cackled with laughter, pointing to the pile of soot and ashes. 'So perish all my enemies!'

One of the kitchen maids burst into tears.

'Don't be such a nodcock,' said Mrs Dawson, sharply. 'His lordship isn't hurt. Look, he's sitting right over there.'

Indeed he was. By this time Nick had made his way to the back of the semicircle of chairs in which the servants sat. He'd ditched the hobbyhorse, and acquired a glass of brandy and a supercilious sneer.

Next to stride onto the stage area was Herbert—who *had* put on a peasant costume. Herbert had never been as high in the instep as Nick, who wouldn't have been seen dead in clothing that didn't mould to his athletic form.

'Good sir, have pity on a poor old beggar woman,' said Nellie again.

Herbert gave a mocking laugh. 'Good God, woman, even when the dibs are in tune I don't waste my blunt on tradesmen, let alone beggars.'

A moment of stunned silence followed his statement. Julia herself could hardly suppress a gasp. Because it was so shocking to hear him admit, during the course of a play, what everyone knew anyway. Herbert generally lived well beyond his means.

'Now, get out of my way,' he said, hefting a cardboard axe. 'I've heard that there's a fortune to be made in timber.'

This time Nellie didn't reduce him to a pile of ashes on the spot. She never got the chance. As Herbert made for the potted lemon trees, swinging his axe in a purposeful manner, there came a bellow of fury from out of the audience. Gatley, who'd been sitting with the other outdoor servants, ran onto the set and tried to wrest the axe from Herbert's hands.

'It's only pretend, you old fool,' Herbert snapped, refusing to let go. 'I wasn't really going to chop down any of your precious plants.'

And then all of a sudden—and it happened so fast that even Julia couldn't see quite how it was done—the axe was in Gatley's hands, and what appeared to be a severed human arm was flying across the stage area. Herbert let out a blood-curdling scream and dropped to his knees, clapping his hand to his shoulder, at which point a fountain of blood went spurting into the air.

This time, all the housemaids screamed. But a couple of the footmen, and one of the under gardeners, cheered. When Herbert leaped to his feet and took a bow, a ripple of applause broke out from footmen, family, and outdoor staff alike. The cheering and clapping increased when he bent down to pick up his 'severed' arm, and flourished it triumphantly, before sauntering off to the back of the room.

'I always suspected that boy had a talent for acting,' said her father with disdain as Herbert ran back to the fake woodland and took another bow, since the footmen were still whistling, and clapping, and stamping their feet. 'But never realised he enjoyed it so much. Perhaps I should have done, considering the relish with which he used to invent stories as to why his allowance wouldn't stretch till next quarter day. If ever he manages to run through his wife's fortune,' he said drily, eyeing Herbert's second retreat to the back row of seats, 'I foresee him running off and taking to the stage.'

But Julia was scarcely listening. Because Alec was making his entrance. Her eyes fixed on the jaunty way he was swinging his telescope as he sauntered up to the 'witch'. She wouldn't react. She wouldn't let anyone guess by the merest flicker of an eyelid what was going on in her mind, in her heart.

The audience was still a little overexcited by the stunning opening sequence, so that Alec had to wait a while for them to quieten down before saying his lines. It gave Julia the chance to make her face freeze into a mask of indifference.

'Good sir, won't you take pity on a poor old beggar woman?' said Nellie, finally, in such ringing tones that it made everyone start nudging each other, and saying *Hush* so they could see what was going to happen next.

'I wish I could help you,' said Alec, shaking his head ruefully. 'But you see, I'm just a poor sailor, cast ashore now that the navy has defeated all England's enemies. I've been walking the length and breadth of the land looking for work, but none is to be had for a man who has spent all his life at sea. I just don't have any skills that are of any use ashore. All I have is this telescope, and half a loaf of bread.' He sighed, a touch melodramatically. 'If I don't find work soon, I will be obliged to sell this...' he cradled his telescope to his breast '...which will be a bitter blow. My captain and crew presented it to me, you see, when I passed the exam which made me a lieutenant. It is my most prized possession.'

He looked so sorrowful as he regarded his battered telescope that she wondered if it was true. And if so, was he trying to make her sorry she'd damaged it?

Well she wasn't! She was angry. Angry that he'd taken advantage of getting involved in the production to say whatever he liked, while at the same time effectively silencing her.

She lifted her chin and gave him a cold stare.

Onstage, he was reaching inside his baggy shirt and drawing out a half loaf of bread. 'Times are hard,' he said. 'And if it is hard for me, with youth and strength on my side, I can only imagine how hard it must be for you. I only wish I had more to give you than a share of my last crust,' he said, tearing the bread in two and holding out a portion to Nellie.

'Isn't it clever,' she heard Benson remark to Simson, 'the way the young ones have adapted the story to fit present company?'

Very clever. Each of the three to perform so far had used the play to show an aspect of themselves. But at least her brothers hadn't attempted to make themselves out to be heroes. At least they'd had the ability to laugh at themselves.

Stephens, who was sitting immediately behind the upper servants, tapped Benson on the shoulder. 'Hush up,' he growled. 'Or we'll miss what's coming next.'

Benson went red in the face at the temerity of the footman's remark. But he hushed up anyway. Nobody argued with Stephens when he got *that* look on his face.

Because Julia had been distracted by the altercation between Benson and Stephens, she was as startled as anyone else by the flash of flame, and the plume of smoke which suddenly enveloped the two actors on the woodland set. But she did see what went on behind its cover. Winifred and Electra dashed up, threw a spangled shawl over Nellie's shoulders and clipped on a pair of gossamer wings, while she tore off her fake nose and wart. When the smoke cleared, everyone applauded Nellie's transformation from hideous witch to beautiful fairy creature.

Nellie waited for the applause to die away before speaking.

'Because you were willing to share what little you have,' she said, 'I shall give you the reward you deserve. What is your heart's desire?'

Julia's heart thumped thickly in her chest.

Alec scratched his chin. Looked pensive. 'Well, all I've ever wanted is a ship of my own.'

Julia flinched. She couldn't help it. He was clearly using the play to convey the message that he couldn't wait to get back to sea. He'd warned her it would happen, and that when he went they would be glad to see the back of each other.

And she'd said she would be far more relieved to see him go than he would be to leave.

She had been wrong. While he clearly couldn't wait to shake the dust of Ness Hall from his shoes, she was going to miss him terribly. Miss what they'd had to start with anyway. Miss what they could have had if only things hadn't gone so horribly wrong.

'Go,' said Nellie, 'to the forest, and dig about the roots of the lemon trees. It is amongst them that you will find the means to obtain your heart's desire.'

The orchestra stuck up a chord, Nellie threw back her head, and launched into a rendition of the song which she managed to get into every production in which she'd appeared that year. At first, Julia couldn't see that it had anything to do with the current play. But then she grudgingly admitted that it was about staying true when appearances changed, and Nellie had appeared first in the guise of an old crone, and then a beautiful fairy princess, and that only Alec hadn't treated her any differently whatever she'd looked like.

Instead of going to search for the treasure, Alec sank down onto the tree stump at Nellie's feet, gazing up at her, apparently spellbound by the beauty of the witch and her mellifluous voice.

She'd had no idea he was such a gifted actor. Although, perhaps he really didn't care how much he was hurting her. Her hands curled into claws in her lap. How could he be so callous?

But then why shouldn't he be? Why should he care in the slightest for her, or her feelings, when she'd trapped him into a marriage he hadn't even wanted? He'd reminded her tonight that he'd had his life all mapped out before he arrived at Ness Hall. And he'd also just told her, in front of everyone, that getting a new ship was still his heart's desire. Was what he'd always wanted. Well, she knew that already. Did he have to ram the fact that their marriage was over, over, over, down her throat?

Fortunately for Julia, the song had tragic associations—since there were rumours it was written for Lord Wellington's wife, when she lost her looks due to smallpox—and Nellie's performance was so moving that most of the ladies were reaching for their handkerchiefs before it came to an end. So she had the perfect excuse for dabbing at her own eyes.

Trust Alec to pick a song that everyone associated with a miserable marriage, she sniffed, blowing her nose as Nellie graciously acknowledged the applause, and wafted off the stage.

Then Alec shook his head, as though shaking off a dream, got to his feet, and went over to the lemon trees. He leaned over the pots, and from behind the larger one, pulled out—to the accompaniment of a duck call from one of the orchestra members—the stuffed duck she'd seen Winifred painting yellow. Only now it had sequins glued all over it, too, so that it glittered.

Everyone in the audience roared with laughter as Alec regarded the duck in distaste.

'Well,' he said, once the hilarity had died down. 'The good fairy said I could use this to gain my heart's desire. So I suppose she meant I should sell it, and buy my ship. I'll go to London and put my case—and my duck—to the Admiralty board.'

The orchestra struck up a sea shanty as Alec set off, whistling cheerfully. The younger boys and girls came running out from behind various pieces of scenery singing along to his whistled sea shanty, and did a little dance she assumed was meant to be a hornpipe. Actually, given the fact that Alec had been so involved with the youngsters over the last few days, it was probably completely authentic.

She was the only person present who didn't appear to be enjoying the performance. Everyone else, even her father, was clapping, or tapping their feet in time to the jaunty music. And when it reached a rousing conclusion, everyone—particularly the proud parents of all those who'd taken part—applauded their performance.

She alone kept her fists clenched in her lap. It was all she could do to hold herself together, never mind pretend she was enjoying a play that, so far as she could see, had been expressly written to hurt and humiliate her as much as possible. He'd isolated her, that was what he'd done, by charming first her family, and now the audience. Everyone was on his side.

Alec stepped out from wherever he'd been lurking while the children performed their piece, and went to stand by the backdrop with the tavern painted on it.

'The day is far spent,' he said. 'I may as well rest here for the night.'

From that point on, the play stuck pretty close to the original story. The innkeeper's daughters, played by Winifred, Electra, and Lizzie, crept into Alec's room while he was sleeping, in an attempt to steal a feather from the golden duck. And became stuck fast, by magic, to its sequinned back. Uncle Henry, as the tavern keeper, berated them for being in a man's room, and, as he tried to drag them out, became stuck, too. And then Aunt Constance came in, accusing him of taking part in an orgy with the tavern wenches, and got stuck to him.

As they all shouted and struggled, Alec woke up and rubbed his eyes as though he couldn't believe what he was seeing.

While they all carried on arguing and struggling, he picked up his telescope.

'I'm off to London, to make my fortune,' he

declared, tucking the sequinned duck under his arm. When he set off, the tavern wenches, the innkeeper, and his wife all trotted along behind him, making increasingly frantic efforts to get free.

'I have to say they're doing this remarkably well,' her father leaned to murmur in her ear. 'To look at them, anyone would think they really were caught in some spell and couldn't break free.'

'Yes,' she replied. 'Especially considering they haven't rehearsed it. Well, not Uncle Henry and Aunt Constance, anyway.'

'Hmm…but then the tale of the Golden Goose is pretty well known. And your Aunt Constance has a fondness for charades and such like. Always shines at this sort of thing. But you have to hand it to your husband. The way he is strolling along, all unconcerned, as though he's barely aware of them…' He chuckled. 'Capital entertainment the young ones have got up, this year. Capital.'

Julia's sense of isolation grew even worse as her father gave his seal of approval to the pantomime which was causing her such anguish. She felt mocked, too, by the servants' gales of laughter at the sight of their betters apparently helpless under the force of the witch's spell.

Only her Uncle Algernon appeared to find the whole thing the least bit unsettling.

'Young man,' he said, from the chair where he was sitting on the sidelines. 'Your behaviour is disgraceful. How could you lead these innocent, impressionable girls into such an escapade? Have you no shame? And as for you...' he turned on Aunt Constance '...at your age you ought to know better.'

For one moment, everyone tried to stifle their laughter. Uncle Algernon's face had gone purple and his jowls were quivering ominously. He had never looked more like a bishop, ranting against the sinfulness of the younger generation than he did in that instant.

'Leave off cavorting in the streets,' he bellowed. 'And return to your home!'

He reached out to seize Aunt Constance, and compel her to do as he bid her. Only some force greater than him appeared to pluck him from his place and join the tail of people magically glued to Alec. The audience laughed even harder than before when they realised that far from condemning the jollity he was, actually, joining in. And Julia finally understood Uncle Maurice's cryptic remarks about Uncle Algernon, in relation to Nellie's ability to make a man do anything.

Aunt Joan stood up next, wringing her hands.

'Have you no thought to your position? What will the archbishop think if he hears you've taken part in a silly jest like this? Sit down, sit down!'

'I only wish I could.' He panted, pretend-struggling to get free.

'Of course you could. Stop this play-acting nonsense at once!'

'If you think I wouldn't rather be sitting next to you,' he said as Alec tugged him towards the fireplace, 'then you are very much mistaken. Instead of acting like a shrew, why don't you try helping me to get free?'

'Oh, this is ridiculous,' she snapped, grabbing his arm as he went past her chair for the second time. And then shrieking as she appeared to get stuck, too. The audience, seeing that Aunt Joan's pious show of outrage was also part of the act, roared with appreciative laughter.

'Frances, Frances,' Aunt Joan wailed, as she was dragged past her sister-in-law's seat. 'Help!'

'Me?' Aunt Frances said, placing one elegant hand on her bony chest. 'I don't see what I could do. But, I suppose…' she sighed with an air of resignation '…I must do what little I can.' She set her face, rose elegantly to her feet, and took hold of the sleeve of Joan's gown. And became part of Alec's human tail, too.

'Stephens,' she cried, holding out her free

hand imploringly. 'You are the only one strong enough to help.'

With an air of determination, the enormous footman surged to his feet as the tail swept past his chair, stepped up behind Aunt Frances, and manfully seized her round the waist. With the inevitable result.

'Take your hands off me,' Aunt Frances protested, trying to swat at him with her fan over her shoulder.

'Sorry, ma'am,' replied Stephens, going rather red in the face, but remaining firmly glued to her back, with his meaty great arms wrapped round her waist.

At that point, even Julia's father burst out laughing.

'Never knew the dried-up old stick had it in her.' He chuckled.

Only Julia sat stony-faced as Alec led his victims round the furniture, in and out of the pillars, and over various obstacles. Because it was clear to her that various members of the audience had been primed to join in, even though they weren't in costume. Or, if not, then they were all just joining in what was swiftly descending into something rather like a cross between a child's game of follow-my-leader, and a riotous, drunken sort of country dance. Everyone, it seemed, was thoroughly enjoying themselves.

Except her.

But at length, Alec came to a standstill in front of the thrones on which she and her father were sitting.

'Your majesty,' said Alec to Papa as he swept a low bow—causing incidental havoc amongst his human tail. 'I have come to London to seek my fortune. Do you, perchance, have a ship I can command?'

It was just as well he was keeping his eyes fixed doggedly on Papa. This was the closest she'd been to him for days. And that time he'd been shouting at her, red-faced and furious. Back then, it had been relatively easy to maintain a sort of dignified indifference. But oh, how hard it was tonight to resist the temptation to slap his face. Could she get away with it, as part of the performance? Probably not. Everyone, but her, seemed to know the part she was supposed to perform. And unless Freddie handed her a card with stage directions on, she couldn't slap her husband without letting everyone know how deeply upset with him she was.

Tremors started up in her stomach, and her knees. Tremors of hurt, and confusion, and thwarted rage. Ruthlessly, she slammed the lid on all her feelings. Reached for the ice she'd imagined flowing through her veins earlier. She would remain cold, and unmoving, no matter what he said or did. No matter how close he stood. No matter how much her hands longed to reach out and…touch him, move him, make him look at her, notice her.

At this point Freddie handed her father a card with a few words written on it.

'Oh. Do I have to say these lines?'

Well at least Papa wasn't in on the jest Alec seemed determined to play on her. Papa clearly hadn't been to any rehearsals, nor had any idea what he was supposed to do or say next.

Papa fished out his spectacles, hooked them over his ears, and peered at the wording on the card. 'I see,' he said, raising his eyebrows and giving Alec a cool, considering look.

'"I do not have a ship for you to command,"' he read aloud. '"Even though you appear to have mustered your crew already."' He eyed the trail of people who were apparently bound to him by some form of enchantment. '"But I have something far better for you. My daughter."' He waved his hand in her direction. '"She isn't happy. In fact, she hasn't smiled for a year and a day. And I have vowed to give her hand, and half my kingdom, to the man who can make her smile."'

Alec stepped back—causing all his magically stuck followers to stagger back like drunken shadows—and looked her up and down.

Julia braced herself. So far he'd used the form of the play to make some very pointed statements. And now he'd got the perfect opportunity to tell everyone exactly what he thought of her. She wouldn't be a bit surprised if this version of the Golden Goose ended with the sailor saying not even a princess and half the kingdom was worth sacrificing his happiness for, and going off to sea with her entire family stuck to the duck he held under his arm.

'Well, it's very kind of you to offer me the hand of your daughter, but—'

No matter what he said next, she would not let anyone know he'd hurt her. She would *not*.

'I don't think I'm the proper sort of husband for her. For she's a princess, and I'm just a poor sailor. Very poor. Too poor to really think about marrying anyone, let alone a princess.'

Benjamin put another card into Papa's hand.

'"You will not be a poor man once you marry my daughter,"' said Papa. '"I have told you, I will give you half of my kingdom."' Just as he'd been obliged to do in real life.

'That's all very well,' repeated Alec with a stubborn glint in his eye. 'But what sort of a man marries a woman just to get his hands on her money? A blackguard, that's who!'

"'Are you by any chance,'" read Papa, "'reluctant to marry my daughter? Do you find some fault in her?'"

Ah. That was a question he'd never asked before. They'd both been so determined, her father and Alec, to hush everything up and avoid scandal, that Alec's feelings about what he had to do had never been taken into consideration. At last he was getting the chance to tell everyone what he really thought about being press-ganged into marrying her.

She braced herself as Alec turned his head, and finally looked at her. Really looked at her.

'No,' he said stoutly. 'I find no fault in her at all.'

What? Julia blinked. That wasn't at all the kind of thing she'd expected him to say.

'She is the most beautiful woman I've ever seen.'

He said it with such sincerity she almost believed him. Except that she could hear a caveat in the tone of his voice.

'It's just that…'

Ah. Here it came. The excuse for avoiding an entanglement with her. She stiffened her spine and gave him her coldest, hardest look.

'Well, how could a simple sailor like me possibly make a princess happy? I wouldn't know how. I've no experience with women, you see, having spent all my adult life at sea.'

As excuses went, it was brilliant, she had to give him that. Just the sort of thing a sensible man would say to a monarch when he wished above all else to disobey a decree without suffering a painful penalty.

Benjamin handed her father yet another card.

'"Then this shall be your quest,"' said Papa. '"You must discover what it takes to make my daughter happy. Or suffer banishment from my kingdom. And deliver up to me, as compensation for my disappointment, the golden goose."'

Alec turned to the tail of people following him. 'Some of you are women,' he said with an air of desperation. 'What do you think would make her happy?'

'Money,' declared Uncle Henry, ignoring the fact that he wasn't a woman.

'Lots of stamina in the bedroom,' declared Aunt Constance, shooting him a withering look.

'No, no, it will be money,' put in Electra, as one of the tavern wenches. 'It was what we wanted, wasn't it? Money to buy fine clothes.'

'Yes, of course it's money,' said Uncle Henry impatiently. 'Though my last mistress told me the only thing that would make her happy was a box at the opera, it was the position of it, which would show I'd opened my purse to her, she really wanted.' Which inflammatory remark caused her Aunt Constance to reach over the tavern wenches and cuff him round the ear.

'You are all idiots,' snapped Aunt Frances. 'Every woman wants to be loved, of course. Tell her you love her, young man, and give her a kiss, and I wouldn't be a bit surprised if that doesn't break the spell holding us here.'

There was a murmur of agreement from his captives, which rippled through the audience, too.

With a sinking heart, Julia foresaw the end of the play. As in the ways of many of these sorts of tales, the kiss of 'true love' would break all the spells, and they would all be supposed to live happily ever after.

The trouble was, this wasn't a story. Well, it was a story, but it was her life, too. And she didn't think she could possibly play-act at the happy ending, when she was pretty certain that her own life was never going to have any such thing.

Chapter Fourteen

'Princess,' said Alec, sweeping her a bow, and thereby compelling his human tail to do the same. 'I love you.'

Freddie handed her a card upon which one word was written.

'"Stuff!"'

'I knew you'd say that,' said Alec.

Freddie handed her another card.

'Of course you did,' she said waspishly—without bothering to even glance at the lines. 'Since you have clearly written the script to suit yourself.'

'Indeed I have. Nevertheless, it is true.'

Freddie nudged her, silently urging her to read the words she was supposed to say once he'd had his turn.

'"You cannot possibly love me,"' she read woodenly. '"We have only just met. You know nothing about me."'

'I know you are beautiful,' said Alec. 'And that everyone here wants you to be happy again. Don't you?' he said over his shoulder to his train.

Some called out 'Oh, yes, your Highness.' Others, 'We do!'

'See? They all love you, too. And not one of us would love you if you didn't deserve to be loved.'

In bewilderment, she reached for the next card Freddie was holding out to her. She could no longer work out what was real, and what was play-acting any more. And, as she looked at the words written there, her eyes began to sting. How could he expect her to speak *these* lines, in public?

But Freddie was looking up at her expectantly, and her father was, too, and so were all the servants. She couldn't simply break down in tears, or get up and run out, as though she had no more backbone than a serving maid.

Lifting her chin, she read the words out loud.

'"The ones I loved the most are the very ones who robbed me of my smile. They put a curse on me."' It was true, though how on earth Alec had worked it out was beyond her. Yet somehow, to-night, he'd managed to make her feel exactly as she'd done as a child. Isolated. Unloved by relatives all too busy fighting their own battles to spare any time for her. She'd been so starved of affection, real affection as a child, she'd snatched at the friendship Marianne and David had appeared to offer. And ended up so fuddled by David's deception she'd ended up trying to compromise him into marriage. And then fallen so hard for Alec, that his rejection hurt worse than anything that had gone before.

'"Beware,"' she finished, her voice fading to a hoarse whisper, '"lest the curse fall upon you, too."'

'It already has,' said Alec. 'I'm bound to you forever. Whether you love me or not. Just as surely as these poor souls are stuck to the Golden Goose.'

'Are you…are you really comparing me to a goose?'

'Oh, hang the goose,' said Alec, tossing it aside. His captives all collapsed in various directions, with varying degrees of artistry. Aunt Frances, she noted, who'd landed firmly in the burly footman's lap, didn't appear to be making any effort to disentangle herself.

'Don't shut me out any more,' Alec said, reaching up to cup her cheek and turn her head in his direction when she would have carried on watching the antics of his newly released prisoners. Anything was better than facing him in the wretched state she was in.

'I know I've been a fool,' he said. 'But if you

would only give me another chance I will spend the rest of my life making you happy.'

'You…' Tears clogged her throat. She didn't know whether Freddie had another card for her or not. All she could see was Alec, standing there looking as though he was playing the part of the romantic lead in a silly pantomime.

'How can you do this to me?'

A look of panic came over Benjamin's face. He searched frantically through the cards in his hand. Alec placed a hand on his shoulder. 'We've got beyond that now, lad.'

'What do you mean?' Her heart was thundering so hard it was making her feel almost ill. 'I don't understand what is going on. How can you use this play to…to…?'

'How could I not?' Alec got a very determined look in his eye. 'I humiliated you in public. Don't you think you deserve a public apology?'

An apology? 'Is that what this is?' She looked from him, to her family members, who were struggling to untangle themselves from the undignified poses in which they'd landed. Apart from Aunt Frances, that was.

'Oh, for heaven's sake, forgive him,' said Aunt Frances, her normally porcelain cheeks turning a surprisingly rosy red. 'Hasn't he grovelled enough?'

Grovelled? How had he grovelled? In which part of the play had he done that? Had they been watching the same performance as her? She pressed a hand to her forehead, wondering if she'd become ill, and this was all part of some fevered dream.

'Tell her, right now, you are sorry you made such a to-do over the kiss,' said Aunt Constance fiercely. 'I told him it was nothing to make such a fuss about,' she said to Julia. 'Everyone kisses everyone at Christmas time. That's what the mistletoe is for. It's just a bit of fun.'

Julia's cheeks were burning. How could everyone speak about the incident with Eduardo, so openly, in front of the servants like this?

But then she caught sight of Lizzie, wringing her hands and looking as though she was about to step forward and say something, too.

And no matter how hurt she was at the way Alec had acted, she couldn't let the girl throw her reputation away. A married woman could get away with a bit of dalliance. But once a girl of marriageable age got a reputation for being fast, it would stay with her, and blight any chance for future happiness.

As she floundered for a response that would neither be a complete capitulation, nor land Lizzie in hot water either, Freddie nudged her, a triumphant grin on his face. Then he handed her another card.

"'I can see that you have gone to a great deal of trouble to prove your love for me,'" she read. "'You have got all my family to help you make your apology.'" She supposed he had. Even Nick and Herbert had taken part in this pantomime. A thing they'd always said was too demeaning before. She looked up from her lines to where her older brothers were standing watching her, their expressions inscrutable. Then across to where her aunts were helping each other up, smoothing down their rumpled gowns, and generally looking very pleased with themselves.

'We all love you,' said Alec, simply. 'And we all felt it was high time we showed you how much,' he finished in a rush.

They…they *all* loved her?

Suddenly, she saw the entire production in a different light. He'd said he was merely a sailor, with no skills he could use on land, with nothing to offer her, in fact. She'd assumed he was saying he was hankering to go back to sea, but, could he have been trying to say he felt worthless? Undeserving? Was that why he'd had her play the part of a princess? And dressed in ragged clothing, and gone on a quest to try to win her hand?

'This whole performance—the duck, and the clowning around—it was all for me?'

There was a chorus of agreement.

'You are such a dear girl,' said her Aunt Frances unexpectedly. 'Always trying to see the best of people. Though,' she finished tartly, 'I've never been able to stomach the way you let people take advantage.'

'It's more a case of never having a cross word for anyone,' Aunt Joan said in her defence.

'You all make her sound like some kind of... pudding heart,' said Nick crossly. 'And she isn't. She's pluck to the backbone.'

'Nicky?' She couldn't believe he'd say such a thing of her. She always thought he'd despised her.

'Don't look so shocked,' put in Herbert. 'We may not like the way Father always favours you over us, but it don't change the fact you are our sister.'

Suddenly she recalled the way Nick had objected to Alec sitting so close to her at the breakfast table, before he'd realised they were betrothed. At the time, she'd just thought he was being his usual quarrelsome self. But he had, now she came to think of it, been sort of...protective.

And both her older brothers had dressed up

and sat in the front row of the chapel when she married, rather than go out hunting, which she was sure they would have preferred. She'd only seen their sour expressions, and recalled the mutterings about her marrying for love, but that didn't alter the fact that they'd put in an appearance.

'Family,' put in Uncle Algernon. 'Nothing more important. We need to stick together. And you young people,' he said, advancing on Alec and her, 'need to patch up your quarrel. We all want you both to be happy. Especially me, since I married you. Don't want your marriage going cold less than a week after you spoke your vows.'

'Yes, come on,' said Nick with a touch of impatience. 'Tell him he's forgiven and make friends. Good God, girl, you don't want to end up with a marriage like mine, do you?'

She glanced across the room to where Ellen had given a stricken gasp. Nick sought refuge in his brandy glass. The way he always did.

But Ellen was watching him with a thoughtful expression on her face.

'Well, what do you say?' Alec asked gently.

'I…I've forgotten what the question was,' she admitted. She could scarcely believe that Alec had managed to get her entire family to help him make a public apology for losing his temper with her. Nor that they'd responded with such enthusiasm.

Her family. Who usually sniped and moaned the entire time they were forced into proximity with one another. All united in the affection she'd never really seen they had for her.

'Why don't you just read the lines I've written for you?' Alec suggested.

In a daze, she looked at the card Freddie was pressing into her hand.

'"Though you are but a poor sailor, and I am a princess,"' she read, '"I do consent to be your wife. On one condition."' She paused, as instructed by the script, for Alec to make his response.

'And that is?'

'"That you never give me cause to regret it."'

'I never shall. Never again,' he vowed.

Then he drew her up out of her throne, and into his arms, and kissed her, to the sound of applause and cheering from the entire cast of players, the audience, and the stage hands.

'And they all,' she dimly heard Benjamin say, 'lived happily ever after.'

She hadn't known how she would react at this point. Had been afraid she wouldn't be able to act at all. And indeed, she couldn't. The moment his lips touched hers—no, before that—the very second he pulled her into his arms, it felt so good that she simply surrendered. Surrendered to the feeling that she was where she belonged again. After being out in the cold, and alone, she'd come home. Home to Alec.

Tears seeped from her eyes as she put her arms round his neck and kissed him back. What point was there in clinging to pride? What use was there in quibbling about the fact that he was apparently forgiving her for something she hadn't even done? What man wouldn't have believed the evidence of his own eyes? When it had come so soon after her previous episode of loose behaviour in that very same place, he was bound to put two and two together and make five.

At least he'd gone to a lot of trouble to make the apology. And had done it in public. And enlisted the aid of her entire family.

How could she help loving such a…forgiving man? Even if he was so wrong about needing to forgive her? Most men were, after all, nearly always wrong about something.

The audience, meanwhile, were not only applauding, and cheering, but, as their kiss went on and on, also whistling and stamping their feet.

It was beginning to go beyond the bounds of what could be considered appropriate.

Alec seemed to think so, too, because he broke off kissing her, gave her a brief, hard hug, and spun her round to face the cheering audience.

'Come, take your bow,' he said, leading her by the hand to where the rest of the cast were forming up into a line.

Once more, she wasn't sure if this was an act, or her real life, or what, as they all bowed several times.

Then the orchestra played a sort of fanfare, and her father got to his feet. He held up one imperious hand, and everyone went quiet.

'Well, I must say, that was a most unusual performance. Something quite out of the ordinary.'

He looked pretty much as she felt. As if he wasn't sure whether he approved or not. But then he appeared to make up his mind.

'But I'm sure you will agree with me that it provided a very fitting end to this season of, er...' He shot Nick a slightly perplexed frown. 'Of goodwill. And now—' he resumed his attitude of total command '—refreshments will be served in the supper room, while the nursery party retire to their beds.'

His cool words reminded the servants in the audience of their duties, and they got to their feet and scuttled off to their allotted tasks, either to serve supper to the family, or to put their children to bed.

The cast began to disperse, too, discarding costumes, laughing, and congratulating the young people, and each other, on a successful performance.

Alec took her by the arm and tugged her behind the woodland backdrop.

'Julia?' He searched her face intently. 'Did you mean it? That kiss? I thought at the time—' He broke off, to wipe away a tear from her cheek. 'But you still don't look happy. I'd hoped this was a reconciliation. I'd hoped…'

It was his own face that he wiped then. Wiped it clear of expression. 'I can see that I hoped for too much. But at least you are speaking to me now. That is a start.'

'I would have spoken to you at any time these past three days if you'd made any attempt to speak to me first,' she hissed. Only a thin screen separated them from everyone else. She could hear snatches of conversation. So she was certain others would be able to hear them, too, if they didn't keep their voices down.

'But you couldn't be bothered. You were too busy…' She waved her hand at the room he'd spent so much time transforming into the set for his pantomime. 'Creating all this!'

'You would have forgiven me, if I'd just come to you and told you I was sorry for the way I spoke to you?'

'I...' She considered. Flung up her chin. 'I might have done.'

'Yes, you might have done,' he said grimly. 'Because you are very forgiving. I saw the way you wanted to make peace with Marianne, in spite of everything, but that wasn't enough for me. You deserve better. I needed to show you that I really, really meant my apology, and wanted to start afresh.' He gripped both her hands. 'And I do want to start afresh, Julia. I know I made a mull of things, but doesn't that tell you something?'

'That you have a hot temper and a nasty, suspicious mind?'

He winced, briefly shutting his eyes. 'Anyone who knows me well would tell you that I'm famous for staying calm no matter the provocation. The fact that I lost it so spectacularly when I saw you in the arms of another man, should tell you that...that...I really do love you.' His face turned a shade of crimson. Which made her blink. He'd said it during the play. But that had only been lines. Now that he wasn't playing a part, he had no need to say what he had. They both knew he'd had no choice, as a gentleman, but to marry her.

And she'd realised, over the last couple of days, that she'd given him plenty of reasons to regret it.

So…for him to say he loved her…in spite of everything…must mean…he really did.

Could it be possible?

He sighed at the baffled expression she was sure must be showing on her face. 'I know I'm not the man you wanted to marry. I know I let you down, badly, the moment we came to our first test. But if you give me another chance then I swear I will make you glad you married me, and not that trainee doctor.'

'But…' She shook her head. He thought she'd been up to no good with an actor, and still he was saying he wanted to make a go of their marriage. He was prepared to overlook something as bad as that?

'You could have just said that, you know. You didn't need to go to all this trouble.'

'You are worth the trouble,' he insisted. 'Besides, I didn't think you would listen to me, after the unjust way I laid into you.'

'It wasn't unjust…not really,' she said, in a spirit of trying to meet him halfway.

'Yes, it was. You know it was. I behaved like a savage. And you just stood there, and took it all, rather than defend yourself. Because all the time you were protecting Lizzie.'

She gasped. 'You knew about that?'

'Not until a day or so after. Looking back, I could see all the signs that you hadn't done anything wrong. Your anger, the way you threw me out of your room, the way you smashed my telescope. And while we're on the telescope, I need to explain that—'

'You did. During the play.'

'No, no—that is, I needed you to understand why I seemed so upset about it, when you broke it. Why I concentrated on it, rather than on you. You see...' He thrust his fingers through his hair, forgetting that he was wearing a stocking cap, so that it slid to the floor. 'It became a sort of... symbol, I suppose. It felt as if you were destroying everything of value in my life. Smashing what I'd begun to think could be so much more than I'd ever dared hope to find.

'And then, when I realised that you hadn't wantonly smashed anything at all, I felt so guilty, I knew that a simple apology wouldn't suffice. I should have trusted you. I should have known you wouldn't go about kissing other men. And then, to hear of the noble way you took all the blame, let our marriage dissolve about your ears, rather than let a single whisper of scandal touch an innocent girl...' He shook his head. 'And then I started to fear that our marriage couldn't have meant so very much to you, if you could let it go so easily. Without even a token protest. Instead, you threw me out of your room, out of your bed, without a flicker of remorse. Then went about your duties the next day as though nothing had happened.'

She considered his way of looking at it. She'd been so determined to hide her hurt. And she'd clearly been more successful than she knew. So successful he had no idea what it had cost her.

'While you,' she reflected, 'went prowling about the place with a scowl on your face like a wounded bear.' She'd thought he was just bad-tempered. But now it struck her that if the marriage hadn't mattered very much, he wouldn't have been in such a bad mood, for so many days. He wouldn't have thrown Eduardo through the window, either. He would have just given her a withering look, and strolled away.

'All that stalking up and down the terrace, scowling at your shoes…you weren't just regretting marrying me? You were…'

'Planning a foolproof strategy for winning you back. Words weren't going to be enough. I did look for some, Julia, but I didn't know where to find them. I've no experience, you see, with wooing a woman. The only thing I am good at is organising boarding parties, and cutting-out crews, or drilling gun teams and the like. And then I saw that in the youngsters rehearsing for the play I had a willing crew. None of them liked the way we'd quarrelled and they all leaped at the chance to help me show how sorry I was. Am.'

'You…you really do care for me, don't you?'

'Yes.' He searched her face. 'Are you starting to believe it?'

She nodded.

'And could you…' he bent to pick up the cap, dusting it down with one hand—anything, it seemed, to avoid looking directly at her '…could you come to care for me, too, do you think? One day? Oh, I don't expect too much, too soon, but if you would at least give as much to our marriage as you did before I made that stupid blunder, then…hang it, what am I saying?' He tossed the cap aside. 'Why should you have to make any effort? It is for me to woo you. To make you fall in love with me. I only wish I knew how to do it. Do you like flowers, Julia? Or jewels?'

Tempted as she was to keep him grovelling a bit longer, she didn't think it would be right. He'd gone to extraordinary lengths already, to prove how much she meant to him. And the nervous way he was fiddling with the cap—this man who always seemed so sure of himself—proved beyond any clever words that she really, really was important to him. More important than his pride.

'I do like flowers, and jewels,' she said. 'But you really don't need to buy me any—'

'Oh, but I do—'

'No.' She placed one hand on his chest. 'You really don't. Because you don't have any need to win me over. I think I'm already as much in love with you, as you say you are with me.'

'You cannot be!'

'Why not?'

'Because I'm not the man you wanted,' he said, clasping her hand to his heart. 'Because I let you down so badly. I drove you away with my nasty suspicions and my hasty temper. After you tried so hard to adapt to marriage, too—letting me in your room, and your bed, and in the end I...'

She placed the fingers of her free hand over his lips to silence him. 'You may not be the man I thought I wanted. But now we're married, I find I really don't want any other man. And as for letting me down—I can see exactly why you did what you did. But what impresses me is the way you went about making amends. Nobody has ever gone to such lengths to win my approval before. Because nobody has cared about winning it. I cannot believe,' she said, with a little shake of her head, 'that you even persuaded Nick and Herbert into joining in the effort to make me feel better. How on earth did you persuade them to take part?'

'It wasn't all that difficult, Julia. Your family all value you. And you heard what Herbert said. They may be jealous of the affection your father showers upon you, when he practically ignores their existence, but you are still their sister. And in their own way they are fond of you. As must be anyone who knows you.'

'Stuff!' He knew very well that Marianne had no trouble at all remaining completely immune to her. And as for David...

As though he'd known what was going through her mind, Alec slid his free arm round her waist. She stepped closer, resting her head against his chest. Relishing the way he cradled her to his heart.

'Besides,' he continued, stroking his hand over the crown of her head, 'getting to know Lizzie has been something of a revelation. She has made me look beneath the surface, to the heart. I haven't had much to do with women before. And I've tended to misjudge them. Well, you and Lizzie, anyway. I thought she was being manipulative and demanding when she wrote that letter to get me here. I accused her of telling lies, and of interfering in my life. When what she had really been doing was inspired by the love she has for me. The only way she knew how to show it was to get me here. And she knew I wouldn't come if all she did was ask me. She… used a stratagem. The same way I would have used a stratagem in battle.'

'Oh. So when your sister does it, it is permissible, is it?' She raised her head, and shot him a challenging look. He met her challenge squarely.

'It is when she does it out of love. And when it makes me see that I need to look beneath the mask a woman wears, to what is in her heart. Lizzie wanted to give me something back. Something to show how grateful she was for all the years when I went without to ensure she could have a genteel upbringing. She said she wanted to give me a Christmas present. At first, I found it hard to accept that the present she wanted to give me was a rich wife. A rich and loving wife,' he hastily amended.

'It all came as a bit of a shock to me. You see, I'm not used to receiving presents. That telescope was the only thing anyone had given to me, as a token of goodwill, for years. Other than that, I've had to work for everything I own. To struggling, if you must know. I've been the provider for my crew, for my sister, for so long that to have something as good as you just land in my lap—it seemed too good to be true. So when it seemed to go wrong, it was easier for me to think it had *all* been false.'

'And now?'

'And now I understand that you are not hard, or fickle, or flighty. Nor any of those things I accused you of. You are noble, and loving, and good. You took the blame for Lizzie's mistake, no matter the cost.'

She sighed. 'It wasn't such a big thing. In this family, there are always scandals. Affairs. Infidelities. Now that I'm married, it's almost expected that I should stray. The only shocking factor was that I appeared to do so, so soon after the wedding. And,' she added wryly, 'with a man of lower class. But if there should be talk about Lizzie, it could have ruined her chances of ever making a good marriage.'

'See? Noble. Good-hearted.'

'What,' she said with a rueful shake of her head, 'am I to do with you?'

He gave her a rather wicked smile. 'You could kiss me.' He looked up. 'There's bound to be some mistletoe around here somewhere. After all, you festooned the place with it.'

'So I did,' she mused. And then darted him a tentative smile. 'Aren't you afraid I hung it everywhere because I'm a designing hussy? Determined to trap some poor unsuspecting man in my toils?'

'So long as that man is me,' he growled, hugging her tighter, 'I don't give a rap.'

'Then let's go and find a kissing bough,' she said, gazing up into his eyes. Eyes which she could finally believe were burning with adoration for her.

'Who needs it?' He bent his head, and kissed her anyway. Without benefit of mistletoe. With her whole family, and the staff, separated from them only by a flimsy screen of canvas.

And for the first time in her life, she didn't care. Didn't care what it looked like, or what anyone thought of her behaviour, or what they might say. She just soared away on a tide of love.

Love for the man who'd finally seen beneath her mask to the girl she truly was inside.

And loved her—just as she was.

* * * * *

MILLS & BOON®

HISTORICAL

AWAKEN THE ROMANCE OF THE PAST

1215/04

MILLS & BOON®

**If you enjoyed this story,
you'll love the the full *Revenge Collection*!**

**Enjoy the misdemeanours and the sinful world
of revenge with this six-book collection.
Indulge in these riveting 3-in-1 romances
from top Modern Romance authors.**

Order your complete collection today at
www.millsandboon.co.uk/revengecollection

'The perfect Christmas read!' - Julia Williams

Jewellery designer Skylar loves living London, but when a surprise proposal goes wrong, she finds herself fleeing home to remote Puffin Island.

Burned by a terrible divorce, TV historian Alec is dazzled by Sky's beauty and so cynical that he assumes that's a bad thing! Luckily she's on the verge of getting engaged to someone else, so she won't be a constant source of temptation... but this Christmas, can Alec and Sky realise that they are what each other was looking for all along?

Order yours today at
www.millsandboon.co.uk

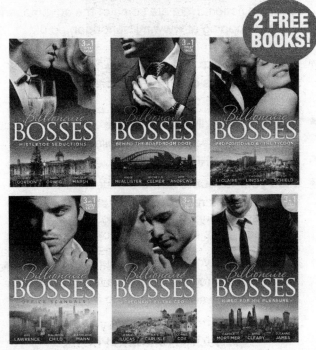